A LIFE
UNAPPRECIATED

A Special Agent Brett Gatlin Thriller/Suspense Novel

Vincent J. Sachar

DEDICATION

*To all those whose selflessness and sacrifice is
often not seen on this side of eternity.*

SPECIAL THANKS

To my wife, Gwen, for her countless hours of collaboration, for being someone I can openly talk with while in the process of writing, and for providing that ever so valuable "first-read" often well into the wee hours of the night.

CHAPTER 1

BLOOD IN THE SAND

*H*e was warned. He was told, before he ever agreed to work undercover, that a day might come when he would be facing death and not
*in a great position to do much about it. For Special Agent Brett Gatlin, that
day had arrived. The pulse of gunfire erupted. Too many shots per second
to do much thinking. Gatlin would now be in total reliance upon his training, his instincts, and some much-needed good luck. Gatlin was fighting
to save his own life.*

*Even so, something deep within him was crying out in terror. The im-
possible was happening. A team of the most highly-trained special ops DEA
agents was being summarily destroyed. The men that Brett Gatlin had
trained with and to whom he had pledged his life and loyalty would not be
lifting drinks in a cantina with him at the close of this day. They would not
be tapping beer mugs together and boasting about how more than four years
of training, planning, strategic advances, and sacrifice had brought them
the victory they hungered for. Rather, the sounds of dirges would rise from
spilled blood in the hot desert sands. Gatlin's team members—every one of
them was gone.*

Arizona's southern border cuts through 100,000 square miles of the Sonoran Desert. Prickly pear, ocotillo, and buckhorn cholla cactus populate the desert. It is home to diamondback rattlesnakes, desert centipedes, bark scorpions, and collared lizards. This desert, the hottest in North America, is inhospitable for anyone or any creature that cannot withstand extreme temperatures. There aren't many reasons why humans would ever want to spend any time there. Natives to the region speak of the various ways the Sonoran Desert will kill you. Special Agent Brett Gatlin was about to witness yet another way.

It was there, in the Sonoran Desert, that this group of well-armed individuals had gathered in the stifling heat to complete one of the largest drug deals ever. It was not uncommon for the exchange of drugs and money to take place out in the desert with guns drawn and individuals on high-alert, watching one another's every move. But, violence at times such as this was rare. These were business deals with everyone having a stake in a successful outcome.

The sellers on this day were all key representatives of Bernardo Damario Garcia, whose drug cartel was the largest and most powerful in all of Mexico. Brett Gatlin was one of several DEA agents present who were working undercover, posing as buyers. The federal agents operated within a process called backstopping—phones trace back to fake businesses that appear to be legitimate, computers have clean IP addresses, vehicles have untraceable license plates, and individuals have false driver's licenses.

Brett Gatlin's cover was that he was Hank Childress, an attorney representing major buyers and often arranging deals combining various parties. Brett Gatlin, Daniel Nguyen, Eduardo Sanchez, Pedro Vargas, Luis Manuelo Gonzalez, and Kenny Manchester were all linked together under DEA Special Agent Max Bradford as members of a covert special ops team called *Subterraneo.*

In his work as an undercover agent, Gatlin didn't always attend the transfer of product and money. But, this deal was so big, it would have looked suspicious were he not present. He claimed to be representing a large contingent of American buyers whose payment was in excess of three hundred fifty million. Their purchase and that of the others present would put a major dent in the stockpile of illegal drugs that Garcia's cartel currently possessed. This deal would also significantly bolster the Garcia clan treasury.

The last group of buyers present on this day were purportedly new to the trade. They were not originally scheduled to be involved in this deal. They called themselves the *empresarios*, using the Spanish word for entrepreneurs. Their title indicated they were organizing, managing, and assuming the risks of a business. These four individuals arrived in a Hummer and a white van that had no windows.

Under this day's plan, a team consisting of both American and Mexican highly-trained federal agents would arrive on the scene. These agents possessed enough firepower and experience to overtake all of Garcia's men. Their presence would assure that this would be the day that Garcia's cartel would be defeated. They would also provide the safety of Brett Gatlin and the *Subterraneo* team.

"We'll take as many of Garcia's key men as we can into custody. This is what we've been aiming for," Bradford reminded his team. "Losing that huge stash of drugs and not getting paid will cripple Bernardo Damario Garcia. And when the word gets out that a team of American and Mexican agents bested Garcia, major buyers will back away from doing business with the man."

Gatlin's eyes, like that of a big cat studying the landscape in search of prey, continued to scan the hot desert terrain. Like rapidly rising cumulus clouds, a darkening sky, and a drop in barometric pressure just before a thunderstorm strikes, Gatlin sensed the tension building. The *empresarios* began to protest the terms of the deal. Their reactions surprised Gatlin. To his knowledge, nothing had changed from the agreed-to terms. Brett spotted tightening body postures, glaring

3

eye contact, and men beginning to place themselves in offensive and defensive positions. Yes, a storm was definitely brewing.

By now, perspiration drenched Gatlin's body. His throat was dry, but his hands were clammy. His heart was beating furiously. One prevailing thought dominated his mind. Where was the army of federal agents? He continued to search in the distance hoping to see this team of agents arrive before things broke loose. Where were they? They should have already been here. Gatlin was beginning to tick off seconds in his mind like the timer on a detonator of an explosive device.

Through the corner of his eye, Brett spotted the doors opening just a crack at the rear of the Hummer and van that the *empresarios* had arrived in. He caught sight of a momentary reflective flash of light. He made a concerted effort to control his breathing and slow his rapidly beating heart. His leg muscles tightened. His body was poised to move quickly. Over the course of time, Brett had learned to pick up signals and understand their meaning. To him, these signals were clear. Weapons were about to be fired. Time was up. Things were ready to erupt.

As shots began to ring out, Brett turned his head towards one of Garcia's henchmen. The burly Mexican had been standing next to Gatlin. Now, he was lying in the scalding white sand bathing it in a pool of red. A few minutes ago, the guy looked like he could lift a truck with one hand. Now, he was motionless with his mouth open and his eyes staring, but no longer able to see. Gatlin quickly grabbed the dead man's automatic weapon and began firing back. He moved deftly, at times only avoiding a leaden missile by a matter of a few seconds or a few inches. The men from Bernardo Damario Garcia's cartel were systematically being dropped like target ducks at a carnival arcade. There was no question that Garcia's men were the primary targets, although anyone else would also do.

Amid the deadly chaos, a rush of adrenaline uplifted Gatlin as he spotted the clouds of dust in the distance. He screamed in triumph and raised a fist in the air. Four Hummers, specially designed for combat by the U.S. military at Fort Huachuca, each bearing six agents, were racing to the scene. They were coming in from four separate directions to surround everyone. Yes! All was not lost. Within a few moments, these agents would quell the uprising and take charge. The Hummers they were traveling in were reputed to be impregnable. No one outside these vehicles possessed a caliber bullet capable of piercing their outer shells.

Gatlin took refuge behind an empty vehicle and waited for the agents to make their move. After four long years, the plan devised by the *Subterraneo* team and its leader, Max Bradford, was coming to fruition. Victory was within their grasp. This was the day, the hour that Gatlin and his team had been waiting for. It was...

In a moment of time, everything changed. A lone man isolated from all the others, out of harm's way, pressed a button with his thumb. Thick clouds of smoke filled with pulsating flashes of red, yellow, and orange rose from each of the arriving Hummers. The blasts were so powerful they generated ground tremors like an earthquake. Shrapnel from the vehicles flew from every direction. The noise was deafening. Gatlin watched in terror as a series of explosions erupting within the approaching caravan of vehicles induced fire and destruction that no living being could survive. Hah, like the cavalry in an old western movie, these agents would take down Garcia's men and gather up the drugs and money. In doing so, they would also cripple Garcia's operations.

But, some well-placed deadly explosives thwarted that goal. In the blink of an eye, everything changed. A lone man pressed a button and the conquerors were turned into fatalities. Garcia's cartel would be irreparably crippled on this day, but not by these agents.

Luis Manuelo Gonzalez was the first of the *Subterraneo* team to die. He had been with several others from Garcia's cartel when a sweep of bullets cut them down. Gonzalez was an experienced federal agent. On this day, he was in the role of a major drug buyer representing wealthy Latin American businessmen, government officials, and law enforcement personnel.

Eduardo Sanchez was *Subterraneo's* most experienced federal agent. He had carefully worked his way to an insider position within Garcia's cartel. In fact, it was Sanchez who convinced Max Bradford that he was in an excellent, though precarious, position to assist a dedicated team in bringing down Garcia's operation.

"You've got me as a trusted insider," Sanchez said. "I eliminate the guesswork and can help mitigate the risks if we play this thing right."

Sanchez was shot to death while he was standing next to Gonzalez. Ironically, two men playacting in roles opposite to their sworn duty were now lying dead in the sand with their bodies touching each other.

Pedro "Pete" Vargas was also in the role of a buyer. He was felled by bullets while running over towards Daniel Nguyen to assist him. Nguyen, *Subterraneo's* nerdy computer whiz, had never attended a drug deal before. Kenny Manchester, another DEA federal agent, was wounded. He fell to the ground and stared up into the face of the man who laughed as he fired a fatal volley of shots into Manchester's body.

On this day, the dead included all of Garcia's men and every member of the *Subterraneo* team present that day, except for Gatlin. The killers bearing the fictitious name of the *empresarios* were members of Caesar Hidalgo Monterro's rival cartel. They would not be accurately identified until later after they rode off with the stash of drugs and close to two billion dollars. The death toll they left in their wake consisted of nineteen key members of Garcia's cartel and twenty-nine federal agents.

During the outburst, Monterro's men continued shooting anyone on the ground who showed any signs of life. Flying debris rendered Gatlin unconscious. He showed no signs of life at the time that Monterro's murderers walked by.

This was to be the day when everything that Special Agent Brett Gatlin and his team had been working for came to a glorious and successful end. Instead, it was a day when everything ended in blood in the hot desert sand.

CHAPTER 2
ESCAPE TO FREEDOM

The bus was old, loud, and offered the riding comforts of a Conestoga Wagon. Even with the windows open, it was unbearably hot. Plus, open windows invited in dust from the unpaved roads and the smell of exhaust fumes. But discomfort, heat, dirt, and odors were the least of Brett Gatlin's problems should those pursuing him discover his whereabouts. He slunk further in his seat, pulled his cap down on his face, and hoped he had made the right move in taking a bus to his next destination. Following the bloodbath in the desert, Gatlin was taking no chances as he headed back towards Mexicali, where he had an apartment that only a limited few knew about.

Gatlin never conducted any business in Mexicali. The city was his place of refuge from his work as an undercover federal agent. No one, other than Max Bradford, his team leader, and whomever Max included on a need-to-know basis was aware of this Mexicali hideout. One night in Mexicali, then Brett would head for the American border in the morning. He would head for Fort Huachuca in Sierra Vista, Arizona and make contact with his mentor, Special Agent Bradford.

That night in Mexicali, as he placed his head on a pillow, the images of the Sonoran Desert bloodbath raced through his mind. He fought hard to dispel those thoughts, but one-by-one he relived the deaths of each of his team members, as well as four Hummers filled with American federal agents and Mexican *Policia Federal* officers. The images replayed in his mind again and again. He could not shake them. Perhaps, he never would.

The sun had just risen. Call it instinct or, perhaps, it was how any man in Gatlin's position would react. Or credit it to the fact that Brett Gatlin was not just 'any man' and never had been. Even before he made his first cup of morning coffee, Brett walked over to his apartment window. From the fourth-floor of his secret Mexicali hideout, he had a view of the street below. On this morning, it told him all that he needed to know. Four, make it five, now six of them were positioning themselves with some remaining at the front and some racing towards the back of his building. The day had finally come. They were here. Gatlin was not sure just who they were. He had no idea how they had even learned about this place. What he did know with certainty was that they had come for him.

Perhaps, Bernardo Damario Garcia, following the major hit he'd taken in the Sonoran Desert, was making a last-ditch effort to show his muscle and send out a message that he was still in charge. Maybe it was people associated with the *empresarios* who were here to finish off the last remaining piece of their slaughter. Gatlin had no idea how anyone had tracked him to this location, but this was not the time to waste trying to figure something like that out. Every life-saving alarm within Brett Gatlin was screaming at him that he was in trouble—big trouble.

The building he was in was old and dingy. There were no elevators, no fire escapes. There was a front entrance with an open stairway that led to an apartment on each side of a floor before turning off into a narrow hallway that led to the back of the building. It had four more apartments, two on each side. The hallway dead-ended to a door that opened to the rear building stairway. This was the building pattern for all eight floors.

Brett Gatlin only had two choices. He could hole himself up in his apartment and shoot it out with these men when they arrived. He was skilled enough to, perhaps, take down one or two of them, but, with automatic weapons and orders from someone to make the kill, these men were not returning home empty-handed. Gatlin's only other choice, and the one he set in motion right away, was to take the stairs upwards. There were four more floors and a door that opened to the building roof. He grabbed his weapon and extra cartridges. He strapped on the small backpack, which he always kept on the ready for emergencies like this. Then, he locked the door to his apartment and ran down the hallway towards the back stairwell. His only hope, and a temporary one at best, was that he would reach the stairwell and begin his ascent unnoticed before anyone pursuing him reached his floor on that same stairwell.

Brett Gatlin did not like functioning under such limited odds of success, but he realized years ago that as a federal agent he would not always be the one to set the terms he would be working under. And this was certainly one of those times when he was forced to react, to move on the defensive, until other circumstances presented themselves.

Gatlin moved with a quickness and nimbleness that he had not lost since his days as a high school all-state football quarterback. He was through the hallway door and headed up the steps before anyone reached his home floor. He could hear what was likely two men racing upwards. He was confident that they did not hear him.

He reached the door to the roof and yanked on the handle. Damn, this was not what he needed right now. Within seconds, Gatlin had a small pick pulled from the front pocket of his backpack and used it to open the lock. After he was on the roof, it took him no time at all to lock the door once again.

For a moment, just a moment, he breathed a sigh of relief. He was safe. He knew that once they realized he was not in his apartment, they would block every exit and send two men up to the roof.

Gatlin moved away from the door and headed towards the large air conditioning unit that once functioned and served to keep the building cool. As he did, a shot rang out from somewhere in the distance and missed him by no more than a quarter of an inch. Damn—a sniper somewhere in the area who would, at a minimum, keep him at bay until all the others joined him on the roof.

Thirty-one years old seemed to be much too young to die.

Caesar Hidalgo Monterro's estate was built like a fortress, impregnable against all outsiders. Tall walls encircled the massive estate and met together where an iron-wrought gate provided the only entrance and egress. A manned guard tower controlled the gate. Two additional towers with armed guards were located at each side of the rear of the property.

On this evening, a great fiesta was being held with the finest foods, wines, and scores of beautiful women. The music played by the band was festive. Monterro, by virtue of his recent victory against Bernardo Damario Garcia's cartel, now reigned supreme as the most powerful drug lord in all of Mexico. Now, everyone involved to any extent in the drug trade would respond to Monterro's beckon and call. His cartel had replaced Garcia's and Monterro would now be recognized as the king among all drug lords.

Monterro interrupted his own celebrating and stepped away from the festivities. The man alone with him in the library of Monterro's estate was a wealthy and powerful American man. At six feet two, the slim American was several inches taller than Monterro. His black wavy hair was perfectly coiffured. His shiny fingernails evidenced the recent manicure he had received and served to highlight his gold diamond encrusted pinky ring. Everything about this man represented American capitalism at his fullest—and everything that Monterro hated. The man told Monterro that his name Frederick Hayes. Monterro did not, for a moment, believe that was the man's true name. Monterro didn't care. He needed the man to assist in destroying Garcia's cartel and eradicating the threat of American and Mexican federal agents in the Sonoran Desert.

"Well, Señor Monterro, we have kept our end of the bargain," the American said. "It is expected that you will do the same."

"But, of course," Monterro said with a smile. "We shall all profit in this endeavor together, yes? Ah, rest assured, my friend. All is well and shall remain as such. Together, we have accomplished what we set out to do. Tonight, we celebrate. You, my friend, need to relax. Come drink some of the finest wine in all of Mexico. Join in the company of the most beautiful women. Eat from the tables filled with food. The blood of Garcia's men and many of your own countrymen has sealed the deal. As I have said, tonight, we celebrate."

CHAPTER 3

THE ONLY WAY OUT

Gatlin could hear the pounding on the roof door as his pursuers sought to break it open. His time was running short. Brett would be in position to pick off a man or two as they entered the roof through the door. With only a handgun and a few clips, he would never be a match for men with automatic rifles and a sniper hidden away somewhere overhead.

Gatlin's SEAL trainer taught him visualization techniques to practice what was referred to as "emergency conditioning." Gatlin had already developed what was called a "trigger" by identifying the most important thing in the world as a motivation to remain alive. He pictured a healthy, smiling Derek, before his brother became involved in gangs and drugs. The memory of his dead brother was the reason Brett was so deeply committed to his role as a federal agent. Then, Brett relied upon what the trainer called a "situational awareness checklist" which included guessing what the people chasing him were thinking or doing, determining the best cover from gunshots, and seeking an exit from where he currently was. His mind was focused upon actions he needed to take and strategies he had to quickly develop. He was in big trouble and he knew it, but he could not permit his thoughts to focus on that. He had to focus on solutions, not problems.

Brett peered over at the building next to this one. The rooftop was at the same height. He estimated the gap between the buildings to be, perhaps ten feet. With a running start, he might be able to make it. But, with a sniper in the area, there was no opportunity for him to get a running start. He would need at least forty feet or more of runway to clear the gap between the buildings. He'd be mowed down well before he ever reached the edge of the roof.

The pounding on the rooftop door was now accompanied by a high-pitched piercing sound—like a screech, as if the door was crying out in pain. The battle between the locking mechanism holding the door in place and the men attempting to break through was fully engaged and Brett knew that the door would soon lose and forfeit its position.

"*First things first, then the next thing.*" The mantra that raced through his mind was something that Max Bradford would say while training his team. It was a reminder that whenever anyone was in a pressured or urgent situation, they had to quickly avoid panic and chaos by mapping out a plan of action.

"You always have time, even if we're talking in terms of seconds, to organize your thoughts," Max would say. "And that begins by determining what the first step you must take may be. Once you focus on step one, your mind will begin a pattern of organizing the more that must be done."

Gatlin focused his thoughts. *Step one is to eliminate the sniper. That's my priority.*

Behind him, there was one building. It was four stories taller than the rooftop that he was on. The sniper had to be nestled somewhere in or on that building.

I've got to draw fire and, this time, evading a bullet is only one of the things I must do. I need to locate the nest. I need to know where this sniper is.

As Brett peered upwards, he counted six windows that were either fully or partially opened and, of course, there was the building roof. With the clock running against him, seven potential locations were not the best of odds, but that was all Gatlin had to work with. He unbuttoned his shirt, took it off, and pushed it out beyond the edge of the large dormant air conditioning unit, which was the only thing protecting him from his assassin. Within seconds, a shot rang out. Gatlin was unable to determine exactly where the shot came from, but based upon what he did see and the trajectory of the leaden missile, Brett could eliminate the windows to the left side of his view. Now, he only had two windows and a rooftop to choose from.

The pounding on the door opening to his rooftop continued. It was now accompanied by a shrieking whine as the door screamed out that it could not hold on for very much longer. It would only take a few more slams before the only barrier keeping those men from reaching Brett Gatlin was gone.

This time, Brett leaned his body out beyond the edge of the unit and spotted the window where the shooter was located as a bullet grazed Gatlin's right arm, tearing his shirt and leaving a stinging bloody scratch on his skin. He had to make his move now. He knew it was time to go all in.

Brett placed his shirt on the tip of his foot. When he stuck it out beyond the metal frame of the unit he was tucked behind, he also raised his body up on one knee from behind the unit and fired simultaneously with the sniper. Using a handgun and having only a second or two to get his shot off before the sniper spotted him, required precise shooting. Brett caught the sniper moving his rifle in the direction of Brett's head and watched as the weapon fell from the shooter's hand. So much for step one.

Brett rose from his hiding place, ran to the opposite end of the roof, and began to race towards the opposite ledge as fast as he possibly could. There were times in years past when he had to escape from the pocket as a quarterback and make some split-second decisions on what his next move would be. This time he only had one choice. He had to run as fast as he could and begin his leap at the edge of the roof. On this day, the stakes did not involve a loss of yardage and being tackled by a body much larger than his own. On this day, failure would result in either a fatal plunge or failing to complete the jump before being shot to death.

As he began his jump, he swung his arms back, jumped at a forty-five-degree angle, and let his arms come forward with his leap. He focused his eyes on where he wanted to land. A bolt of terror shot through his mind when he realized that the gap he had to overcome exceeded ten feet by several additional feet, but he quickly dismissed that thought. He had made his move. There was no turning back now and no room for failure.

If Brett were not entrenched during a jump for his life, he would have heard the rooftop door finally burst open and realized that his pursuers were now on the roof. He was not aware of that. Besides, men chasing after him with assault rifles had suddenly become a secondary threat to his life. A building story might be anywhere from ten to fifteen feet high. Now, a precise calculation was not necessary. A fall from this height onto the cold hard cement below would produce the same result as bullets penetrating his head and heart.

At the midpoint of his jump. Gatlin brought his knees up in front so that his thighs formed a ninety-degree angle with his body. He saw nothing other than the spot on the adjoining roof that he was focused upon. As he neared his landing, he aggressively straightened out his legs and pointed his toes. He had his feet shoulder-width apart and his knees slightly bent. He anticipated that the balls of his feet would make the initial impact and absorb the tension, keeping him stable.

Brett let his torso sink with his legs, placed his hands on the ground, and began to roll diagonally on his back rolling one shoulder to opposite hip. He tucked his head under his armpit, rounded himself into a ball, and rolled.

This would have been a perfect time to rejoice that he had cleared the gap, landed on the adjoining roof, had not, to the best of his knowledge, fractured any bones, and was still alive. And if it hadn't been for the fact that shots began to ring out and quickly put an end to his success, Brett Gatlin would have done just that. Instead, he quickly rose to his feet, ran in a zig zag pattern, avoided getting shot, and entered the door that would take him from the roof. He had no time to rejoice in anything. He did not know if there were others on the ground who would be waiting for him as he exited this building nor how quickly the men on the opposing roof would get to the ground floor.

Even so, as he entered the door that would take him from the roof, he heard a voice bellowing out.

Temporal, mi amigo, temporal. "Temporary, my friend."

As he reached the street level, Gatlin saw no one. He raced through back alleys up and down streets and never stopped until he was some two miles away from his apartment building. He knew that he would never return to that place. He knew that he would continue to be a marked man. But, Brett Gatlin also knew that he had lived to see another day.

CHAPTER 4
WHEN EVERYTHING CHANGED

Brett Gatlin grew up living with his family in Antioch, Tennessee. His dad, Gabriel, was a production engineer in a major recording studio. His mother, Gloria, worked as a nurse in a doctors' office in nearby La Vergne. Brett was five years older than his brother, Derek, and had seven years on his sister, Lucy.

Gatlin, was an outstanding student and athlete throughout high school. At six feet two inches with sandy brown hair, brown eyes, and a well-defined handsome face, Gatlin was one of those guys who seemed to have it all. He played football, basketball, and baseball and graduated with academic honors.

Upon graduating from Antioch High School, Brett attended the University of Michigan on a full scholarship. Upon graduating from Michigan, Brett had been accepted to a number of tier one law schools throughout the nation. He chose Vanderbilt University Law School in Nashville to be closer to his family. His father had suffered two heart attacks and was now on full-time disability. Derek had already been arrested twice for drug possession and was actively involved in a local gang. Lucy was entering her sophomore year in high school and doing well academically. She was excited when she learned she had been chosen for the cheerleading squad.

Three years later, having graduated *summa cum laude*, with his juris doctor degree in hand, Brett was in the process of considering which job offer to accept from several prominent law firms and corporations. Then, came the day that would change his life forever. The police car parked outside of the family home was the first warning that something was wrong. Brett walked in to find his parents and his younger sister all sitting in the living room listening to the Antioch Police Department sergeant and a local pastor who served as a department chaplain. When Brett spotted his parents' swollen eyes and saw Lucy with her head buried in his mother's lap, he knew that what he often dreaded had come to pass. During the ensuing discussion, the family received the few details that were available.

"We believe that Derek's death is linked to a territorial drug war between rival gangs. He was one of three young men who were executed," the police sergeant said.

Drugs, gangs, death at an early age—the whole scenario sickened by the whole scenario. Derek wasted his life from the moment he ended up hooked on illegal street drugs. He was no longer the gregarious young man with a curious mind and a desire to follow in Brent's footsteps as a talented athlete. His bedroom at room remained empty and, for the most part, he had little or no contact with his family. His addiction to drugs was a gateway to criminal activities and allegiance to a local gang. Now, just fourteen days after his nineteenth birthday, Derek's life had ended.

Derek's death devastated Brett. In addition to time spent solacing his family members, Brett spent time alone and could usually be found sitting along the banks of Percy Priest Lake. A day came when Brett's announcement to his parents of a change in his career direction stunned them.

"The way I see it," Brett said, "I couldn't save Derek. He became a totally different person, like a stranger to us, before we all fully grasped what was happening to him. But, I've been doing a lot of thinking. The way I see it, Derek couldn't escape the snare or deathtrap that took control of his life. Maybe there are other 'Dereks' out in the same deathtrap that ensnared my brother. Maybe they can be saved before they end up like Derek."

"That's right, son," his father said. "Maybe, you can become a prosecutor or one of them state attorneys. Then, you can put them bad guys in prison where they belong."

"No, Dad, I don't want to merely be on that end of things. It's too late then. I want to be on the front end. I want to be involved in making sure the stuff never makes it onto the streets. Derek was hooked on heroin, Pop. Once that drug got a hold on him, he was finished."

Once again, Brett sat alone along the shores of Percy Priest Lake, at a spot where he and Derek often walked and fished when they were younger. He pictured his brother, at a much younger age, when he was a carefree young boy who looked up to Brett. Those images were dashed and eventually replaced by a Derek that Brett hardly knew.

What happened to you, Derek? How did drugs and gang members take such control over your life? What more could I have done? What should I have done? God, how I wish I could turn back the clock and get another chance to try and pull you free from all of that or somehow keep you from ever getting involved. I'm sorry, Derek. I'm sorry that I didn't make a difference in your life. I'm sorry that I failed you.

As the tears gently filled and rolled down from Brett's eyes, he vowed that he would do everything in his power to make a difference in the lives of young men and women like Derek. He replaced his dreams of elegant corporate offices and large paychecks with new dreams and hopes. Perhaps, the day would come when he could sit on the shores of this lake and conjure up images of a smiling Derek that didn't fade away and end up in a brutal picture of a premature death.

━━┽┼┾━━

As a federal law enforcement agency under the U.S. Department of Justice, the Drug Enforcement Administration (DEA) is tasked with combating drug smuggling and use within the United States. After receiving a conditional offer of employment, Brett ended up at the DEA training academy in Quantico, Virginia. He was in a class of forty-two trainees immersed in a program that emphasizes leadership, ethics, law, and drug recognition. Brett undertook 122 hours of firearms training that included marksmanship, weapons safety, tactical shooting, and deadly force training. To graduate, Brett had to maintain a minimum academic average of eighty percent, pass the firearms-qualification test, demonstrate leadership and sound decision-making, and pass the rigorous physical-task tests. Upon graduation, recruits earn the title of DEA Special Agent.

Despite his past academic and athletic excellence, Brett did not take anything lightly. He worked hard and, through it all, Brett excelled. He was at the very top of his class in every aspect of his training. The day he graduated, one of his trainers, Special Agent Mike Wright, spoke to Brett about the DEA Rapid Response Teams.

"We've been watching you, Gatlin, and tracking your progress. We believe you have what it takes to be a part of the RRT. They have a stated mission to plan and conduct special enforcement operations. They're designed to work with foreign narcotics law enforcement units. The RRT was originally created to conduct missions in Afghanistan to disrupt the Afghan opium trade. But, now, they've evolved into what is a global arm for the U.S. Department of Justice and the DEA.

I'm not going to lie to you, son. You are clearly a talented guy, but there's no guarantee you'll make it. Selection for RRT is extremely difficult. You'll undergo rigorous daily physical events, including timed runs, timed rucksack marches, obstacle courses, land navigation, and a host of other events. They'll push you. They'll demand more from you than anyone ever has. The process is so incredibly rigorous that candidates don't even know what the standards are for each event. You don't even know what you're aiming at. You're only told whether you've passed or failed.

And more than half the RRT recruits will never make it. And then, if you are one of the ones who make it through, you'll undergo advanced training with emphasis in small unit tactics and close quarters battle."

Gatlin never hesitated.

"I want to go for it. I'm ready to give it all I've got,"

Wright smiled.

"I was hoping you'd say that, Gatlin. We need men like you. Just remember, though, like I said, the odds of making it are not favorable. And, a lot of good men… "

Gatlin put his hand up with his palm facing Wright. He glared at him. His body was tight and tense. He clenched his jaw. Then, as if he hit an inner switch, Brett relaxed a bit and smiled.

"I appreciate your fair warning, sir. I understand. I'll keep it in mind no matter what they put me through."

Brett reached out and shook Special Agent Mike Wright's hand. Wright reached over and patted Gatlin's back.

"I believe in you, Gatlin. I have a greater confidence in you than in any of the young agents I've ever had the pleasure of training."

Gatlin's determination to succeed combined with his athletic prowess and focused mindset caused him to continue to excel in everything that he did. At times he was pushed beyond what he might have thought his body could possibly endure. When thoughts of quitting attempted to invade his mind, Brett would picture his brother, Derek. But, the images he saw were not those of a cold lifeless body lying face-down in a Nashville area alley. Rather, he recalled times when he and his kid brother were tossing a football together or walking along the shores of Percy Priest Lake. He saw Derek before his body and mind were raped and ravaged by street drugs and the powerful addiction of heroin. And every image of Derek propelled Brett forward with a determination greater than any he had previously displayed as a successful athlete or law school student.

DEA Special Agent Brett Gatlin was on a path to save lives. Although he was warned, it was difficult to fathom that a day would arrive when the lives to be saved would include his own.

CHAPTER 5
SUBTERRANEO

Just as he excelled in the DEA training, Brett succeeded through every hurdle he faced as a RRT recruit. That was when Special Agent Matthew "Max" Bradford approached Gatlin. Max's legendary career covered some twenty-two years and landed him a job as a trainer specialist for the Rapid Response Teams. It was on a Friday evening. The orange glow of the setting sun cast its colors into the room when the two men met privately in Bradford's office.

At forty-three-years old, six feet four inches, and a solid body frame, Bradford was an imposing figure. His occasional engaging smile offset his rugged-looking face. Max was the son of an African-American father and Filipino mother. The man was regarded as one of the finest agents in the history of the DEA.

"You've got a drive in you, son, that I haven't encountered in many others over the years. I've checked into your background, Gatlin. It looks to me that right about now you could be making mega-bucks in some big-name law firm or a Fortune 500 corporation, rather than rolling around in the dirt for a lot less money. What's motivating you? What's driving you? Why are you here?"

Gatlin said nothing at first. He sat, made eye contact with Bradford, and took some time to appraise the man. Until now, his contact with Bradford had been limited to Max's role as his train-er. Now, sitting alone with the man, Gatlin made a judgment that Max Bradford was not questioning Brett's commitment nor trying to dissuade him from the career path he had chosen. Bradford had something else in mind. Until now, Brett had never spoken to anyone, outside his family, about the reasons why he decided to become a federal agent.

Gatlin leaned forward in his seat. He fixed his eyes on Bradford.

"I lost my kid brother to drugs and gang involvement. They found Derek with a bullet in the back of his skull, lying face down in an alley just outside of Nashville. Never did find his killer. I tried several times to reach out to Derek. Even so, some-times I wonder if I was so busy pursuing my own career, I didn't do enough. Maybe I could have done more to try to save him. Perhaps, I should have.

You asked what's motivating me. It's not all that complicated. I want to do something to help to prevent others from ending up like my brother. I want to help other families not have to go through the hurt and heartache that my family has endured."

Bradford nodded.

"I'm sorry for your loss, son. I've been around long enough to see far too many young men and women end up on a slab in a morgue while a limited few go on living in splendor from the money they make behind this whole dirty trade."

Bradford relaxed and leaned back in his chair. He lifted a pen from his desk and twirled it in his fingers.

"I asked you to meet with me today for a special reason, Gatlin. In fact, what I'm going to talk with you about is known to an ex-tremely limited number of people. That means it's highly-classi-fied. It's something you're free to accept or reject. But you're not free to talk about it to anyone other than me. Are we clear on that?"

"Crystal clear, sir," Gatlin said.

Bradford leaned forward. His eye contact with Gatlin was strong and sure. He tightened his jaw. He thrust his chest out. His shoulders were back. He sighed before continuing to speak and reveal just why he had called Brett Gatlin into his office.

"I've been asked to start up a new special ops team within the RRT. If you were to join this team, you would be one of six specifically chosen. Each of you will have a specialized role.

The team I am referring to will focus on bringing down a Mexican drug Cartel headed by a man named Bernardo Damario Garcia. You need to know, this is not just any drug cartel. Our intel informs us that Garcia and his folks are the largest cartel in Mexico, as well as throughout South America. By some estimates, sixty to sixty-five percent of all illegal drugs that are trafficked into the U.S. and Latin America come through Garcia. I'm sure I don't need to tell you we're talking about a hell of a lot of drugs and hell of a lot of money.

This will be the first time that a specialized team is entirely focused on one cartel. We will live each day eating, drinking, and breathing based upon what it will take to destroy Bernardo Damario Garcia's gang. Our goal will be to get inside where we can cut off the drug trades. This operation will require absolute precision in our operations and absolute secrecy. Any questions so far?"

"Yes, Sir," Gatlin said. "When you say, 'get inside,' am I understanding correctly that you're talking about clandestine, undercover work?"

"You're precisely correct," Bradford said. "So much so, the team will be named *Subterráneo*. From what I've read in your profile, you're fluent in Spanish, so you know the word means… "

"Underground," Gatlin interjected.

"You got it, son," Bradford said. "We're talking about a secret team consisting of six members, each specializing in specific functions, all working together with the common purpose of cutting off the head of this snake."

Bradford leaned back again. This time he replaced the pen with a paper weight that he lifted from the desk and spun lightly in his large hands. He maintained eye contact with Gatlin, but said nothing more.

Brett Gatlin breathed deeply. His wrinkled his brow and clasped his hands together.

"Special Agent Bradford, it's obvious to me that you're talking about a major operation here. So, why choose a newbie like me?"

Bradford smiled.

"You're smart, Gatlin. You're talented and you're completely unknown out in the field. You've got the smarts, athletic prowess, and an inner drive that all support the makings of an outstanding agent.

Watch your ego with what I'm about to tell you, son, but guys like you don't come along every day."

Bradford paused and placed his hands in a steeple on his desk. Then he sighed, placed both hands behind his head, and rocked slightly back and forth in his chair.

"I like you, Gatlin. Like what I see in you. You remind me a bit of myself when I was your age. Can't say for sure if that's something good or not."

Bradford paused and laughed at his own self-deprecating remark causing Gatlin to chuckle along with him.

"Anyway, I'll give you time to think about this. Give it some serious thought. Understand the full extent of what we are asking you to do and sacrifice. We anticipate this to be as much as a two-year commitment. You'll be hidden away with an entirely new identity. You'll have no contact with your family or friends. No chance right now to marry and raise a family. You better take a liking to Mexican food, beer, and tequila, 'cause you'll be spending pretty much all of your time south of the border."

Once again, Bradford paused, leaned forward, and commandeered Gatlin's full attention.

"From the look on your face, Agent Gatlin, methinks you're comprehending well. This is heavy-duty stuff, my man. This ain't no desk job or hobnobbing with politicians in the nation's capital. It's dark, dirty work that'll make you feel greasy and in need of a shower just about every hour of the day."

"And I would report directly to you?" Gatlin said.

"That's a roger. I'll be your go-to. You and your team members will be committed to each other and working together. But, most of the time, contact among our team will not be in person. It's imperative that no one out there ever knows about *Subterraneo*."

Gatlin was listening intently to every word that Bradford had to say. This sounded exactly like the kind of work he wanted to be involved in when he joined the DEA. If he wanted something calmer and safer to do in life, he could have opted for that better-paying position as a lawyer.

Bradford interrupted Gatlin's thoughts.

"Let me tell you what it's like when you spend time working with and befriending the very people you despise and want, more than anything, to bring down. Guess the best way to describe it is for you to imagine yourself hiding in the slimy dirt under a big rock with creepy, crawly things all around you."

Once again, Bradford paused and left Gatlin sitting in silence. Gatlin continued to shift in his seat. Then, Bradford leaned forward, shrugged his shoulders, and extended a hand, palm up, towards Gatlin.

"So, there you have it, Agent Gatlin. Any questions?"

"This assignment, am I to assume it will start immediately?"

"If you accept, you'll have two weeks leave prior to coming on board. You can visit your family, if you so desire. If you join *Subterraneo*, it's likely you'll not be having any contact with them for quite some time."

Bradford rose from his chair and turned away from Gatlin. He had his hands in his pockets and stared out the window of his office. He spoke without looking back, at Gatlin.

"Son, I want you to know that I will completely understand if you turn this down. Hear me clearly, you have every right to refuse and it will not reflect negatively upon your career with the Agency. In fact, most everybody will never know about it."

Bradford turned back and made eye contact again with Brett Gatlin.

"To be perfectly honest with you, I sure as hell wouldn't blame you one bit if you do say no."

CHAPTER 6

AN END AND BEGINNING

Fort Huachuca Army Base in Cochise County Arizona lies only about fifteen miles north of the Mexican border within the city of Sierra Vista. Its history traces back to 1877 when it was first constructed to keep a watchful eye on the Mexican border and defend US interests from attacks by the Chiricahua Apache Indians. From 1913 to 1933, the fort was home to the African-American Buffalo Soldiers of the 10th Cavalry Regiment. Over the years, Fort Huachuca remained active until becoming the present day United States Army Communications Command and a designated National Landmark.

As Special Agent Brett Gatlin entered the fort, he gave his name, stated that he was anxious to get in touch with Special Agent Max Bradford of the US Drug Enforcement Administration, and did not have any identification papers, other than an ID as Henry Childress. Following a long delay, they granted Gatlin access. A guard ushered him towards a conference room and told him to wait there.

Brett welcomed the sense of security and safety that permeated the room. It was non-existent whenever he was in Mexico. He was finally back in the United States. Bradford had chosen Fort

Huachuca as the place any team member should go to when in need. They were to contact Bradford from the fort. Max Bradford's hybrid special ops team, *Subterráneo*, was known only to a limited few individuals and it maintained its high-level of secrecy throughout these past years.

Framed photographs of the various troops that had been stationed at this fort hung on the conference room walls. Gatlin marveled at pictures of cavalry soldiers wearing the blue uniforms only seen today in western movies. The pictures of the legendary Buffalo Soldiers intrigued him. They were originally members of the U.S. Cavalry Regiment of the United States Army and earned a reputation for their fierce fighting and equestrian skills.

Gatlin experienced a blend of diametrically opposing emotions as he awaited a response from the military personnel that Max Bradford had been contacted. This would be their first conversation following the deaths of all other members of Bradford's special ops team. Just hearing Max's voice would be a source of comfort to Brett. At the same time, the stinging freshness of the debacle in the Sonoran Desert would be the main topic between the two men.

The first person to enter the room was a military police officer. The MP was immediately followed by another man bearing the rank of colonel. The man stood at five feet eleven, had short salt and pepper hair, green eyes, and a square jaw. The MP approached Gatlin first.

"May I see your identification documents, sir?"

The terseness in the man's voice surprised Gatlin.

"I already told them at the gate. I don't have any papers, other than my undercover ID as Henry Childress." Gatlin said. "I was forced to flee for my life from the city of Mexicali."

A second MP entered the room, responded to a head nod from the Colonel, and stood close to Gatlin.

"What's this all about?" Gatlin said. "I'm DEA Special Agent Brett Gatlin. Listen, just contact my superior, Special Agent Max Bradford, at our Arlington headquarters. He'll verify who I am."

The older gentleman stared at Gatlin. He spoke next.

"I'm Colonel Robert Shirley. I am the head of security operations here at Fort Huachuca. Why do you wish to speak to Special Agent Max Bradford?"

"I've already explained to the soldiers at the gate. The special ops team operated under the leadership of Max Bradford. Our team protocol has always been that, in the case of an emergency, we were to come to Huachuca and contact Special Agent Bradford from here. The nature and operations of our team are highly-classified. I'm not at liberty to say much more about that, Colonel. I suggest that you make the contact and permit my Agency supervisor to handle things."

Just then, another man entered the room. The man held the rank of lieutenant. His name plate identified him as Lieutenant James Gilliam.

"Okay, please remain seated," the Colonel said to Gatlin. "Let's see if we can get things sorted out here."

The Colonel and Lieutenant left the room together. Then, Colonel Shirley returned.

"Lieutenant Gilliam will make the first contact to the DEA Headquarters," Colonel Shirley said. "Meanwhile, what can you tell me about your statement that your team members and American and Mexican agents having been killed?"

"We were conducting a major drug deal. I was under cover with my team members. We were in the Sonoran Desert."

Gatlin's eyes drifted off to another time and place. His face was twisted. His breathing was more rapid.

"There was no warning. I watched as all my team members were killed and vehicles filled with American federal agents and Mexican *Policia Federal* officers exploded, killing everyone inside."

Lieutenant Gilliam reentered the room and handed some papers to the Colonel. Shirley quickly read through them and handed them back to the lieutenant. The Colonel clasped his hands loosely behind his back and gazed downward, before lifting his head again and staring at Gatlin. He was hesitant before speaking and appeared to be weighing his words.

"Special Agent Max Bradford is dead. Report we received is that the man suffered a heart attack right there in his office," Colonel Shirley said. "By the time the medical personnel arrived, Agent Bradford was unable to be revived. He was pronounced dead on the scene."

Brett jumped up from his seat. His face was pale. His hands were trembling. His eyes were downcast.

"W-what? Dead? Max Bradford is dead? That can't be right. Max can't be dead."

Brett sat down again and slumped in his chair. He did not even look at any of the others in the room. Dead? Bradford was the most alive guy Gatlin had ever known. The man appeared to be indestructible, someone who would live forever.

Brett lifted his head and stared into the eyes of Colonel Shirley. He continued to shake his head.

"Dead? Are you sure, Colonel? You're sure that we're talking about DEA Special Agent Max Bradford?"

Shirley nodded.

"That is the report we have received."

Gatlin turned away from Colonel Shirley and covered his mouth to help control his rapid breathing.

"Then, they're all dead," Gatlin said. "The entire team is gone, except for me. This can't possibly be happening. This can't be true."

"Colonel Shirley, I am asking you to personally call DEA headquarters. Find out who Max Bradford was reporting to regarding a special team that Bradford headed. That man should be able to identify me and help bring me in. He can verify that I have been working undercover. I need your help, sir."

Once again, Colonel Shirley turned towards Lieutenant Gilliam. The Lieutenant awaited orders from the Colonel. Shirley turned back towards Gatlin, nodded, then spoke again.

"Okay, Gatlin. We'll do what you ask. In the interim, I need you to remain here and remain calm. I will have some food and drink sent in for you. You will be kept under guard until this matter regarding your status is resolved."

Gatlin remained seated as Colonel Shirley, Lieutenant Gilliam, and the two guards left the room. Brett knew that one of the guards would remain stationed outside the door. He didn't care. Based upon what he had just learned, Brett was the sole survivor of the specialized *Subterraneo* team. The roll call of the dead ran through Gatlin's mind. He had already grieved over each of the *Subterraneo* team members. Now, there was Max Bradford, the legendary DEA Special Agent who created and directed this unique team. Gatlin's mind raced back to the day when he sat with Bradford and first learned about the special team that was about to be formed.

I honestly believe I would have followed you to battle in hell itself, Max Bradford. I knew from the very first time I met you and each time I had any contact with you afterwards, that I was in the presence of a legend. Funny, I remember when you told me that guys like me don't come along every day. But, you got it wrong, Agent Bradford. Guys like you are the special ones. Guys like you only come around once in forever.

⊨+ +⊨

Special Agent William Falwell was in his office at the DEA headquarters across from the Pentagon in Arlington, Virginia, when he took the call from Colonel Robert Shirley of Fort Huachuca.

"Special Agent Falwell, am I correct that you are the individual that the late Special Agent Max Bradford reported to?"

"Yes, Colonel," Falwell said. "That's correct."

"Well, please accept my condolences regarding one of your agents."

"Thank you, Colonel. Max Bradford was an outstanding man and agent. He will be sorely missed."

"Then, you, sir, would have knowledge of a special team that Bradford reportedly formed and oversaw? We've got a man here named Childress. He claims to be DEA Special Agent Brett Gatlin. He says he was undercover as a member of Bradford's team. He claims all the team members were killed during a major drug deal. He came to Fort Huachuca to contact Agent Bradford."

Shirley could not see the curled lip nor the shaking head as Falwell never hesitated in his response. He heard the heavy breathing coming from Falwell and knew that the man was not pleased with all that he was hearing. After a slight pause, William Falwell spoke again.

"Colonel, forgive my brusqueness. Let me say that Max Bradford was much too great a man to be used by someone like Gatlin. In fact, Gatlin doesn't deserve to even be mentioned in the same sentence as Max. I can assure you, sir, that Max Bradford was not a traitor, a coward, nor someone who chose to betray his pledge of loyalty and service to his country and the Agency to which he had sworn his allegiance."

"So, you're telling me," Colonel Shirley said, "that Brett Gatlin's statements about working undercover on a team established by Bradford are all falsehoods."

"Falsehoods is too soft a description. They're blatant lies coming from a man who went off the grid years ago. Good and patriotic men are dead because of that traitor. I'll do everything in my power to make certain that a man like Brett Gatlin pays for what he's done."

"I appreciate your candor, Agent Falwell. Based upon the information you have provided, we will hold this man until you can get someone down here to take him into full custody."

"Thank you, Colonel Shirley. Your assistance is greatly appreciated, sir. I will dispatch a team of agents to you the moment I get off this phone."

Falwell sighed. His speech was slow, his voice was tight.

"Brett Gatlin is a highly-trained agent who should not be taken lightly. The man is extremely dangerous. Gatlin disappeared years ago. We suspect that he likely has also become a user, dependent upon the very drugs he pledged to fight against. Unfortunately, Colonel, this certainly would not be the first time a trained agent developed an addiction and became one with the people he was supposed to help destroy. The cartel that Gatlin joined has recently been destroyed by a rival gang. I suspect that Gatlin had to flee in order to save his own life."

Falwell paused. When he spoke again, his message was delivered in a louder voice with an intonation that revealed his anger and disdain.

"Colonel Shirley, Special Agent Max Bradford was fully committed to his role as a trainer for our Rapid Response Team recruits— yet another job at which he excelled. There never was a special ops team formed by nor overseen by Special Agent Bradford."

CHAPTER 7
MAYBE NEVER

William Falwell's hands shook as he punched in the phone number and waited for the call to go through. It was a number that Falwell never called and would only do so in the case of a dire emergency.

The man answered after the fifth ring.

"Yes?"

"Bill Falwell here. I'm calling to inform you that we've got the last of them. Gatlin just showed up at Huachuca."

Falwell waited in the silence that followed. He had delivered the message. It was not his place to say more.

"Well, William, I'm sure that I don't have to tell you what needs to be done."

"No, sir," Falwell said. "I'm on it now. We'll get him out of there. Then, we'll make sure he's the last one to be eliminated. You can be sure that I will personally... "

Falwell heard the click indicating that the person he called had disconnected.

The DEA office in Tucson, Arizona is located slightly more than an hour from Fort Huachuca by way of I-10 East and Arizona Highway 90 South. But, William Falwell did not dispatch any agents from that office to take custody of Gatlin. Two agents from the Arlington, Virginia Headquarters, Michael Palmer and Patrick Nunez, were on their way. They would not even stop at the Tucson DEA office. They would drive to the Fort directly from the Tucson International Airport.

Colonel Shirley was a bit surprised when he learned that the two DEA agents would bypass their agency's office in Tucson and arrive and leave on a commercial flight without reliance on any government channels. Even so, it mattered little to the Colonel. He never had much confidence in federal agencies, anyway. He would uphold his responsibility by holding Brett Gatlin until these men arrived at the Fort to take him away.

Gatlin's efforts to receive some level of communication from Colonel Shirley or any of the Army MPs were unsuccessful. He tried one more time during his last encounter with Colonel Robert Shirley. The Colonel was in the room, along with one of the MP soldiers.

"Colonel, what's going on here? Did you contact Agent Bradford's superior? Did he confirm what I told you?"

Shirley did not respond immediately. As a man in his eighteenth year of military service to his country, Shirley had no regard for someone who had betrayed his oath of service to his country and consorted with the enemy. He was a patriot and regarded someone who would betray his or her country as the lowest of the low. Shirley was familiar with the sacrifices involved in serving in the military or even as a government field agent. If he had his way, anyone betraying their country would be summarily executed. He regretted we no longer had public hangings. Nevertheless, Brett Gatlin was not under his chain of command and not someone for whom he would be responsible to discipline.

"Yes, Gatlin, I spoke with Special Agent William Falwell. The DEA is sending two agents here to Huachuca to bring you back to DEA Headquarters. You can take your case up with them. That's all I'm at liberty to tell you."

Gatlin bolted from his seat. The moment he did, the MP moved between Brett and the Colonel, holding a steel baton upraised.

"Please be seated," Colonel Shirley said. "I'm asking you not to force our hand here, Gatlin. We are complying with the request of the DEA, your agency of authority. As I said, you take up any issues you have with them. I suggest that you sit down, remain calm, and not cause any problems that both you and I may regret."

Colonel Shirley turned and walked out of the room. The MP followed.

Gatlin sat down, put his head in his hands, and took some slow deep breaths.

Why didn't the Colonel get confirmation? The least he should have been told was that I have been undercover on a covert mission, even if this Falwell was not free to provide specifics. Bradford made it clear that the existence of Subterraneo and our mission would be known to a limited few. But, surely his superior would know about it. And I, at the very least, would be identified as active and on-duty. Even if the details of my cover identity and our mission were held as highly-confidential, there's no way anyone at the DEA would think I was AWOL, consorting with the enemy, or whatever else they may be thinking.

⊷✛⊶

DEA Agents Michael Palmer and Patrick Nunez were onboard their first flight. After driving to D.C. and boarding at 5:30 a.m., the two agents had a stop in Dallas and an hour and thirteen-minute layover before their second flight directly to the airport in Tucson, Arizona.

"I still can't figure out what in the hell this is all about," Nunez said. "Why send us all the way to pick up a guy when the Army could fly Gatlin directly out of a fort and have us pick the dude up on this end? Then, they're sending us to Tucson, where we rent a car and drive over an hour to the Sierra Vista area where Fort Huachuca is located. Hell, they've got agents right there in Tucson. Least you'd think they'd do is have someone from that office go and get this guy and bring him to Tucson to hand over to us. I mean this whole thing makes no sense at all."

"Ah, Noonie," Michael Palmer said, using a nickname many of the agents had for Nunez. "You gripe and whine like an old lady. Chill, buddy. You know people in authority in these government jobs ain't necessarily known to be the sharpest tacks on the workbench, eh? Anyway, what's the big deal? We ain't got no other duties than to take a nice trip out west. Then, we hop into a current-year air-conditioned car, drive from Tucson, maybe stop at a nice Mexican restaurant on the way, eh?

This is no big deal, man. All in a day's work, eh? We're on the clock, everything is paid for, the extra hours we put in are accounted for in comp time. Piece of cake, man."

"Yeah, but why are they circumventing the Tucson office? Doesn't that seem strange to you?" Nunez said.

"Everything is strange to you, Patty-my-boy. You see a conspiracy in everything, eh? You probably one of those guys who question whether we actually landed on the moon or maybe believe that aliens from Mars killed President Kennedy, eh?"

Michael Palmer laughed aloud as he punched Nunez lightly on the arm.

"Forget the conspiracies, Noonie. Just sit back and enjoy the trip, man. And, by the way, did you get a look at that brunette flight attendant we got?"

⇒∘⇐

The longer Brett Gatlin sat alone in a locked room, the more time he had to reflect on all that had occurred. Gatlin had a difficult time believing that he was the sole survivor of *Subterraneo*. For four years, the team operated with the precision of a highly-trained surgeon. They worked in situations where there was no room for error. And no matter what the circumstances were, there were no mistakes. They were that good!

The original plan was to bring down Garcia's cartel within two years. Bradford's plan included engaging in smaller deals to establish the team in their various roles, until the day would come when they would arrange to destroy Garcia's gang.

"We're never gonna be able to bring enough manpower into Mexico to destroy Garcia and his operations," Bradford said. "So, what I gotta do is find a way for us to coordinate with the *Policia Federal.*" The Federal Police is a Mexican police force under the authority of the Secretariat of the Interior. They were formed by the merger of four other federal organizations in 1998 and 1999 to better coordinate the fight against the growing threat of drug cartels. Bradford knew that his operation would require finding the right people in America and Mexico who could be trusted to protect the secrecy of these covert actions and work together in the final thrust to bring down Garcia's cartel.

"And what we gotta do," Bradford said, "is, in leading up to the day when we make our big move, we peck away a little at a time. We establish trust with Garcia and his thugs. We work patiently until the day we set up something so big, a deal involving so much, that if Garcia fails, it'll wipe him out. We wipe out a major portion of his supplies, we get some big buyers burned, and, believe me, Garcia will be cooked."

Bradford's plan was solid, but he and the team soon found that Garcia was slick and evasive. If they pushed too hard, too soon, they might lose any opportunity to destroy his cartel. They had surpassed the initial two-year mark and, in fact, doubled it. But, over these past four years, every member of *Subterraneo* held fast.

Now, after more than four years of being hidden away in a world he despised and in a life with absolutely no contact with his family or his former life, Gatlin found himself on the losing end of everything he and his teammates had fought for.

Any info Gatlin received concerning his family came from Bradford and whatever the Special Agent could derive. Attempts by Brett's sister, Lucy, to reach her brother through the DEA eventually landed on Bradford's desk. That was when he learned and passed on to Gatlin that his father had died. By the time Brett learned of this, his father's funeral had been held and the man had been buried. As a result, Brett's follow up with Lucy and his Mom was done indirectly through the DEA.

After four years of no direct contact, Gatlin's sister and mother assumed that Brett was still alive somewhere on the planet, since regular significant portions of his DEA paycheck were deposited in an account to which Lucy and his Mom had access. Brett had arranged for this before he ever went underground. But, beyond that, there had been no contact at all with Brett since the day he left to begin his special training as a member of Bradford's special ops team.

⊨‖ ‖⊨

Palmer and Nunez were seated together at the Railhead BBQ in the DFW airport, having a bite before they boarded their next flight.

"Hey, Noonie, you ever meet this Gatlin guy?" Palmer said.

Nunez finished his bite of a pulled pork sandwich and followed it with a gulp of Diet Coke.

"Nah," he said, as he shook his head and prepared to take another bite of his sandwich. "Never met the guy. They told us he's RRT trained, so, once they get into that, we're not likely to have much contact with them."

Palmer nodded. "Yeah, that's true. That RRT training is supposed to be murder, eh?" Palmer said. "They say it'll bring you as close to death as possible without actually killing you."

Once again, Nunez finished chewing and drank some Diet Coke before responding.

"I knew it wasn't for me," Nunez said. "When I signed up, I agreed to be a DEA agent, not put myself in position for an early death."

Nunez chuckled and Palmer laughed along with him.

"Man, you got that right, Noonie. I like carrying the shield. But, like you, I'm not interested in dying before I start collecting my government pension."

CHAPTER 8

WHAT'S NEXT

The morning sun had risen. Everywhere the distinguished American glanced, he saw people lying throughout Caesar Hidalgo Monterro's estate. The American was seated with Monterro finishing a late breakfast before his flight back home. He dabbed his face with his napkin, placed it down on the table, took his last sip of coffee, and prepared to leave the estate.

"Well, Señor Monterro, I must say that you were a most gracious host last night. It appears as if the attendees at your private party certainly had more than enough to drink. You've got people who never made it home. They're strewn all over this place."

Monterro laughed as he nodded his head.

"Yes, my friend, I am quite sure that they will eventually wake up with heads that feel as if they have been run over by a large truck. Ah, but they are my soldiers, deserving of some additional rewards. These are the ones who work for me, fight for me, serve my every need. It is most important that I let them know that I appreciate their loyal service, yes?"

The American frowned and stared back at Monterro.

"It is also most important, Señor, that you keep me and the people I work with happy and secure at all times."

Monterro laughed aloud, nodded his head, and shrugged his shoulders.

"But, of course, mi amigo. Rest assured that we will do so. We are now *compañeros de armas*, comrades in arms, yes? And you are most welcome here at any time, my friend.

Meanwhile, my people are ready to take you to the airport. I wish for you safe travels."

As Monterro watched the American walk away, he stared at the man and considered how nice it will be one day when he has the pleasure of killing him.

As Palmer and Nunez drew nearer to Fort Huachuca, they were prepared to take the man they were sent for into custody and bring him back to the DEA Headquarters in Virginia. Palmer was driving. Nunez relied upon the GPS in his phone to direct them towards the fort.

"With all the signs we're gonna keep seeing directing us to the fort," Palmer said, "we don't really have all that much need for your GPS, eh?" Then, he chuckled.

"Maybe so," Nunez responded, "but we must never forget that we are federal agents. That means we're supposed to be techie."

The two men laughed.

"Reckon the powers-that-be back home are anxious to get their hands on Gatlin," Palmer said. "From everything I've heard, Max Bradford was one very popular guy. They're not keen on Gatlin trying to justify his disappearance by using Bradford as his mentor and alibi for years of being AWOL."

"Got to hand it to him, though," Nunez said. "If you gonna link your disappearance on another agent, makes sense to pick a dead one, you know?"

"This whole thing stinks, man. Makes me angry. It's guys like Gatlin that give a black eye to all of us," Palmer said. "It ain't fair, but that's the way it works."

Nunez continued to nod his head.

"Yes, I'm afraid so. And what makes it even worse is that the guy had RRT training. Those guys, they are supposed to be among our best, you know?"

"Well, sounds like Gatlin is a man who thinks only of himself and not others," Palmer said. "I'm glad that we're the ones gonna bring this low-life in where he can answer for what he's done. You know, that ain't a bad thing to have on our record."

"Ah, it ain't about looking good on our record," Nunez said. "Getting this dude to pay for what he's done will give some closure for a whole lot of people. And maybe it'll help get things started in restoring public confidence in our agency."

Gatlin heard the scurrying going on outside the conference room door and correctly assumed that the agents were here to take him away. A short while earlier, the MPs had come into the room and fettered Gatlin with cuffs on his hands in front of his body and leg irons attached to his ankles. He would be capable of walking slowly.

"Agent Gatlin," Colonel Shirley said, "Agents Palmer and Nunez are here to escort you back to Virginia."

Gatlin chose not to look at the men.

Palmer moved forward first, checked the cuffs and leg irons, and spoke to Brett Gatlin.

"Our job is to take you back to DEA Headquarters. You don't give us no trouble, our trip back shouldn't be all that complicated, eh? Remember, we ain't the ones you answer to, Gatlin. We just the delivery boys."

"That's right," Nunez said. "We just doing our job, is all. You cooperate with us, we do our best to make this trip back as comfortable for you as possible, all things considered."

Gatlin said nothing. He did not make eye contact with either of the two agents.

Nunez and Gatlin were in the back seat. Palmer drove the car. No one spoke at all. Nunez was careful to keep an eye on Gatlin.

It was shortly before they merged onto I-10 from AZ-90 that everything changed. Palmer was traveling in the right lane. The traffic was light. A deep ocean blue metallic current year Chevy Silverado truck with a driver and passenger sped up from behind them. The truck remained in the right lane and began to tailgate.

"What the heck is wrong with this cowboy?" Palmer said, as he peered in his rearview mirror. "If he wants to go faster, why doesn't he just get in the left lane, eh?"

Nunez turned around. The truck was practically touching their rear bumper.

"Maybe you should just get in the left lane, Mike, and let these guys go."

Palmer shook his head.

"The hell I will. The left lane is for faster traffic or somebody that wants to pass. I ain't moving for these bozos."

Palmer opened his window and signaled for the truck to pass, but it remained inches behind his vehicle. Palmer slowed down.

"You taunt these dudes, you only gonna make matters worse," Nunez said. "Why not just pull into the left lane, man?"

Palmer's grip on the steering wheel was so tight, Nunez could see the white knuckles. He shook his head as he glared into the rearview mirror.

"I ain't going nowhere. I'm within my rights. I'm already traveling over the speed limit. I ain't gonna be intimidated by a couple of yokels."

The truck that was traveling behind them swerved sharply into the left lane, pulled alongside the vehicle carrying Gatlin and the two agents, and stayed in place with them.

"That's right," Palmer said. "If they wanna go faster, get in the left lane and do it, eh?"

Just then, Gatlin shouted and pushed his body against Nunez forcing the agent's body downward. Palmer swerved as the first bullet shattered the rear window, but missed Nunez and Gatlin. A few more shots struck the car's chassis. Palmer tried to slow down and somehow get away from the truck. Shots fired struck both tires on the driver's side. Palmer had the steering wheel gripped tightly in an effort to control the car. Another shot shattered the driver's window, grazed Palmer's forehead and caused him to lose total control of the vehicle. The car swerved off the road onto the dry grass that ran alongside. The car bounced and jerked on the uneven terrain. The bodies of the three passengers were slammed back and forth. Then, the car flipped over and landed with a loud crash that shattered all the remaining windows and crunched in the roof and side doors. The vehicle landed upside down in a ditch.

As the truck sped away, Gatlin was the only passenger awake. Nunez and Palmer were both either dead or unconscious. As Gatlin attempted to clear his head, he heard a pop and loud whoosh that reminded him of times when he turned the propane tank on and lit the barbecue grill in his parents' backyard. He heard a crackling sound that caused his body to shudder. As best he could tell, the fire was somewhere at the front of the vehicle.

My God, fire! The terrain here is so dry, soon everything around us will be burning. We're inside a freakin' time bomb. When those flames spread to the rear gas tank, this thing is going to explode.

Gatlin was relieved when he placed a finger on Nunez' neck and detected a pulse. But, he knew that time was of the essence. He had to get himself, Nunez, and Parker out of this vehicle. Gatlin quickly searched the man's pockets and found keys to unlock his cuffs and leg chains. Once he was free, his first impulse was to flee. If he could exit the vehicle before others were on the scene, he might be able to tuck himself away in a nearby stand of trees and shrubbery. He heard a slight groan from Nunez and made his move. The doors would not open. Gatlin grabbed the agent with both hands and began to drag him out of one of the shattered rear windows. Cars from both directions were stopping. In this age of cell phones, Gatlin was sure that someone would have already called 9-1-1 for emergency assistance.

Gatlin's right ankle and left shoulder ached as he began to move. He exited first, then pulled Nunez through the window and placed him further away on the grass. Brett heard others approaching the scene.

A short, baldheaded man spotted Gatlin and screamed out to him.

"Get away from there now, son. That vehicle is about to blow. Get out. Get away now."

No one drew nearer to the burning vehicle. Gatlin's body ached. His head was spinning, he was nauseous, and his legs wobbled like jelly. He bent his body over in a desperate effort to improve his breathing.

"Look out," another bystander screamed. "Move. Get away from that car."

But, Brett made no effort to get away. Rather, he moved over towards the driver door and began to pull on the handle. By now, the handle was so hot, Brett recoiled from the scalding heat on the palms of his hands. At first, the door did not budge. Then, Brett lifted one leg and braced it just below the top of the door in the area where the door opened. He pulled and tugged on the handle again with both hands. Pain seared through his body and he screamed aloud as he fell backwards to the ground. He looked up to see that the door had opened. He reached in towards Palmer's body and was frantically trying to undo the man's seatbelt. A younger man was now standing with Gatlin. He pulled a jackknife from his pocket and slashed at the belt until he cut through and freed Palmer from his restraints.

"Here, let me help get him," the young man said, as he and Gatlin pulled Palmer from the burning vehicle and moved him away. Then, Brett Gatlin stepped back and fell to his knees. Within minutes, the vehicle was transformed into a large hot orange and yellow ball of fire with flames and columns of black smoke lifting up into the sky.

Gatlin barely remembered seeing that before he passed out into unconsciousness on the nearby grass.

CHAPTER 9

WHO'S THE HERO?

A deep ocean blue metallic current year Chevy Silverado truck had exited ahead and made a U-turn back towards where a vehicle with blown tires had crashed and been upended off the road. But, now, AZ-90, which shortly before had sparse traffic, looked like a used car lot for vehicles traveling in either direction.

"Dang," the passenger said. "They got several ambulances, fire-trucks, and troopers swarming all over the place. It ain't looking good, Charlie. Ain't looking good at all."

Charlie Hough grimaced. He kept his focus on the road again, as demanded by the stop-and-go traffic they were immersed in. His mind was racing as he considered what their options were. Leaving these men alive, especially Brett Gatlin, was not something they could permit.

"Okay, okay, Luke, just stay calm. From the looks of things, there ain't a thing we can do about it right now. So, you and me, we got to come up with a solid Plan B. And for all we know, they might all end up dead or be dead anyway. We just gotta keep our heads clear and be ready for what else we might need to do."

Luke Munson was rocking in place in his seat, shaking his head, muttering, and blowing out a series of short breaths.

"You know there ain't no room for failure for me and you, Charlie. They ain't never gonna accept nothing short of Gatlin on a slab. And those other two guys might be able to identify us, Charlie. If those guys live, especially that Gatlin, you and me gonna... "

"Stop, Luke, just stop it, man. Take a deep breath and chill, will you? We ain't finished yet. All we gotta do is find out where they taking these dudes and we'll be there. If any of 'em survived, we gonna take care of that and end this deal once and for all. Like I said, we ain't finished yet. We ain't finished by a long shot."

Charlie reached over and squeezed Luke's arm.

"Listen to me, Luke. Listen to me. I need you to stay calm so's we can finish this job. You hear?"

The ambulances quickly entered onto I-10 and made the decision that they could cover the forty-minute or so trek to Carondelet St. Joseph Hospital in Tucson in about half that time. With each of their patients already having been administered IVs and stabilized, the EMTs wanted to get these men to a full-fledged hospital, rather than a medical center along the way. State Trooper Carlos Aguilar, after discovering that at least two of the injured men were DEA federal agents, was following the ambulance to the hospital. Meanwhile, Aguilar had contacted the DEA office in Tucson informing them that two of their agents were being rushed to the Tucson hospital following a major vehicle accident. Aguilar and the other emergency personnel were not yet aware that the auto wreck was the result of attempted murder and gunfire.

Aguilar was at the hospital, currently staying out of the way of the medical staff as they attended to the three newly-arrived patients. He would wait before continuing his investigation into the accident. When one of the nurses learned that the trooper was there because the injured men were federal agents and that other agents were on their way, she arranged for Carlos to stay in a small private room just off the ER. Within a short period of time, two DEA Special Agents, Martin Gaela and Rick Watkins, were ushered into the room with Aguilar.

"The lead doctor is a woman named Shamorie," Aguilar said after the agents introduced themselves. "She assured me that we would receive an update on the condition of the three patients as soon as they complete their preliminary diagnoses."

"Thanks," Gaela said. "Do we know what caused the accident?"

"Not yet. When I left, we still had firefighters putting out the flames. With the terrain so dry, the fire was spreading throughout the area. Once the passengers were all rescued, there was still a major job to be done to get things under control."

Aguilar then provided the agents with a report on what he did know and had seen at the accident site.

Just then, an orderly entered the room.

"Trooper Carlos Aguilar?"

"Yes, I'm Aguilar."

"We have a man here who arrived shortly after you and received some first aid treatment for minor burns and an inhalant to help with his breathing. The man was at the accident scene that involved the federal agents. Doctor Shamorie said that you left word that you would like to speak to this man before he left the hospital."

"Yes, I did leave those instructions."

Aguilar turned to the two agents.

"I was told at the scene that a young man who helped free one of the passengers from the burning vehicle needed some medical care and would also be taken here."

The trooper turned back to the orderly.

"Please send him in," Aguilar said.

Aguilar estimated Walter Vaughn to be in his early-twenties. He stood at six feet two, was slightly built, had a scraggly beard and moustache, wore his hair in a ponytail, and had tattoo sleeves on both arms. When he arrived, he had bandages on both hands.

Aguilar introduced himself and the two DEA agents that were with him.

"How're you doing, son?" Aguilar asked.

"Aw, no big deal. Just a few minor burns. I may have to miss a gig or two, but, otherwise, I'll be okay."

The trooper nodded.

"What is your name, son?"

"My name is Walter Vaughn, but pretty much everyone calls me 'Woody.' "

"Woody?"

"Yeah," Vaughn said. "It's kinda like a bad joke. When I was fourteen I drank some wood alcohol thinking it'd give me a buzz. Ya know? Anyway, I ended up at the emergency room getting my stomach pumped."

Walter shrugged and smiled.

"Since then, my friends all started callin' me 'Woody'."

Aguilar quickly moved on from that point.

"You mentioned missing some gigs," Marty Gaela said. "I take it you're in a band?"

"Yessir," the young man said. "Just a local group. We call ourselves 'Illegal Weed.' I play lead guitar. In fact, two of my buddies in the band are headed here now to help me…" Woody raised both bandaged hands and smiled, "get home."

"Well, you take good care of those hands," Agent Gaela said.

"Yes sir, will do."

"Okay if we ask you a few questions?" Trooper Aguilar said.

"Sure," Vaughn responded. "Glad to help if I can."

"Did you by any chance see the accident occur?" Aguilar asked.

"No, sir. By the time I got there, the car was already upside down in a ditch and I could see flames and smoke. People were standing around shouting and stuff."

"I understand that you pulled one of the men from the burning vehicle just before the vehicle exploded," Aguilar said. "That was very brave of you. You likely saved that man's life."

Vaughn didn't acknowledge the trooper's praise.

"Is everybody that was in that car gonna live?"

"Well, son, we don't know," Aguilar said. "We're waiting for the doctors to give us an update. What we do know is that all three men were alive when they arrived here."

"And," Agent Gaela said, "from what Trooper Aguilar has told us, you are responsible for initially saving the lives of at least two of the men."

Walter Vaughn shrugged.

"Well, I ain't the real hero here. When I got there, one of the men from in that car had already pulled one man out. Then, when people all around was screaming at him to get away, he did the opposite. He went over to the driver's door, towards the fire, to save the man still in there.

I seen the guy struggling to get the car door open and nobody else would go closer to the car. The guy was already a mess. Had blood running down his face from a gash on his head and seemed like he was in a lot of pain. Like I said, nobody else did nothing. I ain't no hero or nothing, but I couldn't just stand by and watch. I'll tell ya, if that man hadn't been there trying to save the driver from being burned to death or blown up, well, I don't know. Maybe I wouldn't have done nothing. But, watching that man, injured as he was doing whatever he could to get that door open, affected me. If there's a real hero, it's that dude. All's I did was help him. Let me tell ya, that dude is the bravest man I ever seen in my life."

⇒+ +⇒

Just after Walter Vaughn left the room, Special Agent Gaela took the call from the DEA Tucson office as State Trooper Aguilar and Special Agent Rick Watkins chatted quietly. When he disconnected from the call, Gaela got the attention of the trooper and his colleague.

"Well," Gaela said, "I'm not sure what to make of this."

He turned towards Watkins.

"That was Martha following up on our request for additional info on the agents involved in that accident."

Gaela turned towards Aguilar.

"Martha's another one of our DEA Agents stationed here in Tucson."

Gaela turned towards both men interchangeably with what he had to say next.

"The two agents, Palmer and Nunez, come from our headquarters in Arlington. Seems our hero is a man named Brett Gatlin. He's a trained DEA agent who disappeared years ago and is suspected of having linked up with a notorious drug cartel. Palmer and Nunez were coming from Fort Huachuca where they picked up Gatlin and were escorting him back to the DEA Headquarters in Virginia."

"Whoa," Watkins said, "didn't see that coming."

"You know what that means. Our job just made a radical switch here," Gaela said, "We just increased our job from checking in on injured agents to also keeping an eye on a prisoner until he is back safely in Virginia."

⇒+ +⇒

What happens when a bus filled with middle school students and teacher-chaperones is involved in a wreck that sent everyone and everything within the bus thrown all over? The nearest hospital ER becomes jam-packed with young people, teachers, and some school administrators and parents.

The emergency room at Tucson's Carondolet St. Joseph Hospital was buzzing. The phrase "standing-room-only" was inadequate.

For most people, the sight of an ER that chaotic and filled would be, at the very least, disconcerting. For two men who parked their blue Chevy Silverado in the lot and entered with a desire to remain inconspicuous, the overcrowded room was a welcome sight.

Charlie Hough and Luke Munson were the only two people in that room who were not interested in receiving assurance that the people they came to see were not seriously injured nor dealing with something life-threatening.

Each man carried a knife tucked away.

"Hey, Charlie, we got us a problem. We don't really know what these guys look like," Luke whispered to Charlie.

"Check your phone, Lukester. I just sent you pics of the guys we're looking for that I pulled from the Internet. Listen. Like I been telling you, man, just stay calm. I'll find a nurse or someone who can direct us to 'our dear friends' who came in from a serious wreck on AZ-90 where their car caught on fire." Charlie chuckled. "Odds are no one else came in here under similar circumstances. Just remember, Luke. We move quietly, quickly, then get out of here."

CHAPTER 10

MISSION ACCOMPLISHED

DEA Special Agent Patrick Nunez was the father of two little girls. Angela was five and Priscilla was three. His wife, Marissa, had not yet been notified that her husband had been in an auto accident. At the time, Marissa was scurrying about preparing for Angela's sixth birthday party to be held the following day.

"Is Daddy gonna be at my party?" Angela asked her mother, as Marissa walked out of the grocery store with the girls in tow.

"Oh, my goodness, of course. Your daddy would never miss something so important."

Angela's face beamed with a smile that only a young daughter could bear when thinking of her daddy. "Oh, good," Angela said, as she clapped her hands. "Then, it will be perfect."

As she drove back home with her little girls, Marissa could not help but smile as she reflected upon her marriage. Patrick's job as a DEA agent was the only drawback she had when they started dating. The demands of his job and the potential danger concerned Marissa.

"Ah, not to worry, Marissa," Patrick had said. "I would never let a job, any job, take away from the time I spend with my wife and the children we will have. I love my job, but, remember, baby, it's still just a job. It's not my life, you know? And, to be honest, I don't expect to ever be put in dangerous situations very often, if at all."

Marissa did not particularly like when Patrick left to go to Arizona and escort a suspected criminal back to Virginia.

"No problem, my sweet," Patrick said. "It's a routine matter. Mike will be with me. Me and him go and get the guy. Then, we fly back with him and drop him off at headquarters. No big deal, my love. All in a day's work."

Marissa smiled at the thought that Patrick would now be on his way back home. She never called him when he was on-duty. He'd check in with her. He always did. And Patrick had already scheduled the next two days off from work.

"The first day will be for our little Angela," Patrick said. "The second day is for you and me."

On that second day, the girls would stay with Marissa's mother. Patrick and Marissa had a day of massages, pedicures, lunch at their favorite Italian restaurant, and some time shopping in the mall.

Yes, life was good.

Michael Palmer and his wife, Constance, divorced slightly less than two years ago. But, they maintained a friendly relationship and were both involved in the lives of their three children. With two children already in high school and a third finishing up middle school, there was a considerable demand on the schedules of their parents.

"Don't these kids ever stay home?" Michael said, when he last arrived at the house in time to take Richard to his baseball practice. Constance was taking Marjorie to her dance lessons and their youngest, Kevin, to taekwondo.

"Don't ask me," Constance said. "Everything's such a blur, I have no idea."

Mike and Constance had already dated each other twice over the past month and had gone to three counseling sessions over the past several months. They were considering the possibility of getting back together again. It was something they both wanted to do.

⟞⟝⟝

State Trooper Carlos Aguilar and DEA Special Agents, Martin Gaela and Rick Watkins waited patiently for a medical update on the three men. They were thankful that they had been given a private room to stay in while they waited.

When the doctor entered the room, the three men turned their attention to her.

"Gentlemen, I am Doctor Shamorie. Thank you for your patience. I'm sure you are aware that we are having quite the day."

"How are things with the youngsters who were on that bus?" Gaela asked.

"Much better than everything could have been," the doctor said. "We've got a broken arm, ankle sprains, bruises, bumps, and, perhaps, a concussion or two. But, considering what could have happened, things are not all that bad. We still have several patients being examined."

"That's good to hear, all things considered," Aguilar said.

"Now, as to your three agents, I am pleased to say that we also have fared better than what could have been. Agent Gatlin has been treated and stitched up for a severe gash in his scalp, just above his hairline. He dislocated a shoulder, sprained an ankle, and is currently undergoing x-rays on his left knee to enable us to gauge the damage he has suffered.

Patrick Nunez is conscious now. Seems he was subject to smoke inhalation for a lesser period than Michael Palmer. We've just about completed the treatments on his lungs. He has minor burns on his face and neck, but as long as someone keeps a watchful eye on that, he should recover fully.

Michael Palmer remains unconscious. He was exposed to smoke inhalation longer than the other two men and has more severe burns on his arms and legs. I've called for a pulmonary specialist to come in and do an examination. Palmer's vitals are relatively strong considering the trauma, so let's all just keep our fingers crossed. He's got a cut on his forehead that didn't seem to penetrate. We haven't figured out yet how he got that."

"Thanks, doctor," Aguilar said. "Will we be able to speak to any of these men?"

"Well, I'll make sure we get word to you when Gatlin is back from x-ray. And, once we complete Nunez' breathing treatments, you should be able to speak with him. We'll have to wait and see with Palmer."

Just then, one of the ER nurses entered the room.

"Excuse me, Doctor Shamorie. Doctor Martin would like to speak with you?"

Shamorie nodded, then turned to the three men in the room.

"Gentlemen, if you will please excuse me."

Charlie Hough and Luke Munson were shocked when they originally spotted a crowd of people standing outside the hospital emergency room and entered a room filled with others. With so much activity and so many people requiring medical attention, it was nearly impossible for them to ask someone where they might find the men who were injured in a highway car wreck.

Charlie quickly learned about the bus accident.

"We split up," Charlie whispered to Luke. "Just start looking. From what I can see here, most everybody getting treatment is gonna be a kid. Our guys shouldn't be that hard to find. Just remember, we gotta be quick about this. I ain't seen no trooper or anybody else that could be feds here. But, believe you me, they gotta be around here somewhere."

"I don't like this situation at all, Charlie," Luke said. "Makes me real uncomfortable. There's too many people crawling all over this place."

"Stay calm, Lukester, and chill, man. You can always hide in a crowd. Now, c'mon. Man up. Let's get this done and get outta here."

Charlie and Luke may have failed in their initial attempt to execute Brett Gatlin and the two agents who were bringing him back to Virginia. But, these two men were skilled when it came to getting in and out of places. Before they graduated to the level of hitmen, Hough and Munson had scored well as professional burglars. In fact, the amount of money they made from their exploits would have had them sitting pretty right now, if gambling habits, drugs, booze, and women hadn't greatly depleted their stash in a relatively short period of time.

Charlie was the one who found Nunez lying in a bed surrounded by curtains. Nunez was hooked up to some kind of breathing machine. Patrick, despite being groggy, smiled assuming that Charlie was one of the agents from the Tucson office. Charlie's moves were silent and swift. He pulled the breathing mask away from Nunez' face, replaced the mask with a pillow, and pressed down. Nunez twisted, turned, and fought to get free, but Charlie's leverage and Nunez' weakened condition settled the score on this early on. Patrick Nunez thought of his wife, his two daughters, and a birthday party that he would miss just before his body slackened and his breathing stopped. Then, Charlie placed the mask back over Nunez' face and slipped out.

Luke had a much easier task in suffocating Mike Palmer, since the man was already unconscious when Luke found him. Palmer never woke to even know that his life was being snuffed out. Mike and Constance had never stopped loving each other and had been so close to reuniting. Now, that dream would end underneath a pillow blocking Mike's supply of oxygen.

Within minutes, Luke and Charlie were together again. When they entered the area where they expected to find Gatlin, the bed was empty. They stepped outside of the enclosed area. Just then, Trooper Aguilar came out from the room in search of a cup of coffee. Charlie spotted him and pulled Luke with him back into the draped area with the empty bed.

"We gotta get outta here, Luke. We're assuming that trooper and any feds don't know who we are and ain't never seen us, but guys like that have a way of picking suspicious looking people out of a crowd. Anyway, it ain't worth our wearing out our welcome."

"What about Gatlin?" Luke said.

"We ain't got time to search around," Charlie said. "Maybe the dude's dead and they already removed him from here."

Charlie was not at all convinced that was true, but he was sure that they needed to get away from there now. In fact, Charlie believed it was time for he and Luke to get as far away as possible, even if it meant leaving the country. He knew that they were dealing with people that no one should trifle with. If Gatlin was not dead, Charlie and Luke would soon be, once the ones that hired them found out they had failed to complete their job. If they hadn't needed the cash so badly and the pay was not so good, Charlie would never have taken this job. He didn't have specific names of the people who hired them, but he knew that he and Luke were dealing with people who played for keeps.

As Charlie ushered himself and Luke from the ER, that old song about knowing when to hold 'em, fold 'em, walk away, or run, flashed through his mind. It was definitely time to run.

CHAPTER 11

MISSION ACCOMPLISHED

Special Agent William Falwell suspected something had gone awry when he had not heard from Charlie Hough or Luke Munson. His suspicions grew when he could not reach either of the two men by phone. His heightened suspicions were converted to knowledge when he received the phone call from Special Agent in Charge Barb Hennessey of the Phoenix office. The Tucson office was also under Hennessey's direct supervision.

"That's correct," Hennessey said. "Two of my agents out of the Tucson office are still at the hospital now. They will be prepared to take Agent Gatlin into custody once he is released by the hospital doctors."

Hennessey had already provided notice of the deaths of Agents Nunez and Palmer and expressed her personal condolences to William Falwell. Although Hennessey and Falwell had attended a meeting or two at the same time, they did not know each other. By now, however, they were communicating with each other on a first name basis.

"Bill, I must be honest with you. I'm rather surprised that we were not notified that a rogue agent was in custody at Fort Huachuca and that two of your agents were coming into our state to apprehend this man. I'm sure I don't need to tell you that would be standard protocol."

"Uh… yes, you do have my apologies, Barb. Not exactly sure how that slipped through the cracks. You most certainly should have been informed," Falwell said.

Slipped through the cracks? Right! An agent suspected of consorting with the lord of a major Mexican drug cartel shows up in Arizona? An agent who has been AWOL for years? We're told that one of the biggest drug deals in history turned into a bloodbath in the Sonora Desert. There are reports of a major shakeup of the Mexican cartels. Word is that American and Mexican agents have all been killed. And none of this put Falwell and his people on a heightened alert?

The hospitalist at Tucson's Carondolet St. Joseph Hospital cleared Gatlin after x-rays showed that the injury to his knee did not involve any break or tears. He was still a bit disoriented and gimpy. The stitches had closed the gash on his head and a strong dose of antibiotics would continue the fight against infection. Martin Gaela and Rick Watkins temporarily booked Gatlin in the Pima County jail, pending further instructions from DEA headquarters in Virginia.

Gaela and Watkins were shocked when they learned that the two agents from Arlington had been found dead in the hospital ER. Gatlin was spared because he was undergoing x-rays and not present in the ER when the agents were murdered.

When she learned that agents Michael Palmer and Patrick Nunez were found dead by the hospital personnel, Special Agent in Charge Barb Hennessey of the Phoenix office contacted Gaela and Watkins. Doctors on the scene preliminary identified the causes of death for both men to be asphyxiation. A local coroner confirmed that shortly afterwards.

"How in the hell do two of our agents end up murdered right under your noses?" Hennessey said.

"We'd not yet been given access to these men while the medical staff were tending to them," Gaela said. "In fact, we'd just been told that Nunez was conscious and we and the state trooper working on the accident would be able to see him shortly. Palmer was not yet conscious. Gatlin was having x-rays taken. Then, the next thing we hear is that Palmer and Nunez are dead. There were people all over the place following an accident involving a bus full of kids and their chaperones. The place was pretty much pure chaos."

At first, Hennessey did not respond to Gaela's statements. She, along with Gaela and Watkins. She and her two agents were all stunned at this turn of events. While the two dead agents were on a mission to bring a man suspected of wrongdoing back to Virginia, there was nothing yet to indicate that Gatlin or the other two agents were being targeted by anyone. Barb knew that Gaela and Watkins had not been derelict in their duties. Medical personnel attending to Nunez and Palmer did have priority. The welfare of the agents was priority. Gaela and Watkins were correct in not interfering.

Initially, Hennessey directed her agents to place Gatlin temporarily in the local jail pending her discussions with officials at the Arlington DEA headquarters. The decision from Arlington was that Gaela and Watkins would escort Brett Gatlin to Virginia.

State Trooper Carlos Aguilar did not have an opportunity to talk with Brett Gatlin before he was taken to the Pima County jail. Nevertheless, Gatlin would not have said anything to Aguilar. Brett was shocked when the Colonel at Fort Huachuca never received confirmation of Gatlin's status as an undercover agent working with Max Bradford. But now, his fears and confusion had escalated. Gatlin was convinced that he, not Palmer nor Nunez, was the primary target of the shooter on the highway. The truck the shooter was trying to get Palmer to pull over in the left lane. If

Palmer had done so, the shooter would have had a clearer shot directly at Gatlin. If that was true, it meant that Brett was the reason why two federal agents were now dead.

Gatlin's mind was racing, filled with a myriad of thoughts. Why would someone be trying to kill him? Who was behind this? None of it made any sense at all. Brett needed time to think all of this through. He was missing something. He had to be. But, right now, he had no idea what that might be. As a result, Gatlin decided to remain silent while he tried to make sense of these perplexing things.

Gaela and Watkins were headed to the local jail to take Gatlin into custody when Gaela received a call from State Trooper Carlos Aguilar.

"Hey, just want you both to know that I received an initial report from our accident reconstruction team. They're not even close to finishing their investigation," Aguilar said, "so technically I'm not supposed to talk about their investigative work, but something came up that they agreed we all need to know about right away."

Gaela asked Aguilar to wait a moment while he placed his phone on speaker so that Watkins could hear firsthand what the trooper had to say.

"Like I said," Aguilar continued, "they're nowhere near finished with their reconstruction work, but from what they've already found, this thing has taken a whole new twist. I'm talking about bullet holes."

"Say what?" Gaela said.

"Yeah, from what I've been told, our guys are telling me that shots were fired at the vehicle which we would assume caused the driver to lose control."

"What in the world is that all about?" Gaela said.

"Got no idea," Aguilar said, "I was as surprised as you are, but, it gets even more strange. Seems the shots were fired from the left lane of the highway. Now, I'm just speculating here, but if the agents were the targets, you'd think the shooter would have fired at Palmer who was driving. But, again we're speculating here, more shots were fired at the rear seat where Nunez and Gatlin were seated.

This is just a bunch of conjecture right now, but it's very possible the shooter was more interested in the back seat of that car.

"Gatlin?" Gaela said. "You thinking somebody might have been after Gatlin? Maybe somebody who didn't want him to make it back to Virginia?"

Aguilar paused for a moment.

"Look, I'm admitting this is pure guesswork right now. Everything I'm saying could completely change, but like I said a minute ago, things just seem to get even stranger.

Now, if you picture this with me, Nunez was seated behind the driver, so he would have been hit first. But, the shots missed him, as well as Gatlin. That means that either Nunez saw the shooter, screamed out a warning to Gatlin and they both ducked down seconds before the shots rang out. Or... "

"Oh, my God, or," Galea interrupted, "Gatlin spotted the shooter and pushed Nunez down out of the line of fire with him."

"Why in the world would Gatlin do something like that?" Watkins said.

"Well, hell," Aguilar said, "why would a man cut himself loose from cuffs and leg irons, then, instead of clearing out of there, hang around and risk his life trying to save the guys who had him chained up to begin with?"

Everyone was silent.

Gaela and Watkins stared at one another before Watkins returned his gaze to the road. Aguilar broke the silence.

"Listen, before you guys take Brett Gatlin out of the area, I sure would appreciate an opportunity to chat with that man along with the two of you. What do you say?"

Aguilar could have raised the issue of jurisdiction based upon a possible attempted murder in the State of Arizona, but he did not. He hoped that the federal agents would cooperate with him. Besides, Carlos' adrenaline was soaring. A highway accident had just unexpectedly become an attempted murder investigation.

Gaela nodded his head. Watkins whispered his agreement.

"Okay, Carlos," Gaela said. "We'll hold tight outside the jail until you get here. Let's get to work and find out what this is all about before Gatlin leaves Arizona."

CHAPTER 12

MISSION ACCOMPLISHED

William Falwell had already spoken with Barb Hennessey and authorized the Tucson agents to escort Brett Gatlin to Virginia. That was a call that Falwell originally did not anticipate he would have to make. If all had gone as planned, Gatlin would already be dead. That was why he sent Palmer and Nunez to Arizona and had them pick up Gatlin at Fort Huachuca. He hired two professional men. No one would be expecting a highway ambush. This should have been an easy task. Instead, Hough and Munson failed to execute. Hell, the only dead people from that entire ordeal were his two agents. Falwell could have gone either way with whether Nunez and Palmer live or die. But, there was no option with Gatlin.

Falwell's hands shook as he prepared to make the call that he dreaded the most. He knew that the fact Special Agent Brett Gatlin was still alive would more than upset the man. The man and others would be livid. And, something about the man had already convinced Falwell that being the focus of his anger was definitely not the place to be.

Falwell had done his best to falsify classified documents prepared by Max Bradford. He added false allegations by Bradford that Gatlin had defected and aligned himself with a drug cartel. Falwell's official report cited the claims against Gatlin.

"We have evidence that Gatlin is using drugs he was sworn to fight against. After consultation with Special Agent Matthew Bradford, we have concluded that in exchange for access to illegal drugs and any other favors provided by the drug cartel, Gatlin has been working to offset the DEA efforts against the drug trade in Mexico and the United States."

Bradford's signature was also on Falwell's report. Of course, Max ever knew what Falwell had done. And, after Max was poisoned, in such a manner that foul play was never even suspected, his death assured that he never would know.

The fact that Gatlin was on his way to Arlington provided Falwell with his last hope and opportunity. He had to be sure that Brett Gatlin was executed and he was prepared to do that himself. He would not fail this time. His life depended upon it.

As he thought about the position he was now in, Falwell began to shake uncontrollably. He bent over as one in pain would do gasping and expelling breath. He knew better. He should never have gotten involved, regardless of the money. His motivation had been greed. He sensed that the man and others had much deeper motivations—motivations for which they'd be willing to kill.

Hah! Talk about irony! The ways things were headed, Gatlin could possibly end up living longer than Special Agent William Falwell.

"I don't know, Marty," Rick Watkins said, "Gatlin has me confused."

As promised, Martin Gaela and Rick Watkins were waiting outside the Pima County jail for Trooper Carlos Aguilar to arrive.

"Yeah, I hear you, Rick. You and me both."

Gaela stared off through the windshield of the car that he and Watkins were seated in.

"The guy knows he's being brought in for criminal charges that'll put him away for a long, long time. He's supposedly a user, but he remains calm and poised under some dire circumstances—like being upside down in a vehicle likely to blow any minute."

"Exactly," Watkins says. "He manages to free himself from cuffs and leg irons and instead of running away before anyone arrives on the scene, he stays and risks his life, pulling two men from the vehicle."

"And think about it, Rick," Gaela said, "why'd he show up at Huachuca to begin with? If his life was in danger from a drug cartel and he fled back into the States, why not just hide away somewhere, rather than turn yourself into the authorities? I mean the guy was RRT trained. Those guys know how to hide and how to survive."

"Yeah, that's what I'm saying, Marty. I've been racking my brain when it comes to Brett Gatlin and I just can't seem to make the puzzle pieces fit."

Gaela nodded his head, then turned towards Rick Watkins.

"So, let me make this whole thing even more confusing, my man," Gaela said. "What if Gatlin was the one who first spotted the shooter in the vehicle traveling alongside them? That'd mean he was the one who pushed Nunez out of the line of fire and initially saved the man's life."

Watkins sucked in some air, made a whistling sound, and shook his head.

"The guy sure doesn't sound like a rogue agent who'd turned to the dark side."

⟢ ⟣

Gaela and Watkins sat across from Gatlin. Aguilar was at one end of the table. Since Gatlin was in the custody of the federal agents, Gaela had the authority to insist that Brett not be cuffed as they sat together. Before they even entered the jail, the three men spent a few minutes setting a basic strategy on how they would handle things and what they hoped to learn from a time of interrogation with Gatlin.

"Special Agent Gatlin," Gaela began, "we would like to spend a little time with you before we have to escort you to Virginia. This is not a formal interrogation session. There will be no record kept of anything we say here. We will not be recording anything. This will only be between you and us. No one else will hear what we discuss during this time."

Gatlin sat quietly without making eye contact with any of the three men.

"Sir," Aguilar began, "my responsibility relates solely to the highway accident that you were involved in. Once again, I would like to ask you a few questions, if I may. The Arizona Highway Patrol has a highly-trained team of troopers who specialize in accident reconstruction. As you may know, accident reconstruction is scientific in nature and has a goal of determining why an accident occurred. When we learned that three federal agents were involved in this accident, a decision was made to deploy our team."

Gatlin remained silent and continued to avoid making any eye contact with anyone.

"Agent Gatlin, I'm interested in what caused the accident. We've discovered something alarming. Let's talk about the fact that shots were fired at the vehicle you were traveling in. We believe that someone driving in the left lane fired shots at you and the two agents transporting you. And, this would have caused the accident you were involved in. How am I doing now, sir?"

Aguilar paused for a moment to let his words sink in.

"Is that what happened? Someone started shooting at the car you were in?"

Gaela interjected.

"Can you tell us why that occurred? Why someone would shoot at the car you were in? Did you recognize the shooters?

Agent Gatlin, we now have two federal agents who were murdered in the hospital where the three of you were taken by ambulance. I dare say, you only escaped that because you were taken away for x-rays."

"Right," Aguilar said. "And now my investigative responsibilities have escalated from a highway accident to possibly an attempted homicide."

"As my partner said," Watkins was the speaker now, "all of us here are dealing with a double homicide. We've got two of our DEA agents murdered by somebody who followed them and you here to the local hospital. You know, Gatlin, these men had families who, without warning, will have to go on through life without them. Their wives and children will need closure, also."

"Can you help?" Gaela asked. "Will you help us?"

Now, for the first time, Brett Gatlin lifted his head. His jaw was tight. He made eye contact in turn with each of the three men. But, he still did not say a word.

Martin Gaela was an experienced federal agent who had seniority over everyone at the Tucson office. Gaela's peers regarded him as a straight-shooter, a man who carried himself with integrity. He maintained a balance between the authority behind the shield he carried and a humility that permitted him to remember his roots.

Gaela decided that he would not hold back with Gatlin. He realized that this might be his only opportunity to ever question this man. As a dedicated agent committed to his sworn duty, Gaela wanted to know, needed to know, if Gatlin had betrayed his oath. If so, he wanted to try to understand why, after undergoing such extensive training, a man would do so.

"Agent Gatlin, this may well be our only opportunity to speak with you. Not only do I want to know what happened leading to the demise of two of our agents, I want to know about you. We know that when that car landed upside down in a highway ditch, you freed yourself from the chains that bound you. But, you didn't take the opportunity to get away. Why stay there and risk your own life to save two men who were bringing you in to the agency headquarters?"

Gatlin made eye contact with Gaela. He knew that these men were not his enemies and he believed they had no part in anything sinister. Gatlin spoke for the first time.

"I may very well be the reason why those two federal agents are dead."

Gatlin hung his head, stopped speaking, and breathed deeply.

"So much of what is going on with me relates to something highly-confidential that I'm prohibited to speak about," Gatlin said. "I'm sorry that I cannot say more."

Gatlin's jaw tightened and his hands curled into fists. He stared deeply into the eyes of each of the men.

"What I can tell you is that I've never betrayed my oath nor my country."

Gatlin's facial expressions softened and his body posture slackened. He was struggling to find the right words and had his hand pressing against the back of his neck.

"I went to Huachuca thinking that I'd be in touch with Max Bradford and regroup with him. I barely escaped alive from Mexico and had no idea how everything we'd planned and worked on for years had all fallen apart. I wish I could say more. I wish to God I knew more than I do."

Gatlin focused upon Carlos Aguilar.

"Trooper Aguilar, you and your people are correct. It was a metallic blue Chevy Silverado—double cab. I believe it was a current year vehicle. There were two men. I only got a momentary glance at the man in the passenger seat. Caucasian, dark brown hair, medium build, facial hair in the form of a light beard and moustache. He was wearing aviator sunglasses.

He opened his window and I saw him lift his gun and point it at us. I pushed Agent Nunez down, along with myself. Shots continued to ring out. At some point, some of the shots struck our tires on the driver side. Palmer was screaming out at us to take cover and told us when he could no longer control the vehicle. During all this time, my head and Nunez' head were down low. We couldn't see anything. Then, our car began to swerve, spin, left the road, rolled over a few times, and ended upside down in a ditch.

As to who these men were and why they fired at us, I have no idea. Originally, they were pushing us from behind and I believe they were trying to get Palmer to move over to the left lane. That leads me to believe that I was their primary target, since if they were in the left lane, Nunez would have me blocked."

Gatlin paused, took a deep breath, and, once again, took a moment to make eye contact with each of the three men.

"Gentlemen, that's all I know."

CHAPTER 13

DISCERNING THE TRUTH

"Look, there's just so much I can tell you. Remember, I'm in Phoenix. They're in Tucson. All I know is that Gaela and Watkins are responsible for bringing Gatlin to Arlington. I got me a friend at the Pima County jail. He says Gaela and Watkins showed up to take custody of the man and they've got a State Trooper with them. They're all sitting with Gatlin now."

Agent Marianne Pacheco had been working out of the Phoenix DEA office for nearly three years. Following a recent divorce, she was now functioning as a single mother of a two-year-old girl. Money was tight.

When they first approached her about an opportunity to make some much-needed extra cash, the offer seemed too good to pass up. All they wanted was someone to be "eyes-on" and pass on information on things she would see or hear.

She suspected that the whole thing was rather shady, but she didn't know anything specific. Nor was she aware of what their motives were. Besides, why should she care? Her pay level as a young DEA agent was not all that great. Her prospects for advancement as a female seemed rather limited. It was just information. Nothing more. What was the big deal in doing that? It was of no concern to her what they did with the things she passed on.

When the reports about Special Agent Brett Gatlin began to surface, Marianne became increasingly suspicious that all of this had something to do with that man and what he had purportedly done. So, maybe that was a good thing. Perhaps, they were working quietly behind the scenes, since a rogue agent was such a black mark on the Agency.

Pacheco didn't really believe that. She knew that federal agents do not get paid on the side for doing their job. But, she decided to just go with the flow and enjoy the unexpected windfall. And, who knows? Maybe her willingness to do this now will open doors of opportunity to her in the future.

Aguilar liked what he heard when Gatlin described the vehicle from which the shots were fired on the highway. He knew that the Silverado 1500 double cab comes in what they call a deep ocean blue metallic and there's an extra charge for that color. He'd start a search.

"That helps. As far as I'm concerned," Carlos said, "having something is always better than having nothing. You never know when you might get lucky and come up with something more."

Gaela continued in his effort to get Gatlin to open up even more.

"Brett," he said, using Gatlin's first name, "you say you showed up at the fort to get in touch with Special Agent Max Bradford? So, you didn't know that he was dead?"

Gatlin shook his head. His eyes were downcast. His lips were pressed together in a slight grimace. For the first time since they'd all been together, he seemed to be engaged in a struggle as to whether he should speak, and, if so, just what he should say.

"No. No, I didn't know. I still can't believe that. Just two days earlier we had our last team call with Max. We were poised for a major cartel takedown in the Sonoran Desert, but everything went wrong. As a result… "

Gatlin ceased speaking. He took several deep breaths before attempting to say another word.

"They're all dead. Everyone… all the members of my undercover team. I fled to another city in Mexico, but I was followed there by men from a cartel set out to kill me. I escaped. Our instructions were clear. If we were ever in serious trouble, we were to do everything we could to get across the Mexican border to Fort Huachuca. From there, we were to contact our team leader at the DEA. When I was at the fort, I first learned that Special Agent Max Bradford was dead. Then, someone at DEA Headquarters reported me as missing-in-action. They claimed I had defected. They denied that Bradford ever had a team he was overseeing. All of this makes no sense to me at all."

No one said a word as they considered all that Gatlin was saying. If what he had told them was the truth, the man had just lost every member of his team and had now learned that the agent who headed up the special ops team was also dead. Beyond that, it also meant that right after he risked his life and likely should have been killed with all the others, he was being declared a traitor.

"One last question, Agent Gatlin." The speaker was Marty Gaela. "From everything we have just heard, it sounds as if someone is trying to kill you. Who would that be, sir? And why do they want you dead?"

Gatlin's eyes were fixed on Gaela. He shook his head, shrugged his shoulders, and raised his hands with his palms facing up.

"That, Agent Gaela, is the foremost question in my mind. It's the question that is tormenting me. I've tried to make sense out of any of this. And, all I can tell you is that I haven't got a clue."

Carlos Aguillar drove away from the jail. Gaela and Watkins had some time alone while Gatlin was being discharged from the jail for release to the two federal agents. By the time the session with Gatlin was over, none of the three men who had questioned him knew what to think. Rick Watkins had never seen Gaela come out of an interrogation and appear so confused. He was hesitant to even broach the subject with his mentor, but Marty had always insisted that Rick never hold back on anything.

"What is it, Marty? I've never seen you look like this. You look like you don't know what to think. You normally come out of an interrogation session looking like you just solved a puzzle and got a whole lot of answers."

Gaela did not smile. His gaze was distant and clouded. A slight head shake was accompanied by blowing out his cheeks, then releasing the air.

"I don't know what it is, Rick. I just can't seem to get a handle on this guy. Nothing about Brett Gatlin seems to fit the profile of a drug-using traitor who turned his back on everything he trained for when he joined the DEA. And, I'll tell you, Rick. Either Gatlin is the best liar I've ever encountered in my life or the guy was telling the truth."

Marty Gaela paused. He appeared to be hesitant to say what was really on his mind. But, he had always promised Watkins he would be honest with him. This was not the time for Marty to change the rules. Rick had taken a chance and opened a rather difficult conversation with the man he considered to be his mentor. The next move was Marty's and he knew it.

"Okay, the way I see it, Rick, you can't have it both ways. I mean, if Gatlin's not who they say he is, if the man is telling the truth and hasn't done the things they're accusing him of, then... then, something's got to be big-time wrong back in Arlington."

The look on Watkin's face acknowledged that the seeds of the same concerns, the same doubts, had already been planted in his mind.

"That's what I'm thinking, Marty. All of this has my head spinning."

It was clear that Gaela did not particularly like where this conversation was headed. Yet, at the same time, he was concerned that his young partner was being pulled in several directions by the confusion he was experiencing.

"Look, Rick, I know that no federal agency is perfect and we're always going to have some bad apples in every government grouping. But, I don't know, man, I'm just not settled when it comes to Brett Gatlin. And, I'm only going to say this one time. If ever I'm confronted with a choice between my job and my personal integrity, I will not sell my soul for a paycheck."

Watkins reached over and placed his hand on Gaela's shoulder.

"I believe you know this, but there's no one I'd rather walk with than you, Marty."

Gaela smiled. He put his hand out for a fist bump with Watkins.

"We keep our eyes open, Rick. We don't let ourselves lose sight of anything. Right now, all we've got is some uncomfortable feelings about everything. We don't have enough to react either way."

"I hear you, Marty," Watkins said.

"Anyway, guess it's time for us to do our job," Gaela said.

"Well," Watkins said, "at least our job is simply to get the guy back to headquarters and let them sort everything out."

But, Watkins' comments triggered an onslaught of unspoken thoughts in the minds of both these men. There was a serious question whether their DEA superiors could or would sort things out properly and honestly.

CHAPTER 14

ARLINGTON OR BUST

Gaela, Watkins, and Aguilar agreed to remain in contact, share insights, and work together on an auto accident turned double homicide. Watkins asked Gaela about whether it was time to share what they had learned from Gatlin with Barb Hennessey.

Gaela was grinding his teeth and fighting against the nausea that enveloped his body. He did not like the fact that he no longer was sure who could be trusted in his own Agency.

"Let's hold off for a while until we've got more," Gaela said. What Marty Gaela was saying was that he wanted to be more confident that Hennessey was someone they could trust and would not be conspiring with or unwilling to challenge the powers-that-be at the DEA Headquarters.

The trek from the Pima County Jail to the Tucson International Airport was a fifteen-minute jaunt that covered just slightly more than eight miles. They would be on I-10 for about two miles before exiting onto Kino Parkway South, then East Benson Highway, before taking South Tucson Highway directly into the airport. Piece of cake! Or so it would seem.

They never made it.

The Woodmont neighborhood of Arlington, Virginia is close to main Washington, D.C. arteries, such as the metro and the George Washington Memorial Parkway. It was also the area where William Falwell's condo was located.

Falwell gasped, clutched at his chest, and drew his arms back to his body in a protective flinch when he spotted the tall, thin, black-haired man with the dark mole on his face standing in the doorway of his bedroom. The suitcase placed on the bed and the open bottle of Jim Beam bourbon painted a clear picture of Falwell's intentions and the man's current state of mind. His hands were shaking, his brow was covered with perspiration, and his pulse was rapid.

"Are we going somewhere Agent Falwell?"

The man's sinister smile raised his pencil-thin mustache. Then he winked at Falwell.

"H-how'd you... how'd y-you get in here?"

The tremor in Falwell's voice betrayed any effort to disguise his fear.

"W-what d-do you want? You need to leave here before..."

"Haha, before what Billy-boy? Before you call the police and have to explain what you've been involved in and why you have certain people very upset at your lack of performance? Is that what you're gonna do, William?"

"L-listen to m-me. Th-this isn't my fault. I can't control every-thing that happens somewhere across the country. Plus, it wasn't me or my people that let the guy get away in Mexicali. I had noth-ing to do with that. They can't pin that on me."

Falwell regained a bit of confidence as he continued to talk to the tall thin stranger.

"I just need a little more time. That's all. You tell them that I'll still take care of things. Like I said, I just need a little more time. I've got everything worked out. The guy will be here soon. I'll get things done."

The same wry smile was on the man's face as his eyes shifted to the suitcase sitting atop Falwell's bed.

"What were you planning, Falwell? Were you thinking maybe you'd fix things from some other country. Was that it?"

"Look," Falwell said, "I-I wasn't thinking clearly. I'll stay. Okay? I'll stay and get things done, just like they want."

Falwell's eyes shifted to the gun, replete with a sound suppressor. The man now had it pointed directly at Falwell. William Falwell also spotted the latex gloves that the man wore.

Falwell grimaced at the pain that was throbbing in the pit of his stomach. His lips quivered and his legs shook.

"Listen to me," Falwell said. "Hold off and listen to me. Will you? I've got money. I can pay you well. I'll double whatever they offered to you. All you gotta do is let me live. What do you say, man? Think about it. What's in it for you to kill me? Huh? What you want is to get paid. Well, I'll top whatever you'd get from them."

The man lowered the handgun and smiled.

"You know, you got a point there, my man. After all, money is money. I mean you are so right about that. What do I care about the reasons why they want you dead? That's of no concern to me. What you're saying sounds like a good business deal. I mean, if I'm for hire, then I ought to listen to the highest bidder. I mean that's kind of like my right. Don't ya think?"

"Yes, yes, of course that's true. Yes, I'll pay you more. What's going on between me and them is not your issue. I'll get the money for you now. I can make a wire transfer to any bank anywhere in the world. Just say the word. You won't be sorry, my friend. Just a good business decision, you know?"

"Yeah, I do know," the man said.

The man's moves were so sudden and quick, he had Falwell by the throat before the special agent ever saw it coming. He squeezed tightly with the gun pressed against Falwell's forehead.

William Falwell struggled to speak. His face was distorted. His words were garbled. The man eased up a bit on his grip to give Falwell an opportunity to say what was on his mind.

"Wait, wait, I-I'll pay you more than double. More than… "

That same wry smile appeared on the man's face and he winked again at his victim.

"Aw, I was just having a little fun with you, Falwell. Letting you live ain't a good business decision at all. Not in the least. You see, if I let you live then I become their target no matter where in the world I may be hiding. You see why that ain't a good business decision? And these people, well, let me tell you what you already know, Special Agent Falwell. These people we're talking about, man alive, they got the resources to find someone no matter where you go."

The man's eyes narrowed. His grip was steady and true. Tears flowed from Falwell's eyes. His body shook uncontrollably. Two rapid sounds, much like that of a staple gun, ended all the movement and trepidation.

Special Agent William Falwell had been correct. Brett Gatlin had, indeed, outlived him.

⊨⊨ ⊨⊨

Watkins was driving. Gaela was seated in the front passenger seat and Gatlin was in the back seat. First, Gatlin got his arms around Gaela's neck and ordered the agent to unlock the cuffs that had Gatlin fettered. Then, Gatlin, displaying lightning-quick moves, relieved Gaela of his weapon.

With his left arm tightly fastened around Marty Gaela's neck and the handgun pressed against the man's temple, Gatlin ordered Watkins to toss his gun and his phone on the floor at Gaela's feet.

"Give it up, Gatlin," Watkins called out. "You got no place to go, man. You're a federal agent. You know you can't hide forever. Don't be stupid."

"Just do as you're told, Watkins, and nobody gets hurt," Gatlin said. "Pull over here."

Gatlin chose the far end of a strip mall in front of an empty building that once housed a wholesale food outlet of some sort. He made Rick Watkins get out of the car, leave it running, and come to his side of the car.

"Now, unlock these leg irons, Watkins. And, be nice and careful about it. We wouldn't want this gun to go off and put a big hole in your partner's head."

Watkins did as he was told.

"Now, step away from the vehicle. And keep going until I tell you that you can stop."

Then, Gatlin ordered Gaela to drop his phone on the floor and step out. Gatlin hopped out of the back seat while keeping the gun still pointed directly at Gaela.

"Agent Gaela, I'm going to need you to go stand next to Agent Watkins."

Watkins and Gaela could do nothing as Brett Gatlin got behind the driver's seat and drove away.

The band was practicing. Walter Vaughn was with them, even though his bandaged hands kept him from doing anything other than singing, helping to adjust the sound, and running out to the van to fetch something. That's where he was now, bent over into the back of the van when the man with the plumber's wrench approached him from behind. Walter never knew the man was there. The man started to raise the wrench positioned behind Walter's skull when one of the band members stepped outside. The man quickly withdrew the wrench and held it to his side.

"Hey, Woody, you find it yet?" the band member shouted, as he came closer to Walter.

"Naw, hey, here it is. Got it. Hey, who are you?" Walter said, as he spotted the man standing behind him.

"Oh, sorry, son. Thought maybe you were having problems with your van and came by to see if I could help."

"No, I was just looking for a piece of equipment for my band. But, thanks anyway, sir."

Walter ran back inside with his friend, unaware of what he had just escaped.

Brett Gatlin had chosen his location well. Not only was the store he made Gaela and Watkins stop at empty, the next two were also out of business. The *Palace of Nails* salon was still in operation, but the first few staff members the two agents encountered and flashed their badges to were fluent in Vietnamese, but not in English. They eventually did get the use of a phone, called in the emergency, gave a description of Gatlin, and the car he had taken. Now, they were waiting for a car to pick them up.

"Well," Rick Watkins said, "Gatlin ain't gonna get far driving around in one of our cars with a BOLO transmitted all over the city. Just a matter of time before they nab his butt."

Gaela stood quietly with a grin on his face.

"What are you smiling about," Watkins said.

Gaela turned his head, stared at Watkins, then looked away and off somewhere.

"You're underestimating that guy, Rick. If I were a betting man, I wouldn't be putting my money on anyone catching up with him anytime soon."

"I don't get it, Marty. Not too long ago, this Gatlin was the one guy, in all the years I've known you, that you were having a real hard time trying to figure out. You saying you got him solved now?"

Gaela laughed as he turned back towards Watkins.

"Not by a long shot, Rick. But, I'll tell you a few things I believe. When Gatlin had that gun pressed against my head, you were right in following Agency procedures and putting the safety of a fellow agent paramount. But, the truth is, I don't believe there was any chance whatsoever that Gatlin would have ever pulled that trigger. From what I could see, he didn't even have his finger on the trigger."

Gaela chuckled.

"That guy never had any intention of killing either one of us."

Watkins shook his head. His jaw was tight. His eyes stared off into the distance.

"I've been thinking a lot about what we talked about earlier. You know, about whether there's something wrong going on behind the scenes at DEA Headquarters," Watkins said. "That scares me, man."

Gaela lowered his voice to a whisper, breathed deeply, and expelled his breath slowly.

"Yes, Rick. You got that right. That's something we should be scared about—like very damn scared."

CHAPTER 15
BRING IN THE CLEANING CREW

It began as a national news story then soon escalated into a front-page report. "Rogue DEA Special Agent Responsible for a Multitude of Deaths" was the headline of one major newspaper. Another read, "Special Agent Brett Gatlin: Mass Murderer in One Day." The media infatuation with the story surrounding Gatlin soon grew into an obsession. The major networks chose names such as, *Blood in the Desert, Betrayal in the Sand,* and *The Death Trail of a Traitor* to describe the saga of what occurred in the Sonoran Desert. The story continued with the fact that an armed and dangerous man was still at large.

The reports stated that DEA Special Agent Brett Gatlin began working with the Monterro Drug Cartel in Mexico. It alleged that he provided information that eventually led to the deaths of twenty-nine federal agents. This was a well-designed strategic move to describe Gatlin as a traitor to his country and a killer. It also guaranteed that others would now be engaged in the search for him. Beyond that, the message was clear. Gatlin need not be captured alive.

As the daily reports continued, CNN, MSNBC, FOX News, and others competed for viewers. They sent people to film the area in the Sonoran Desert where the failed drug bust occurred. They presented the profiles of the dead American federal agents who were killed in the line-of-duty. Experts provided insights and details on the various Mexican drug cartels. Panels of experts were employed to talk about the scourge of drug trafficking and the roles of DEA agents. There were other panels that provided suggestions as to how the convoy of American and Mexican agents may have been destroyed by well-planted explosives.

Brett Gatlin's face appeared on national television and in newspapers and magazines across the country. One major magazine referred to Brett Gatlin as "the most hated man in America."

Through it all, Special Agent Martin Gaela tracked the news with a questioning attitude that supported his personal profile of Brett Gatlin. At the same time, Kerry Anderson, a young, rising reporter with the Washington Post, began to cover the story. Anderson would write an initial article that was about to impact in ways she could never have foreseen.

DEA Special Agent William Falwell's Woodmont condominium showed no signs of anyone having been killed in the bedroom or any other room. The suitcase that had been on top of the bed was gone. Clothes and several other personal items were missing. Money had been withdrawn from one of Falwell's personal bank accounts.

Everything pointed to the fact that Falwell was on the run, perhaps even out of the country. This neatly-arranged cleanup job gave the authorities another person to search for as the saga of Brett Gatlin continued to unfold. Some experts conjectured that Falwell had been involved with Gatlin. When investigators learned that Falwell had an infusion of funds in an overseas bank account, it seemed to support the idea that the man had been involved in some illicit activities. Some speculated that as the spotlight on Brett Gatlin intensified, Falwell feared that his culpability would soon be discovered. He was now more than likely attempting to distance himself.

⇥ ⇤

Local police found the car that Gatlin had taken from Agents Gaela and Watkins. It was in the parking lot at the Tucson International Airport. But, there was no clue as to whether Gatlin had flown out of the area or wanted others to believe that he had. Federal agencies, local police, and private investigators with direct orders to shoot and kill, were all searching for Brett Gatlin. By the end of the first week since he had last been with Gaela and Watkins, no one had any idea where he was.

"The man's like a freakin' ghost," Andrew Gotschild, the chief private investigator said. Gotschild was on his update call to someone no one else even had access to. "There's no doubt he's good at coverin' his tracks. Looks like you boys done trained him real good. But, don't you worry none, sir. It ain't all that surprising at first that someone is able to evade me and my team. But, that don't last long." Gotschild chuckled before continuing to speak. "They always slip up. And believe you me, we got more'n enough nets set out there when they do. I got some of the finest men situated in different regions of the country. The moment we catch wind of where this here Gatlin is, we'll be takin' the boy out and I'll be comin' to you for the rest of our money."

There was a pause of silence after Gotschild finished speaking. He claimed he didn't know the man he was speaking with. He never met him and didn't even know the man's name. The phone he called was a throwaway that could not be traced. But, in

91

the few times that they had communicated, the man spoke slowly, carefully, and often generated gaps of silence. Gotschild was not easily spooked, but the man he was dealing with did make Andrew very uncomfortable. The money Gotschild would receive was extremely generous. He was used to being well-compensated. So, Andrew tolerated the discomfort he experienced in dealing with this man.

"I am not inclined to be patient when it comes to matters for which I and my colleagues are expending a great deal of money," the man said. "You are reputed to be the very best. I expect you to live up to that reputation."

The man never added the words "or else" to the end of his sentence, but Gotschild seemed to hear them anyway. He shivered as the man disconnected from the call. All the money in the world was not worth the risk taken if Andrew Gotschild and his thugs failed in their mission. Unfortunately, it was much too late to step away from the commitment he had made. He now had to deliver "or else."

Kerry Anderson, despite being very attractive at five feet eight inches, blond hair, captivating green eyes, and high cheekbones that accented her dimples when she smiled, was still single at twenty-eight years old. She had already developed a reputation for being a top-notch reporter with a unique ability to dredge out the truth. Before she wrote her first article and garnered front-page status, Kerry flew to Arizona and spoke with Colonel Shirley at Fort Huachuca. It was primarily after she spent time speaking with Agents Gaela, Watkins, and State Trooper Aguilar in Tucson that her curiosity and suspicions began to fester.

"Based upon the information I received and my own observations," Aguilar said, "Gatlin, for whatever else the man may be, was a hero. The man initially saved the lives of the two federal agents who had him in custody. He displayed incredible courage and self-lessness, disregarding concern for his own safety."

Aguilar spoke about the fact that Gatlin pulled two men to safety from an upside-down vehicle that had become nothing more than a time-bomb death trap. He confirmed what he had learned from additional insights he received from Walter Vaughn, the young man who assisted Gatlin in pulling Agent Michael Palmer from the burning wreck.

Gaela and Watkins were much more careful with their words. Nevertheless, Kerry was astute enough to sense that both men had their doubts when it came to the reports that Gatlin was a man who had betrayed his oath and aided the enemy in the deaths of so many federal agents. She intended to reach back to them, particularly Agent Marty Gaela, but would wait to do so. She knew that if either or both men had doubts, their opinions could reflect negatively on their own Agency. She would have to handle this area of her investigative work gingerly. Kerry also planned to reach out to Brett's mother, Gloria, and his sister, Lucy.

By the time Kerry wrote her first article, she had still not been able to get a response from Brett's mother or sister. Her Washington Post article was prominently placed on the front page, despite not being the lead story.

REPORTS ABOUT ROGUE AGENT HAVE MANY CONFLICTING PARTS

Are we witnessing a rush to judgment? Special Agent Brett Gatlin is said to be a man who betrayed his oath as a DEA Special Agent trained in the Agency's specialized Rapid Response Team operations. Yet, now such claims are fraught with conflicting reports. Some depictions of the man are raising major questions about the veracity of all that has been said...

Anderson's article stated that Gatlin showed extreme courage and a disregard for his own safety in initially saving the lives of the two federal agents who were transporting him to the DEA Headquarters in Arlington, Virginia. She reported that Gatlin had every opportunity to flee from the scene on that day. Instead, he chose to stay. She told how he pulled the two men from the burning car. Kerry quoted statements from Arizona State Trooper Carlos Aguilar and Walter Vaughn. She chose not to include any direct statements from Special Agents Martin Gaela and Rick Watkins. She did offer her own observation that the two men were neither killed nor injured by Gatlin after he had overcome them prior to his escape and disappearance.

Kerry Anderson's article cited Colonel Robert Shirley's statement that Gatlin claimed to have been working undercover on a special ops DEA team and had fled to Fort Huachuca to reach his supervisor, Special Agent Max Bradford.

Anderson's story was the first to even hint that the man everyone had identified as a dangerous criminal might not be so. As a result, news of her article spread like wildfire across the media scene. Suddenly, Kerry Anderson was in demand by every major television news program and national magazine.

Hidden away, still undetected by those seeking him, Brett Gatlin learned about the reporter for the Washington Post who was the first person to openly cast doubt on his guilt. Also, hidden away in darker secrecy, there were others who learned about Kerry Anderson's article and knew that they now had a new challenge facing them.

CHAPTER 16
STORY WITH TWO SIDES

Andrew Gotschild had a prominent career even before he ever established his own specialized and elite private investigation agency. He began his career as a Marine Raider, a special operations combat force of the United States Marine Corps. He received a Purple Heart and was decorated for bravery in combat. But, the injuries he suffered cut short his time as a Raider. While recovering, Gotschild earned a college degree and afterwards successfully earned a position as a special agent with the FBI.

Gotschild, now retired from the Bureau, located his agency in Bethesda, Maryland. It was elite, expensive, and geared primarily to work for people in government positions. The case he was overseeing now was so selective and secretive, the payments to Gotschild were off the books. There would be no official record of this current engagement. Andrew understood fully well that he and the people paying him were stepping across the boundaries of legality. This was also the first job Gotschild ever took where the people paying him were anonymous.

Andrew understood that people in the government sometimes had to work very discreetly. Over time, he noted that many things that government people did were not capable of being categorized as black or white, good or bad. As a result, Andrew learned not to ask a great deal of questions. He simply set his teams in motion to get the job done.

The news that two of his men had found Gatlin staying at a rooming house in Rockford, Illinois, some ninety miles west of Chicago, was heartening news for Andrew. It was time, more than time, to end this job.

Gotschild positioned two men outside the building where Brett Gatlin was housed. At his command, two additional men were on their way to that location. Andrew was awaiting word that Gatlin was dead. Mission accomplished.

After Lucy Gatlin heard about Kerry Anderson's article suggesting that Brett might be innocent, Lucy spoke to her mom. Lucy, at twenty-four- years old, was a respiratory therapist who worked out of a clinic associated with the Saint Thomas Midtown and Saint Thomas West Hospitals. She was engaged to be married, but, currently, still lived with her mother, Gloria.

A blurb on one of the televisions at the clinic caught Lucy's attention. She and her mom had been distraught over the news about Brett. Now, for the first time, there was a reporter who was taking the position that Brett might not be guilty of the things he was being charged with. Kerry Anderson's article mesmerized Lucy. Afterwards, Lucy spoke with her mother.

"Mom, Kerry Anderson is the reporter from the Washington Post that has been calling us and trying to get us to meet with her. She's claiming that it's possible that Brett is innocent and all these things they're saying about him are not true. She's getting a whole lot of attention on this. Mom, I'm thinking that maybe we should meet with this reporter."

Gloria Gatlin was a kind even-tempered woman whose vivaciousness abated after she lost her youngest son and her husband. Beyond that, she and Lucy had no contact whatsoever with Brett for more than four years. Now, suddenly, her son was front-page news being accused of crimes that led to a multitude of deaths.

"Well, of course, Brett is innocent," Gloria said. "He'd never do the things they say. You know, Lucy, those things would be the very opposite of why he ever became a federal agent to begin with. It'd be like a slap in the face against Derek and his memory. Anybody who knows Brett would know there's no way he's done any of these things they're accusing him of."

"I know that, Momma. But, we're not talking about whether Brett is innocent or guilty. We're talking about a reporter who wants to speak with us and is publicly taking Brett's side in all this. Maybe we should agree to speak with her. If we can help keep her positive and saying good things about Brett, we should do that. Lord knows no one else seems to have anything good to say about him."

Lucy was haunted at times by the fact that no one in the family had heard a word from Brett in more than four years. What if he had changed? What if he somehow had to work with people who were indirectly responsible for someone like Derek being killed and Brett just couldn't handle that anymore? Could it be that the same seeds of an addictive personality that existed within Derek were also in Brett? Maybe they had been dormant in her older brother for years while he was in school and nowhere around illegal drugs. Was it possible that those tendencies finally caught up with him now?

Despite the fears and doubts that battled for control of her mind, Lucy refused to yield to them. Brett would never yield to drugs and would never betray his oath as a federal agent. She knew her brother. She'd always respected and admired him. She just could not believe that the Brett she grew up around would completely sell out and change, even over the course of four years.

Lucy sat alone on the banks of Percy Priest Lake, perhaps in one of the very same spots where her two brothers once sat.

I know you, Brett. I don't believe, I won't believe what they're saying about you. You could be sitting now in some fancy office somewhere making really good money and far removed from the kinds of dangers you likely have faced in recent years. God, how I wish I could talk with you and even see you again. Mom's heart aches for you, Brett. She never openly talks about it, but I know she grieves for you. Hold on, Brett. Don't quit or let them get to you. There must be, there has to be some way out of this mess.

Neither Andrew Gotschild nor any of his men had any idea how Brett Gatlin had made it from Arizona to Illinois nor whether there was a pattern to where he was headed. A homeless man, known to be a substance abuser called one of the toll-free phone numbers left by Gotschild's agency offering a five-hundred-dollar reward for anyone who aided in finding Gatlin. Initially, they questioned the accuracy of a man who was likely never completely sober. Nevertheless, in line with orders passed down into his network, Gotschild had demanded that every lead, no matter how trivial, be followed up. When one of his men kept eyes on the area, he spotted a man walking from a small local bodega. He snapped a few pics with his phone camera, sent them to Gotschild, and was shocked at the response he received. They had found the elusive Brett Gatlin.

While the two men awaited the backup being sent by Gotschild, Gatlin spotted them sitting in their car. It concerned him that someone must have spotted him before this and he had failed to notice anyone in the area. Regardless of that slipup, Brett was now on full alert. Unlike his incident in Mexicali, there was no alternate stairway, no access to a rooftop and no adjacent building to leap to. Moreover, Brett did not have a weapon. None of that mattered. It was time to take action. He quickly devised a plan, considered each step he would have to take, and appraised the risks involved. He would use the primary advantage that he possessed. He knew these two men were there. They did not know that Brett was aware of them.

Brett came out the front door of his building and began walking as if he was, once again, making a quick jaunt to a local store. The car that had been waiting outside began to follow, moving slowly along the street. Brett kept himself in positions where should someone want to shoot at him from the moving vehicle, something always blocked him and denied a clear shot. He did not believe they would risk being identified by firing shots from a moving car, but he was not taking any chances.

Brett had not been in this area for very long and had no intention of remaining here much longer, but he had already familiarized himself with his surroundings. There was an alley located two blocks ahead. He set that as his target. Brett began to run and crossed over a street against the light. The two men spotted him as he turned down the alley. They had no choice but to leave their car and chase after him. The two men had guns drawn as they proceeded cautiously, but quickly down the alley. They covered for each other when they passed a series of dumpsters, expecting Gatlin to be hiding somewhere behind or alongside them. He was not. The alley ended with a back alley that was perpendicular to the one they'd been traveling on. But, when they reached that end, Brett was not hidden at the corner nor did they see him running either to the right or to the left. Gatlin seemed to have vanished.

It is sometimes only a fraction too late when someone realizes the error they have made. The two men were so busy looking to the right and left, they never considered looking upwards. Brett had found a way to climb up the cement block wall of the building to their left and grab hold of an overhang. He dropped directly down on one of the two men. As the man fell to the ground, he struck his head on the cement and was rendered unconscious. The second man whirled with his weapon pointed directly at Gatlin, but, by then, Brett kicked his weapon from his hand, then struck him several times with lightning-quick punches to his throat.

In less than one minute, Brett rendered the two men unconscious. He grabbed each of their weapons, emptied their wallets, took the car keys, and drove away in their vehicle before the two backup men ever arrived on the scene.

CHAPTER 17
GUILTY OR INNOCENT?

Andrew Gotschild did not reveal to anyone that he and his men had located Brett Gatlin in Illinois. He did not want the people who hired him to know that his team had failed when they had Gatlin within their grasp. When the two backup men arrived at the scene, they could not find Gatlin nor their two associates.

The two men that Gatlin had rendered unconscious eventually came out from the alley minus their weapons, their money, and their vehicle. Their awareness was further heightened by the repercussions of failure when the order came down from Gotschild.

"Eliminate them," Gotschild said. "And make sure that you don't leave a trail."

They buried the two men in a remote swampy area outside the city. It would be a long time, if ever, before anyone ever discovered their remains. Andrew Gotschild paid his team members extremely well, but the cost for failure was also exceedingly high.

※

At first, Kerry Anderson's article met with some strong opposition from other journalists who had covered the story. Edmund Foley, a reporter for the Chicago Tribune, claimed to have first-hand reports that Walter Vaughn was a reputed substance abuser whose stories about himself and Gatlin had been greatly exaggerated or completely fabricated.

"Gatlin was neither a hero nor someone who made any attempt to save the lives of the two federal agents who were transporting him to the DEA Headquarters," the reporter stated in his rebuttal article. "Walter Vaughn, a key witness to the events of that day, has been identified as a substance abuser who is currently out on bail pending drug charges. One person familiar with Vaughn stated that he made up the stories about himself and Gatlin in the hope they might benefit him in his own criminal trial."

Anderson sought to get others who were at the scene that day to corroborate Vaughn's claims that Gatlin was, in fact, a hero, along with Walter. Unfortunately, she was not able to get a statement from anyone. Most of the onlookers never responded to her phone messages. One older gentleman swore that he could not see well from where he stood and could not provide any valid insight as to what occurred. Kerry suspected that a few of the onlookers did not want to be identified as someone who did not come forward and make any attempt to save the lives of people trapped in a vehicle and a lone man who was trying to save them. Others did not want to appear to be favorable towards a man who everyone said was responsible for the deaths of loyal federal agents.

But, there were several key media personalities on CNN and MSNBC that remained fixated on the validity of the questions raised by Kerry and invited her to appear on their programs. Kerry Anderson had raised sufficient suspicions that a United States federal agency might be involved in a conspiracy or a cover-up of some sort. As a result, the slaughter of federal agents and members of Garcia's cartel in the Sonoran Desert resurfaced as front-page news along with the continuing saga of an at-large DEA agent.

⚊⚌ ⚌⚊

Brett Gatlin continued to trade off vehicles as he made his way closer to the nation's capital. His nights were restless. Over time, Brett had learned how to never permit his emotions take charge. He could control his breathing, fight against negative thoughts, and keep his mind active and alert. But, he did not have the power to control his dreams. Once he reached that necessary REM level of sleep, his mind traveled wherever it preferred to go.

Brett's dreams included sitting with his deceased father and discussing how Gatlin's role as a special ops agent kept him from seeing his dad for years before the man died. Brett never even attended his father's funeral. Gatlin's dreams also conjured up images of his dead brother with Derek laughing about the fact that Brett and his team had utterly failed in their mission to destroy major drug trafficking out of Mexico.

"Hah, you gave up everything for nothing, Bro," Derek said in a dream. "You could've been sitting pretty, man. Now, the very people you sacrificed for and lost more than four years of your life serving, are all against you. You got suckered, Brett. And you think I latched onto the wrong people?"

After more than four key maturity years of not seeing his sister, Lucy, Brett no longer knew just what she looked like. And, his heart ached for his widowed mother who, along with Lucy, had always loved him unconditionally.

These thoughts, images, visions, and distortions passed through Gatlin's mind while he slept, leaving him as a captive to watch them. He awoke each morning with that proverbial dark cloud hanging over him and a sense that he had not gotten a refreshing night of sleep. Antioch and Nashville seemed like places of fantasy to him now. And he dared not even consider going anywhere near his mother and sister. He was sure that people looking for him would expect that he might desire to see his family members. Gatlin considered the strong possibility that the phones of Gloria and Lucy Gatlin were tapped. His greatest expression of love for his mom and his sister would be to stay as far away from them as he possibly could.

The people pursuing him wanted Gatlin dead. To his mother and sister, it was as if he had already died.

⊨⊣ ⊢⊨

The diner where Marty Gaela and Rick Watkins were to have lunch with Carlos Aguilar was a place where the two federal agents and the state trooper would have the ability to talk privately.

"So, tell me again, Marty," Watkins said, "Aguilar just calls you out-of-the-blue and asks if you and me would be willing to meet and have lunch with him?"

"Yeah, Rick. Like I already told you three times, he said he wanted to discuss a few things related to the highway crash on ninety that've come up since we were last together. Look, I know we aren't officially investigating that whole deal and even the murder investigations of the two agents at the hospital are being handled by others. But, we were somewhat involved in that whole mess once we showed up at St. Joe's Hospital. I'd like to hear what Carlos has on his mind."

"No, no, don't get me wrong, Marty. I'm interested too. You got no idea what's on his mind?"

"Nah. I figured we could both hear what he has to say when we're together."

Marty Gaela was astute enough to suspect that Carlos Aguilar was aware of the article released by Kerry Anderson and the

104

responses that arose afterwards. Aguilar took the lead in questioning Walter Vaughn and was the only one of the three men meeting today who had spoken with some of the bystanders at the scene of the accident. Gaela and Watkins were never at that scene. Their involvement began when they arrived at the Carondelet St. Joseph's Hospital.

⊷ ⊷

Neither Carlos Aguilar nor either of the two federal agents had any reason to believe that anyone had an interest in their meeting. They were wrong. The man discreetly sat at a table shortly after they arrived. The device he had and the earbud inconspicuously embedded in his ear provided him with all the access to their conversation that he would need.

Aguilar waited until after they greeted one another and ordered their lunches before he revealed what was on his mind.

"My emphasis has been where it should be. I've been focused upon the accident that occurred and the fact that shots were fired at the vehicle before it crashed. We located the vehicle described by Gatlin. The truck was found at the airport. The vehicle was apparently stolen from its owner sometime before the accident took place. No prints, no forensic evidence whatsoever was found in the vehicle indicating we're dealing with pros."

Gaela listened attentively and nodded his head. But, he knew that nothing that Aguilar said thus far constituted the reason why they were all together.

"Listen, I'm not gonna pull any punches here. You guys were both with me when we questioned Walter Vaughn. I had no reason to doubt that young man then and no reason now. In my opinion, that boy was not only telling us the truth, he had injuries consistent with his story. If you guys know something I don't, I'm all ears. Something just isn't right here. Somebody knew that two DEA agents were transporting Gatlin from Huachuca to Tucson. They knew that exact vehicle they were in. Somebody was willing to take quite a risk showing up at a hospital where they had every reason to believe that federal agents were present and, hell, my state police vehicle was sitting outside the emergency room in plain sight.

Now, somebody gets uncomfortable when a reporter starts questioning whether Gatlin is the monster that your Agency helped say he is."

Gaela and Watkins remained silent.

"Look, I understand that you both have to play things close to the vest when it comes to questions raised about the DEA. But, that doesn't apply to me. I'm sure you both are fully aware that there's a jurisdictional tussle between the DEA and Arizona State Police over the investigation of the murders of two of your agents. And what ought to, at least, have some degree of cooperation doesn't have any when it comes to your people.

I just want you fellas to know that I'm not on any kind of crusade against the DEA, but I'm not wearing this here badge to simply turn my head and pretend that something doesn't smell right when that's clearly the case."

The gap of silence that ensued seem to last for a long time before Marty Gaela spoke.

"Speaking for myself, Carlos, I'm not comfortable with what I'm seeing. No, we don't know anything more, but I'm ready to dig deeper. Hold tight and let's see if there can be a greater degree of cooperation between you and us."

Aguilar breathed what appeared to be a sigh of relief. Then, he turned his head towards Rick Watkins.

"Yeah, Carlos. You can count me in, too."

CHAPTER 18

TRUSTABLE

When Brett Gatlin survived the bloodbath in the Sonoran Desert and made his way to Fort Huachuca, he would have cited only three people in the entire world that he could trust. Two, his mother and sister, were unapproachable lest he put their lives in danger. The third person was Max Bradford and, while at the fort, Gatlin learned that Max was dead.

As Brett Gatlin was drawing nearer to Washington, D.C., the issue of trust was paramount in his mind. Kerry Anderson had written a newspaper article that was, at least, somewhat favorable towards Brett. But, in and of itself, that did not qualify Kerry as someone he could put his trust in. Besides, she was a reporter. If he dared to contact her, how could he possibly believe she would keep that confidential? Being contacted by the guy who was either a rogue agent responsible for a slew of innocent deaths or the victim of a conspiracy was surely a major story. How could he ever believe a reporter would be able to keep such a contact a secret?

Gatlin knew, only too well, the remarkable difference between being alone and being lonely. For more than four years, Brett Gatlin worked by himself and spent a great deal of time isolated from others. He was alone. But, he always knew they were there.

He had a team he could count on in an emergency. He knew that he could call on Max Bradford any time of the day or night.

Now, for the first time in his life, Brett Gatlin was lonely. He had no one in his life that he could turn to. Colonel Shirley stated that Special Agent William Falwell was the man that Bradford reported to. Shirley never provided Brett with any specifics regarding his conversations with Falwell. But, it didn't take a genius or a wizard to discern that whatever Falwell had to say was not favorable towards Gatlin. The fact that Brett left Huachuca bound in cuffs and leg irons and in the custody of two federal agents from Virginia was more than enough evidence of that.

Everything Brett was dealing with now was compounded by the fact that he had absolutely no idea what was going on. He entered the Sonoran Desert as a member of a Special Ops Team on the verge of fulfilling a four-year strategic plan to defeat a major cartel. He escaped the bloodbath that ensued alive, but since that time everything had completely fallen apart. Gatlin needed help. He needed someone who could move about more freely than himself if he was ever going to figure out what was happening.

It was time to trust. And, Brett knew that there was one and only one person he could completely trust. That person was himself. It was time to trust his own gut, rely upon his own instincts, and get increasingly proactive. His life depended upon it.

In his career as a DEA special agent, Marty Gaela worked hard honing his skills when it came to learning just who could be trusted. After years of experience, Gaela could read body language in a person he was interrogating so well, some of the other agents called him the "human lie detector." He was guarded in his dealings with other agents. He did have a strong trust in Rick Watkins. It was birthed from the fact that he mentored the guy. Throughout that time, he had opportunity to develop a uniquely close relationship with him. But, even now, when a key question was burning in Gaela's mind, he knew that Watkins would not be capable of providing any meaningful insight and answers. He simply did not have enough experience. If Gaela was going to resolve this, he was going to have to do it by himself.

The problem was he simply did not know her well enough. She had only been in the position of Special Agent in Charge of the Phoenix office, with authority over Tucson, for just short of four months. If anything, Marty Gaela had a strong impression that Barb Hennessey of the Phoenix office was a straight shooter who took her job seriously and was not known to play games or politics. But, was she willing to stand firm, even if it meant challenging some of the bigwigs in the agency that provided her with a job? Was she trustable enough for Gaela to go to her with questions and doubts that were searing in his own mind? He could be wrong. He realized that. But, was he willing to raise doubts and questions about some people somewhere within his own agency? To make matters worse, he would be questioning things with little more than circumstantial evidence and gut feelings? Could he go to his superior with this?

Until now, Marty Gaela always had a comfortable balance when it came to knowing who and when to trust someone. This time, he wasn't comfortable at all.

<hr>

Lucy Gatlin was, by nature, a friendly, trusting person. But, the nationwide story that her brother had betrayed his sworn oath and was working with a Mexican drug cartel shook her to the core. She did not believe that Brett would ever do such a thing, but there were occasional doubts that haunted her. She feared drugs. Lucy was much younger at the time, but she had witnessed what a drug dependency had done to her brother, Derek. The Brett that she had always known would never do what they were saying. But, was Brett still that same person she had known before he disappeared from her life?

"Please, Ms. Gatlin," the reporter's voicemail message stated. "I'm anxious to know more about your brother. I've already raised some serious questions about all the accusations being thrown at him. The public only knows the Brett Gatlin that others have described in negative ways. I need to be able to introduce them to the Brett Gatlin that you know. I have a strong belief that you and your mom can give us a completely different picture. I'm asking you to trust me."

Trust? When Lucy finally responded to Kerry Anderson's requests to meet with Lucy and her mom, Lucy had finally taken that proverbial leap of faith. Yes, she and her mom did have the ability to introduce the real Brett Gatlin to a world that only saw him in a negative light. The more Lucy thought about things, she made the decision that if Kerry Anderson was trustworthy, she and her mom would have their opportunity to talk honestly about Brett. If it was a mistake to trust Kerry, then what difference would it make? Her brother was already being condemned by a world that had been fed so many negative things about him.

When they met with Kerry Anderson, Gloria and Lucy Gatlin told the story of an achiever who excelled academically and in sports. Despite the passage of years, they both wept when they spoke about Derek's murder and how it radically changed the direction of Brett's life and future.

If Kerry Anderson had noted major contradictions in what she had learned about Gatlin prior to meeting with his mother and sister, her questions increased geometrically. Armed with the knowledge that Gatlin cast aside wealth and comfort to wage war against the things that helped to destroy his kid brother, Kerry was even more determined to uncover whatever was beneath the surface in the reports related to Brett Gatlin. She knew a thing or two about what it means to base your life's career on a strong underlying principle.

Kerry's father, a corporate chief financial officer, was accused of embezzlement of corporate funds. Kerry was a journalism major in college at the time. Fortunately for everyone concerned, the accusations were disproved due to the astute work by the FBI in uncovering a criminal ring. When a local reporter took the time to not only cover the story of the illegal activities, but also to extensively write an article fully clearing her father's name and reputation, Kerry was elated.

Kerry recalled how swiftly some of her father's friends turned away from him and would have nothing to do with him when the accusations were not yet disproved. She saw her mother shed tears when some of her women friends also disappeared from her life. And, through it all, she watched as her mother, despite her lack of sophisticated knowledge in the financial work her husband engaged in, believed in him and supported him throughout the ordeal.

"I promise you, Daddy," Kerry said back then. "When I become a journalist, I'll never lose sight of the human element in any story. I'll always seek truth over sensationalism."

When the story about Brett Gatlin broke, Kerry did not set out to take a questioning position. But, when she began to hear conflicting reports, she held true to her promise. She began to doggedly pursue the truth over all else. Now, after spending time with Brett's mother and sister, Kerry was even more intrigued. Yes, she understood that if Gatlin somehow became hooked on illegal drugs, that addiction could take precedence over all else. But, his actions at the scene of the highway accident and what she heard from medical personnel at the hospital did not fit the profile of a substance abuser.

The more Kerry Anderson learned about Special Agent Brett Gatlin, the less the initial reports about him made sense. She determined, more than ever, to do whatever it took to uncover the truth. What she did not know, what she could not possibly know, was just how costly that might be.

CHAPTER 19
MOVING ON

FBI Special Agent Marion Ortega assumed the primary responsibility in the search for Brett Gatlin. Ortega worked out of the Bureau Headquarters on Pennsylvania Avenue in Washington, D.C. Her team also coordinated closely with a designated team at the DEA Headquarters in Arlington, Virginia. It was at a Monday morning meeting when Ortega's team members shared updated info together.

"So, what we're saying," Agent Aaron Yates said, "is we see a pattern that indicates to us that Gatlin may be traveling east, heading possibly towards the State of Virginia."

"And what is your basis for this?" Ortega said.

"I'll let Monty respond to that," Yates said.

Agent Monty Richards projected a map from his laptop that highlighted several cities from Arizona on into Illinois. Richards and Yates placed markings on the map where, in each instance, a car theft had been reported.

"But, in every instance," Monty Richards said, "the stolen vehicle is eventually discovered in another state than where it was registered and stolen from."

"Right," Yates said. "The vehicle is completely undamaged and left in an area where it will readily be discovered. You get the impression that the thief borrowed the vehicle in order to get to another location."

"And, in every instance," Agent Tamako Yamamoto said, "the vehicle is clean. No prints."

"More than that," Aaron Yates said, "after we began tracking these auto thefts on what was initially not a whole lot more than a hunch, we dispatched a team to go over the last vehicle. It was found in an area near Springfield, Illinois. We had our guy run a search before the vehicle was turned back over to its owners. Whoever had been in that vehicle knew how to make sure that not a thread of forensic evidence was left behind."

"Like a professional car thief?" Ortega said.

"Like somebody even better trained than that," Yamamoto said.

"And just what does that mean?' Marion Ortega said.

"It might mean," Agent Yates said, "we're talking about a special ops trained individual. Someone like our friend, Brett Gatlin."

"Excellent work," Special Agent Ortega said. "Okay, so until now we've been behind these car thefts and have gained knowledge once the vehicle is dumped somewhere. We've got to notify jurisdictions nationwide starting with states heading eastward as we suspect. Let's see if we can get notice of a theft and be tracking things before the car is dumped. It's a longshot, I realize, because we are also relying upon when someone even reports a theft. We need to have every law enforcement agency send out an all-points bulletin identifying the vehicle and identifying Gatlin as being the possible thief. We go hard on this. We rouse everyone on what is a whole lot more than just a car theft."

Everyone nodded. Ortega chose Agent Tamako to spearhead the APB plan by preparing an advance communication that will only require the addition of a vehicle description and plate number before being transmitted to a slew of law enforcement agencies.

"May sound a bit crazy," Ortega said, "but it just might be that our boy is headed home, back to Arlington. Maybe, he has an ally or two there who he needs to hook up with. Regardless, this time, we get him."

⊷⊷ ⊶⊶

Gatlin was traveling a route that would take him from an area north of Springfield, Illinois to Norfolk, Virginia. Once he was in Norfolk, he would refine his plans on finding a way to reach into the Arlington Headquarters to hopefully gain more insight on what was going on. Perhaps, he could find a way to reach Special Agent Mike Wright, the man who had trained Gatlin, then steered him towards the RRT. He would consider trying to find Wright away from the DEA offices. Mike had been known to be particularly close to Max Bradford.

Gatlin was leery of his approach of stealing vehicles to take him from one place to another for fear that FBI investigators might pick up on the pattern and be able to track him down. But, using any form of public transportation was out of the question. He was sure that the authorities were monitoring every airport, train station, bus station, and other means of livery.

Gatlin would be spending this night in Ripley, West Virginia. That placed him less than seven hours from Norfolk. He would continue traveling the next day. This time, he left the last vehicle he had stolen in a more remote location. He wanted to delay its discovery until he had replaced his transportation needs in the early morning and left the area.

After abandoning the car, Gatlin walked more than seven miles to a seedy section of town where he'd find a room to get a few hours of sleep. Traveling like this made him realize even more so how much easier it would be if the human body did not require sleep nor food and drink.

The streets he was walking on were dark, dirty, and currently appeared to be empty. Of course, it was very possible that people who frequented areas such as these were always lurking about in a dark corner or alley for one nefarious reason or another. He kept a watchful eye as he walked along. Funny how even in the darkest area, there were shadows.

Gatlin walked another few blocks when he spotted two individuals up ahead at the front of a dark alley. He would have no choice but to walk past them, but before he reached the spot where they had been, they entered the alley. He braced his body for a possible ambush. But, when he reached the entrance to the alley, no such attack occurred.

As he peered into the darkness where the two men had gone, he could hear them laughing, grunting, and cussing. Despite the darkness, he discerned that they were kicking the body of some-one who was lying prone against the alley wall.

"What's the matter, old man, you so drunk you can't even try to get away when we kick you around like a damn football?" one of the men said. And, they both broke out in laughter.

"I don't want no trouble." Brett heard the old man say. "Just leave me alone. Don't hurt me. Leave me be."

"Aw, listen to the old boy begging," the same man said. "He don't want no trouble, he says."

"But, we are trouble," the other man said, followed by a chuck-le. "That's exactly who we are. We always been trouble. We always gonna be trouble. Hey, let's see which one of us can break the most ribs. You think we can hear when a bone cracks inside the old gee-zer's body?"

Gatlin stood and stared. The men were laughing and enjoying themselves so much, they had no idea that Brett was even there. He prepared to move on.

This is not any of my business. I've got enough of my own problems to deal with. I don't need to mess around in anyone else's. Much too risky. I need to just go about taking care of me.

"Go away. Just leave me be," the old man cried out. "I ain't done nothing to you. Leave me be."

"I got me a better idea," the first man said. "Forget the ribs. I'm gonna kick him in the head. Maybe I can break the old drunk's freakin' neck."

The second man reached down and grabbed the old man by the throat, squeezing tightly as the man's face turned scarlet.

"Okay, man, I'm gonna be the holder. You be the placekicker. I'll make sure this head is nice and steady for a good solid and clean kick."

Brett was there before either of the men even fully realized that he was. As the man began to lift his leg, Gatlin grabbed the man's ankle and threw him against the back wall. The second man let go of the old man's throat and lunged towards Brett. Gatlin dropped him with a punch to the stomach, an uppercut when the man doubled over, and a solid left hook to the man's temple.

The first man recovered enough to come towards Brett with a switchblade knife that he pulled from his pocket. Gatlin let the man come forward, then grabbed his wrist and twisted until the knife fell to the ground. Brett threw a series of solid punches that the man tried to defend against to no avail. Within less than a minute, both men were unconscious on the ground.

Brett stared down at the old man.

"You okay? Look, I can't stay here. I've got to go before... "

"Before the police show up?" the old man said. "Here, help me up, son. I got a place we can go to where the cops don't never come. C'mon quick now."

Brett pulled the old man to his feet. He could smell the strong scent of whiskey and heard the empty bottle clang as it fell from the man's lap onto the ground. The old fella might be inebriated and he wobbled and staggered a bit, but he was able to walk swiftly with Brett. He took Gatlin farther down the alley, made a left and traveled along a back alley, then turned right down yet another alleyway. If at all possible, this corridor between buildings seemed even darker and dirtier than any of the others. More than halfway down the alley, they reached a gray metal door. The man opened it and turned to Brett.

"Place has been empty for years. They say they gonna tear it down someday, but that day ain't never come yet. You got others that stay here. They won't give no mind who you are and what your situation may be. This here place got a code even stronger than what they say about that Las Vegas city. What happens here stays here and who is here stays here and nobody talks about nobody."

Brett hesitated. Then, he considered his options, which were not all that extensive, and entered the old building.

CHAPTER 20

A HIDDEN WORLD

B rett's mouth fell open. He instinctively slapped his hands against his cheeks. He had followed the old man rather blindly into an old abandoned building. He hadn't had the time to even consider what he would see once he was inside. But, he never expected to see what he now did.

The room was immense. The ceiling was at least thirty feet high. The walls consisted of cement blocks painted gray. The concrete floor was also painted gray. Light from outside entered the room through a series of thin clerestory fixed lite windows placed some twenty feet above the floor.

It appeared as if the place had once been a factory of some sort. But, now, it was home to more than forty homeless people. Like a line of separate booths at a flea market, each person had their own spot along the walls of the long open room. As it was now dusk and darkness was moving in, Brett spotted lanterns, candles, and some flames burning in outdoor barbecue grills. Some of the designated areas belonging to an individual had a covering of some sort. Some had old chairs, others had boxes or crates to sit on. Brett spotted an old bureau that was missing two drawers. There were old couches, love seats, rocking chairs, and various pieces of furniture that a previous owner had likely discarded. There were some tables, wooden barrels, and even a hammock or two. They used the grills to heat up food, as well as provide some light by containing open flames. A variety of beads, old rugs, quilts, or tapestries graced some of the locations. The one consistency that Brett noticed was that each person's location evidenced a sense of care and pride from its inhabitant.

Gatlin spotted a few circles of individuals sitting and chatting together. There were some who were playing cards or some other game. A solitary man plucked very quietly on an old guitar. Brett was amazed to see a sense of order in a building that had otherwise lost its identity and purpose years ago when the enterprise it once housed moved out.

"C'mon," the old man said to Brett. "Got somebody I want you to meet."

Within minutes, they were standing in front of the spot belonging to an old woman. She groomed her gray hair tightly in a bun. Her face bore the strain and markings of life's challenges, but her eyes sparkled and her smile was warm and friendly. She was one of the people who had a grill in front of her station. In fact, she was currently heating up something in an old pot that was clearly larger than what she would personally need to feed herself.

"Well, Zachary," the woman said, revealing the old man's name to Brett, "I see ya got this here nice-lookin' feller taggin' along with ya, huh?"

Zachary turned towards Brett.

"This here's Miss Molly. Best durn cook we got in this place. Everybody's responsible for their own food and drinks, but lots of us get stuff from out there and bring it over here for Miss Molly to work her magic. We do share food and meals from time-to-time."

Molly smiled revealing a good number of empty spaces in her mouth where teeth once existed.

"Well now, anybody's like to be hailed as a good cook when ya got a bunch of vagabonds who act like anything's a feast when they're good and hungry. We do okay in here, but lots of time we eat kind of catch-as-catch-can. Ya know? Don't always have a lot ta eat every day. But, like I say, we do all right."

"My friend here," Zachary said, referring to Brett, "just saved my life from a couple of monsters who was fixin' to break all my ribs and then snap my neck. Can't tell you how grateful I am he come along when he did or my spot and my stuff in here would have been up for grabs."

Zachary took a bit more time to provide Molly with the details of all that occurred in the alley.

Molly shook her head as she continued to stir the contents in her pot.

"World's getting rougher and rougher out there," Molly said. "There was a time when people didn't just come along looking to hurt others for no reason at all."

Molly turned more directly towards Brett.

"Exceptin' fer the fact he drinks too much at times and, when he does, he snores loud enough ta wake the dead, Zachary here is a good man. Wouldn't never hurt nobody. Always helpful ta others. Always respects other people and their stuff.

Well, you need ta know that any friend of Zachary is automatically on my good person list. Stew's just about ready to eat and I believe it's a good one tonight. Gibson's grocery gave up some vegetables that was fresh, just not quite fresh enough fer the buyin' folks. And they gave us two good size pot roast bones that still had enough meat on 'em to flavor this thing up real good."

"We'll eat," Zachary said to Brett. "And, I got room for you to sleep over at my place. Matter of fact, you can stay long as you'd like."

The stew was delicious. Brett joined Zachary afterwards in chatting with some of the "residents," as Zachary called them. No one ever asked Brett his name nor anything about his personal life. They did not have any televisions in this abandoned warehouse. They didn't even have electricity, but it was possible that some of the folks inside would have seen Brett's picture somewhere while wandering around town. Brett considered that he spotted a look of recognition on the faces of a few of the people he met, but no one ever said a word. No one would.

That night, Brett learned that the residents had some form of structure that they all willingly adhered to. Zachary brought Brett to Millard, the man they all called "Mayor." He was sitting with a lit pipe between his teeth and playing chess on a board placed atop an old oak barrel. The residents referred any disputes to Millard. He also had a panel of "advisors" who assisted with more serious matters or decisions. Miss Molly, for example, was an advisor.

Many of the residents had established good contacts with stores and restaurants outside the walls of this building. They were able to pick up supplies and items that were for the common good. Some received otherwise disposable food items from restaurants or grocery stores. The local bakery gladly gave the residents older bread and baked items that were still edible. One resident, whom they all called "Our Hero," worked out a deal with a local store where he emptied their trash into dumpsters at night and they gave him supplies of toilet paper rolls in return. Amazingly, a cistern and a well in the old building were still functional. The city had turned off the water some time ago.

Mayor Millard always found ways to reward those individuals who did things to the benefit of the entire community.

Brett did spend the night there and slept well, despite Zachary's occasional snoring. Gatlin woke up early to find that most everyone was still asleep, except for Miss Molly. He found her brewing a large pot of coffee. She greeted Brett with a warm nearly toothless smile and a cheerful whisper of good morning. Molly poured a cup of coffee for herself and Brett.

"I'll be heading out now," Brett said. "I don't want to wake Zachary. A couple more hours of solid sleep will do him well."

Molly nodded and leaned a bit closer for Brett to hear her without disturbing any of the others.

"Ya look like ya got the world on yer shoulders, son. I seen it in yer eyes, even last night. Jus' remember, the Good Lord, he don't lose track of nobody, even when we sometimes wonder where he is when we're in the midst of things. Keep yer head up. I got me a feelin' yer a man who knows how ta survive. Hold tight and God speed."

A tingling in his skin and a fluttery feeling in his belly crawled through Brett's body. He was amazed that an old woman in a makeshift homeless shelter displayed more wisdom and awareness than so many others he had ever encountered. He had no idea whether Molly had any idea who he was, although he suspected that she did. Regardless, he was also sure that she would never tell him, nor anyone else.

As Brett reached over to take Molly's hand before leaving, he placed the wad of five one hundred dollar bills in her hand.

"I thought maybe giving this to Zachary might not be the best idea. You know, he could get tempted to invest it in some liquid entertainment. I hope you'll use this wisely for whatever you think is best."

Molly's mouth fell open.

"Ya know ya don't have to… "

Brett lifted his hand with his palm forward like a traffic cop signaling drivers to stop.

"It's not payback. It's not given in pity. It's my personal investment in a group of people who have found a way to rise above their own struggles and misfortune and provide some degree of meaning to their lives. Thank you, Miss Molly."

Brett turned and started walking away. Then, he turned back.

"And, yes, your stew last night was delicious."

Then, he smiled, turned, and walked out of the building.

⇌ ⇋

His next stop would be Norfolk, Virginia, which would bring him even closer to the Arlington area. Right now, his plan to try to reach out to Special Agent Mike Wright was sketchy. But, everything in his life was confusing with no guarantee at all that anything would ever make sense again and ever turn out well.

He reflected for a moment on the resident community tucked away in an underground world on the periphery of normal society itself. In one sense, those people had nothing. In another sense, they likely had much more than he and many others possessed.

CHAPTER 21
GOTTA KNOW

Norfolk, Virginia placed Brett within three hours of Arlington or Washington, D.C. He considered that those two cities were places that held answers that he desperately wanted. With his hair much longer and dyed black and a beard and mustache providing some cover to his face, Gatlin had taken steps to disguise his appearance. Even so, unlocking doors to the next places he desired to go would take a whole lot more than some changes in physical appearance. He dumped the car he had driven and was quickly walking the downtown streets with a goal to find a homeless shelter.

Brett was startled when the first police car whizzed by him. He was thankful that it had quickly passed. Two more police cars heightened his awareness. He spotted more police cars stopped ahead, dealing with some kind of altercation. The local bar that he neared was filled with people and had a band playing music. Brett went in.

Gatlin found a spot in the far corner of the bar, where he sat and ordered a beer. They did not serve food in this bar, so the sweet fruity smell of beer permeated the room. The local band had many in the crowd dancing and singing along, which helped make a guy like Brett even less conspicuous.

A man sitting nearby nodded, then moved closer to where he could better converse with Gatlin. Brett pegged the man to be somewhere in his early forties. His body was lean and tight. His medium length sandy brown wavy hair added to the relaxed look the man bore. His facial hair sported some light silvery patches. His green eyes added to his friendly demeanor.

"How goes it, my friend?" the man said. "You local or just passing through?"

Brett was not anxious to engage in conversation with others, but he did not want to draw attention to himself by appearing to be brusque or impolite.

"Nah, just in town for a night. Figured I'd stop and have myself a cold one and enjoy the music. The band's pretty good."

"Well, to start with, we have something like fifty breweries here in Norfolk with a slew of local labels. Good stuff. So, yes, the beer here is really good. Then, we've got some good local musicians throughout this area. Norfolk's known for having talented artistic people. Good beer, good music—can't go wrong with that combo."

The man laughed and Brett laughed along with him. He turned more directly towards Brett and extended his hand.

"Roger Clark," he said.

"Paul Williamson," Gatlin responded. "Nice to meet you. So, you're from around here?"

Gatlin figured that tossing a few questions at the stranger would keep the focus on Clark rather than himself.

"Originally from Des Moines," Clark answered. "College, a dream to fly, and a few lucky breaks got me my wings as an Air Force pilot. Was one of the first pilots to fly the Raptor."

Gatlin was familiar enough with the F-22's reputation as the greatest warplane ever created to at least converse with the man and further assure that things were not focused on him.

"Never been in the military," Brett said, "but read quite a bit about the Raptor having such stealth technology and high-tech features that federal law has banned the export of those birds."

Clark smiled, nodded his head, and took another sip of his draft beer before speaking again.

"The Raptor does things that a plane isn't supposed to be able to do, while you're cruising along at speeds up to 1,500 miles per hour. The F-22 is said to be the first operational aircraft to combine supercruise, supermaneuverability, stealth, and sensor fusion in a single weapons platform."

"Sensor fusion?" Gatlin said.

"Yeah, well just consider that you're combining data from multiple sources and what you get is one much better picture of just what you're dealing with," Roger said. "Guess the best way to describe what it's like to be in the cockpit of the Raptor is to say that no matter how many times you fly it, the rush, exhilaration, and the shock at what that plane can do is there every single time."

Gatlin smiled.

"Sounds awesome to me. You still fly now."

Roger Clark's demeanor changed. He breathed in deeply before responding. His head was lower, his lips pressed tightly together, and his shoulders were slumped.

"No. Not anymore. I'm out of the service."

Gatlin remained silent, providing Clark with the opportunity to continue speaking if he wanted to do so.

Roger finished his beer, signaled the bartender for a refill for himself and Gatlin, then shrugged his shoulders.

"What can I tell you?" Clark said. "Developed some major problems with my eyes and a bit of rheumatoid arthritis in my left shoulder. Got myself grounded and, after a while, realized I was never gonna get back in that cockpit."

Clark paused as the bartender served up two more beers. He raised his mug to a toast with Gatlin, took a sip, then spoke again.

"They offered me positions as a flight instructor, but, I don't know, man. I always believed I was born to fly. I figured if I continued to hang around guys who were getting to do what I no longer could, I'd either go crazy or end up wanting to strangle someone."

Clark laughed and, again, Gatlin laughed along with him.

The moment changed when Brett spotted two uniformed Norfolk police officers enter the building. They stared in the direction of where Gatlin and Clark were seated and headed that way. Brett's body tightened, he angled his face away and sipped at his beer. The police officers slowly moved past Clark and Gatlin to an area where the restrooms were located.

Clark turned towards one of the officers and nodded his head in greeting. He placed his body in a position that further blocked Gatlin from the police officer's view.

"How's your night going?" Clark said.

"Aw, doin' okay. You know, on nights like this we get a whole lot of folks here in the downtown area. Nice weather today. Folks been cooped up all week and just want to get out and let off some steam."

"Any trouble out there?" Clark said.

"Nah, folks tend to get more boisterous when they've been drinking. Had to break up a few skirmishes." The officer started laughing. "First one was between two females. Second one involved a lady who was about to kick some serious butt on a guy that set her off."

"Haha," Roger said. "Sounds like you saved that guy from a whuppin' and a major loss of dignity."

Clark and the police officer were both laughing now.

As his partner exited the restroom, the officer excused himself from Roger Clark and headed in. Roger grabbed Gatlin's arm.

"Come on. Let's get out of this place," he said.

Within minutes, the two men were out in the night air.

"My car's parked around the corner," Clark said.

<hr />

"I am sure that I am not alone in the expectation that you and your team would have apprehended the man by now, Andrew. I am also sure that you are aware that the clock is running, my friend, in a rather unfavorable manner towards you and your folks. I am doing my very best to keep others calm, but you need to understand that I am simply one man. My position and influence may be rather strong, but even I cannot keep everyone at bay forever."

The man always made Andrew Gotschild uncomfortable. Andrew dreaded hearing about clocks running and people getting increasingly impatient. Of course, Andrew was much too smart to ever reveal his distaste for the man's subtle threats.

"I appreciate your indulgence in providing us with additional time, sir. We know that Gatlin is headed east. He might be attempting to reach Agency Headquarters in Arlington. Believe me, we'll be ready for him, no matter what his plans are. The man is highly-trained, but my guys are the best there are. We'll get him, sir. Don't you worry about that. I assure you, we'll get him."

"Well, I most certainly hope that you do, Andrew. I most certainly do hope so."

Gotschild suspected that the man and his cohorts already had a backup plan to replace him with another investigative team and make sure that Andrew would never be in a position to talk with anyone about the job he had failed to complete.

⤙⤚

"I've got a place not far from here," Roger Clark said, as he drove his Jeep out of the downtown area.

"You can drop me off anywhere," Gatlin said.

Although nothing specific was ever said between the two men, Brett was aware that Roger Clark knew who he was and had already taken a step to get a known fugitive out of the downtown area.

"You don't need to be wandering around at night putting yourself at risk," Clark said. "You'll be safe in my condo. I live alone. Nobody ever comes around."

"No need to get you involved in my affairs," Gatlin said. "Not sure why you'd want to anyway."

Clark pulled off the road for a moment, kept the car running, and turned towards Gatlin.

"I read those articles that lady journalist for the Washington Post wrote. Read about what happened to your brother and why you chose to become a fed. So, let me take a moment and tell you a story. It's about a boy whose mother was pregnant at a time when his father was flying bombing missions over Cambodia at the close of the Vietnam War. The boy's father died when his plane was shot down. The man never got to see his son."

"I take it," Gatlin said, "that you were that boy."

"I was," Clark said, "and as I grew older, I wanted to know everything about the father I never had a chance to know. There was even a time when I tracked down some of the men in his squadron that knew my dad. You might think that I'd be bitter towards a country and branch of the military that cost me ever getting to know my own father. But, truth is, I moved in the opposite direction. At a very young age, I decided that I wanted to be like my father. And, I wanted to finish what he started and never got to complete.

Let me tell you, Gatlin," Clark continued, revealing that he definitely knew Brett's identity, "there were times whenever I was down, struggling a bit, questioning whether I'd ever make it as a pilot. There were times when I wondered if I'd ever get past the politics and games people play and be one of the pilots chosen to fly the Raptor. "

Clark fixed his gaze deeply on Gatlin.

"No matter what I went through, no matter what anybody ever threw at me, I never lost sight of my dad, the reason why I became a pilot in the first place and the personal mission I was on. That carried me time and again and it was the one thing I would never forget or betray."

Brett Gatlin's head dropped down. His eyes were no longer locked on Roger Clark. His eyes were misty. Clark reached over and placed his right hand around Gatlin's left arm, causing Brett to lift his head again.

"A man doesn't lose sight of the deep personal motivation that spurred him to take action in the first place. When I heard about your brother and your personal motivation, I knew there was no way you'd line yourself up with the very people who represented the reason why your kid brother is dead. I don't know what this whole thing is about, but I'm betting that the doubts raised by the lady reporter are a hell of a lot closer to the truth than all the other stuff that's been said.

When I'd fly the greatest fighter jet ever made, there were many times I had to make a decision in a split second. I learned to trust my instincts. And my instincts are telling me now that you need a friend."

CHAPTER 22
HELP NEEDED

The two men were positioned outside One Franklin Square at 1301 K Street NW in Washington, D.C., where the Washington Post has its offices. They would spot her as she left the building. They knew she was in today after Roger Clark called the Post offices and asked for Kerry Anderson. Gatlin and Clark discussed whether they should initially speak to Kerry over the phone, but they ruled it out.

"We're taking a gamble that we can even trust the woman," Gatlin said. "Giving her advanced notice could blow up in our faces."

They considered the extra time they expended in learning her pattern, once she left the office, to be worth the investment they made. The plan they devised was simple. Assuming Anderson was alone as usual, Roger would link up with her while Brett remained in the Jeep. Her opportunity to meet with the man whom she'd been writing about was an immediate, one-time- only proposition. The choice was hers, but only under the terms offered by the men approaching her. She would not be free to call anyone. There would be no pictures taken, no recordings made. This was

Kerry's single opportunity to meet the illusive, ghost-like man that she was familiar with only in theory and based upon the opinions of others.

The moment Clark spotted her, he quickly signaled Gatlin. He walked behind the attractive woman whose news articles about Special Agent Brett Gatlin had garnered a captive audience with a voracious appetite for more. There were those who regarded Anderson's reports as nothing more than the ramblings of a woman entrenched in the mindset of the liberal media. But, even those who disputed the alternative scenarios proposed by Kerry, nevertheless, waited for her next installment.

Roger Clark now walked alongside Kerry Anderson ready to make his move. He and Brett had taken the position that they were in control of everything in their take-it-or leave-it proposition for Kerry Anderson. Yet, as Roger prepared to make his move, both he and Brett hoped above all else that this woman would take their offer. Now that Roger was with him, Brett had deviated from his original plan to contact Agent Mike Wright. Kerry Anderson could possibly be of great value to them.

One Franklin Square, a twelve-story building with more than 625,000 square feet of space, is located five blocks northeast of the White House and four blocks from Metro Center, the hub of the nation's capital mass transit system where Kerry was headed. Clark intended to approach Anderson before she entered the Metro Center. He spoke to her as the two walked closer to the metro hub. Kerry stopped to acknowledge Clark.

"Hello, Ms. Anderson. Find your articles on Special Agent Brett Gatlin of great interest."

"Why, thank you."

Kerry started to turn back towards the station entrance.

"Before you walk away, I'm assuming you might be interested in meeting the man you've been writing about?"

Anderson froze. She tilted her head to the side as she gazed with focus at the man. Her mind quickly shifted between whether his question was simply rhetorical or he had something to offer.

"Listen, mister… "

"Clark. Name's Roger Clark, Ms. Anderson. And you've got about ninety feet to the entrance of the metro station and less than a minute to decide whether you're interested in meeting Brett Gatlin. It's just that simple, Ma'am. Not any more complicated than that."

"You're telling me that you can arrange that meeting?" Kerry said.

"Indeed, I am," Clark responded. "The terms are simple. The meeting happens now, at our choice of location, in complete confidence. You hand me your cell phone, so I can be sure that you neither call anyone nor record anything. You agree to these terms, I make it happen. As I said a moment ago, it's as simple as that."

Kerry did not move. She stood still and stared at the man. There was limited time for her to further appraise him and no time to consult with anyone else.

"Listen," Kerry said, "how do I know that you…"

Clark interrupted.

"You don't, Ms. Anderson. You don't know. You don't know anything except a man has approached you on the street and is telling you he can bring you to Brett Gatlin and give you the opportunity to talk with the man. That's all you know. Take the offer or go catch your train."

Kerry continued to stare at Roger Clark. If the man was telling the truth, if he could arrange this meeting…

Clark spoke gain.

"Listen, Ms. Anderson, we're talking about a man who's being sought by every law enforcement agency in the country. We're talking about a man who will tell you that he is innocent and that your perspective on this entire matter is the correct one. There's no room here for advanced notice of a meeting or arranging to meet at a place of your choosing. You're likely focused upon whether you can trust me. But, I assure you, trusting you is the real issue here. It's also a major gamble on Agent Gatlin's part.

So, if you'll pardon my brusqueness, I need your answer now, Ms. Anderson."

Kerry smiled, nodded her head, and shrugged her shoulders.

"You've got a deal, Mr. Clark. Drop the Ms. Anderson tag, call me Kerry, and lead on."

"Great. You just made what is likely the best decision any reporter could make," Clark said. "Call me Roger and," Clark extended his hand out with his palm up, "I'll take your cell phone right about now."

The two men were eyes-on poised outside of Kerry Anderson's condo in a white, non-descript van. Scott Lambert was the first of the two to unwrap his subway sandwich. His partner, Leo Sawyer, was still adjusting the devices that would enable them to hear and record any conversations that Kerry would have inside her own place of residence.

"Quit messing with that stuff," Scott said. "You keep fooling with it, you're gonna screw it all up. Get away from there and come eat your food, man."

Lambert was a former military career guy and he certainly looked the part. At six feet four with a square jaw, buzz cut brown hair, and large biceps, Scott looked like someone the average person would not want to tangle with.

Leo Sawyer was the techie of the two. He was six feet two inches, lanky, with brown hair that seemed to have a mind of its own, a scruffy beard, and wire-rim glasses. Sawyer was the one to create a schematic for the placement of bugs throughout Kerry's condo.

Leo picked the lock to get them in. Leo's instructed Scott on how to turn off the home alarm system. Once they finished with their work inside, they returned to the white van. Now, they would sit and wait for Kerry to return and eventually tip them off to her plans.

"Gotschild's gonna be real pleased with the way you set things up, Leo. That reporter lady so much as breathes and we'll know it," Scott said.

"I'm hoping," Leo said, "that once we latch onto her cell phone, I'll be able to get us permanently linked onto that device. Then, we've got her no matter where she is."

Scott Lambert smiled and high-fived his partner.

"You're a good man, Leo. Glad that you decided to use your skills to benefit the dark side," Scott said, followed by a laugh.

⊨ ⊨

Once Roger was sure that they were not being followed, he led Anderson to the covered parking lot where the Jeep was parked. She climbed in the back seat. Clark hopped in the driver's seat. Brett, seated in the passenger seat, turned around and nodded in greeting to the one person who first openly expressed doubts that he was the criminal that people, worldwide, believed him to be.

"Nice of you to drop in," Gatlin said, evoking a smile from Anderson. Brett was somewhat taken aback by the fact that Kerry Anderson was even more attractive in person than the pictures of her he had seen. He sought to distract himself from staring at the young female reporter by turning to Roger Clark and thanking him for his successful mission in getting Kerry to come with him.

Clark smiled, nodded his head, and fist-bumped Brett.

"Well, you know, you're the star of the show she came to see."

Roger Clark provided Kerry with a brief synopsis of who he was and why he was here with Gatlin. Then, Brett turned back towards Kerry Anderson.

"I'm going to provide you with as much time as you want to ask questions," Brett said. "But, how about we begin by having me provide you with my side of the story?"

Brett began by telling Kerry about the death of his brother Derek, which was the reason why he joined the DEA. Although Kerry was aware of this from a conversation she had with Brett's mother and sister, she said nothing. As Brett spoke, he was confirming all that his mother and sister told Kerry. Although Gatlin continued to preserve the name and details surrounding *Subterraneo*, he did mention that he was in an undercover role as a member of special ops team supervised by Special Agent Max Bradford.

"The original plan was that we would remain undercover for two years, but the time extended to four years. I went to Fort Huachuca because that was our sanctuary destination where we were to contact Max. But, I never received confirmation from DEA Headquarters supporting my role as an undercover agent involved in a major covert mission. I have no explanation for that Kerry. It makes no sense at all."

Gatlin mentioned DEA Special Agent William Falwell as the man that Max Bradford apparently reported to.

"If Max reported to Falwell, the man had to know about our special ops team."

"Agent Gatlin," Kerry Anderson said, "based upon what you have told me and what I picked up from the original police report of the accident in Arizona, it appears that someone is trying to kill you. Do you have any idea why?"

"Please, call me Brett. No. I have no idea. The threats against my life started in Mexicali when somehow a group of Mexican thugs discovered a place I had there—a place only known to Max

Bradford. At the time, I assumed it was a follow up of some kind to the Sonoran Desert drug bust."

"How did your team in Mexico communicate?" Kerry asked.

"One of our guys, Danny Nguyen, had us communicating with encrypted messages."

Kerry was thorough and quick with her questions. Brett was already impressed.

"You speak," Kerry said, "as if everything that you have experienced is a mystery to you—things you simply have no explanation for. Is there anything in particular, anything out of the ordinary that you, perhaps, have thought of after everything that has occurred?"

Brett paused for a moment before deciding that he would reveal to Anderson something that had been troubling him.

"I told you that we were in the Sonoran Desert and that the plan was to have a small army of American and Mexican federal agents come to the site where we were meeting."

"Yes," Kerry said, "and you said that the convoy was annihilated by explosions that killed everyone."

Gatlin's eyes seemed to be focused on another time and place.

"There was so much going on all around me," Gatlin said, "so I realize I could be mistaken... but... I never saw anything strike those Hummers. I didn't see anything launched at them. Besides, it would have taken some powerful weaponry to penetrate those vehicles. The other thing I noticed was that every vehicle exploded simultaneously."

Anderson's face was ashen as she considered what Brett was saying.

"Are you saying that the explosives seemed to be inside each of the vehicles that the federal agents were in? That would mean... "

Gatlin stared deeply into Kerry Anderson's eyes. He nodded his head as he spoke.

"Yeah, it would mean that the Hummers were rigged. It was an inside job."

CHAPTER 23

A MEASURE OF INTEGRITY

Caesar Hidalgo Monterro wasn't pleased when the word came down from the United States that, in the future, the exchange of money would take place in America.

"Your people will be granted safe passage over the border into Sierra Vista, Arizona," the distinguished American informed Monterro. "There will be no problem there, whatsoever."

A decision had been made that nothing would be placed on a computer or other device. During a meeting of representatives from Monterro's cartel and the Americans, Monterro's people would provide a full monthly accounting and the exchange of money would be in cash. Even bank wire transfers would not be utilized. An initial meeting to divide cash from the Sonoran Desert incident would be held soon.

"These Americans," Monterro said to a few of his key men, "they are extremely cautious. That means, of course, that they have far more to lose than getting caught for being involved in the drug trade with our people."

Monterro laughed. He lit up a cigar and took his first puff before speaking again.

"Sometimes, I think these *gringos*, they have such a sense of superiority they believe we here south of the border are simply not all that bright. Ah, but that is something we may always use to our advantage. When an American has a fear that exceeds the criminal charges for involvement in the illegal drug trade, it means he or she is a person of great importance and position. Yes? And, already, we have those who assist us across the border who will soon reveal to us the very people who think they can hide their identity from us."

Monterro paused again, puffed on his cigar again, and followed that with a sip from his wine glass. He then lifted the glass and invited his men to join in a toast with him.

"*Salud!* To your health, my friends, we shall prosper together for years to come."

Monterro smiled as he placed his glass down on the table. These men stimulated a loyalty in him. He could envision remaining faithful to them into the future and making each of them wealthy in their own right. As for the Americans, he would bide his time until the day he would have the great pleasure in bringing them down.

Kerry Anderson listened intently to everything that Brett Gatlin had to say. As expected, his version of things was drastically different from what the DEA and other segments of the media were saying. Yet, at the same time, it was consistent with all that Kerry had been uncovering in her investigative work. As she pieced together things she had heard from Agents Marty Gaela and Rick Watkins, along with State Trooper Carlos Aguilar and even things that Walter Vaughn had to say, Gatlin's version was consistent with them. When she recalled what Gatlin's mother and sister told her, Brett was also saying the same things as they did.

Beyond that, Kerry Anderson was particularly astute at perceiving verbal and non-verbal communications. One of her college roommates and closest friends, Delonda Wilson, had gone on to become an agent with the FBI. Delonda, an attractive African-American woman, was originally from the Bronx borough in New York. At six feet two inches, she was a starting guard on the university women's basketball team and still managed to graduate with high honors.

"When you're interrogating someone," Delonda once said as she shared some of her FBI training, "you've got to look for two categories of validated behavioral indicators. One is entirely verbal and used to differentiate a lie from the truth. You know, things like the fact that lies consist of fewer words, omit more information, are less plausible, structured, and logical. The second category includes what we refer to as nonverbal behaviors where a person is communicating emotions and cognitions through things like facial expressions, voice tone, gesture, body movement, and posture."

Kerry learned a great deal from Delonda. Anderson was astute enough to realize that the insights shared by her friend were not foolproof, but, time and again, she relied upon what Delonda had taught her. The results, far more often than not, proved to be accurate.

Delonda was currently stationed in Seattle. Shortly after Anderson's first Washington Post article was published, Delonda called her.

"I'm proud of you, girl," Delonda said. "You never were one to simply follow the pack. You know, I envy your freedom. You can express what you believe without the concern that a federal agency is weighing every word. Just remember, Kerry, I'm here for you, even if I have to work behind the scenes."

Now, as Kerry had the unexpected opportunity to question the man she wrote about, she applied everything that Delonda had taught her. As Gatlin spoke, every indicator suggested that the man was telling the truth. When she looked deeply into Brett Gatlin's eyes, she saw integrity, convincing her even more so that her initial instincts were correct. This man was not a rogue agent who had betrayed his country and his oath. These were not the eyes of a man hooked on illegal drugs.

When she stared into Gatlin's eyes, Kerry saw something else. She saw a strong attractive man who caused her blood pressure to increase and her heart to flutter. But, no! If she were to help this man, it had to be based upon a belief in his innocence. She was a journalist, a professional. As a member of the *fourth estate,* Kerry was committed to pursuing truth for truth's sake. As an unbiased reporter, she was bound to follow the evidence that she unearthed and discovered, wherever it would lead. If she agreed to assist Gatlin by taking steps he could not take himself, it had to be on the basis that she was answerable only to herself and an uncompromising agreement to reveal the truth, regardless of the consequences in doing so. It also could not be based upon any personal attraction she might have towards him.

Kerry fought the hidden battle to push aside any attraction to Brett Gatlin. Besides, if, as she currently believed, Gatlin's innocence was eventually substantiated, the prospect of getting to know him on a more personal basis was certainly something she could then consider. At the moment, the man's life and future hung precariously in the balance between what so many others were saying and the words written by Anderson.

Kerry Anderson was seated across from what had all the markings of a once-in-a-lifetime story. The man in front of her represented a potential Pulitzer prize in journalism, a best-selling book, a reputation as a reporter that would greatly impact on her future, including future earnings. As she stared at Brett Gatlin, the image suddenly changed. Seated across from her was a man who was the subject of a gross betrayal, a man whose life was in jeopardy as already evidenced by bullets fired at a vehicle traveling on an Arizona highway. She saw a man being pursued by those who were not hesitant to kill. Two federal agents never returned to their families in Virginia when their bodies were discovered in a Tucson hospital emergency room.

Brett Gatlin was not a great story that would further launch Kerry Anderson's career and future. He was Kerry Anderson's opportunity to test her own mettle and discover just how deeply she was willing to fight for and expose the truth. He was how Kerry's own conscience and personal integrity would be measured.

⇒⊹⊹⇐

Attorney General of the United States, Floyd V. Harrington was the head of the United States Department of Justice. As a result, his authority extended over several law enforcement agencies. Included were the Federal Bureau of Investigation and the Drug Enforcement Administration. No Attorney General has ever been elected President of the United States. Bobby Kennedy may have come the closest before an assassin's bullet ended his quest for the Democratic Party nomination. Floyd Harrington intended to end that presidential drought.

Norman Finley ran his fingers through his black wavy hair. His gold diamond encrusted pinky ring glistened in the overhead lights of Harrington's office. The man was careful with his words for fear that Harrington was secretly recording their conversation. In fact, Harrington was doing exactly that. Then again, when dealing with a man as powerful as Harrington, recordings would certainly not be the greatest threat one would ever face.

"So, Norman, you're satisfied that we'll have the full cooperation of Señor Monterro going forward?" Harrington said.

"Yes, absolutely. I am fully satisfied. The man is no fool. Despite his lack of knowledge as to who he is specifically dealing with,

Monterro knows, by virtue of the assistance he's already received and the clearances in getting the products into the U.S., that he's dealing with powerful people in our government. Besides, it's much too sweet a deal for him to cross anyone."

"I want you to stay on top of him, Norman," Harrington said. "Sweet deal, notwithstanding, I don't trust Monterro and believe that only a fool would do so. We've got much too much at stake to let some Mexican gangster mess things up for us."

"I understand," Norman said. "I'll keep tabs on the guy. Matter of fact. I'll be back at Monterro's estate in less than a week."

"Good to hear," Harrington said. "Nicely done, my friend."

As Norman Finley left Harrington's office, the Attorney General made a quick phone call.

"He's leaving my office now," Harrington said before ending the call.

Serving at the pleasure of a president whom Harrington regarded as too weak and gutless to take a strong stand against anyone or anything, the Attorney General would permit crimes, especially drug-related crimes, to increase making this president appear ineffective. In due time, the AG would find a way to make it clear that he would have taken a stronger stance, but he was held back by his boss. The money that Harrington and others derived from a relationship with Señor Caesar Hidalgo Monterro would be of great benefit when Harrington and several others campaigned for strategic government positions.

As a Harvard Law grad and a reputed expert on US constitutional and criminal law matters, Harrington would never attempt to describe his actions as being within the realms of legality. Floyd was, however, a secret proponent of *consequentialism,* an ethical theory that the consequences of conduct are the ultimate basis for any judgment about the rightness or wrongness of that conduct.

When Harrington would be seated in the Oval Office and the government righted as a large ship being put back onto its proper course, all the actions leading into Floyd's election would be properly justified. Indeed, the end would justify the means.

CHAPTER 24
KERRY'S ASSIGNMENT

"So, just what is it that you want from me?" Kerry asked. "I'm sure that you gentlemen did not bring me here just to convince me that I'm on the right track, since I've shown no signs of changing my stance on this whole matter."

Roger Clark spoke first.

"When I chose to help Brett, I did so because I was convinced he is innocent. I knew that, to some extent, I could help be his eyes and ears. But, there are people, places, and things that are unapproachable to me. If I even try to reach out to certain people, I would have great difficulty explaining why I'm so involved in the life and welfare of a man I supposedly don't even know."

"But, you," Gatlin interjected, "as a member of the media do not have that problem. Anyone you approach would see you as a reporter doing her job. You may not get any further than Roger would, but, at least you can get in the door."

"Okay," Anderson said, "so what doors are we talking about?"

Gatlin shrugged. Then, he leaned in towards Kerry and made strong eye contact with her.

"Hold on, Brett," Roger Clark interjected. "I think we need to know where Ms. Anderson stands before we say too much more."

Roger turned towards Kerry.

"If we're wasting our time, if getting involved deeper is not something you desire to do, we should know that now before we reveal too much more."

Anderson's narrowed her eyes. She clenched her jaw. Her head was shaking before she ever uttered a word. She made eye contact with both men in turn as she spoke. Her facial expressions were strong and tight.

"When you brought me here," Anderson said staring at Clark, "you told me what your terms were. I agreed to them and will abide by them. Now, here are my terms."

Gatlin was listening attentively as Kerry Anderson spoke. At the same time, he was impressed with her delivery. She was feisty, strong, and steadfast as she delivered her message. Her beauty belied her strength. This was one formidable woman and Brett liked what he was seeing.

"If I assist, I do so on my own terms. You're free to suggest and I'll keep you apprised on everything that I learn, but I run my own show. You don't tell me what to do or not do. I do things my way on my own timing. Are we clear so far on that?"

"Crystal clear," Gatlin said and he worked hard not to smile as he said it.

Roger Clark was not quite as willing or able to curtail his emotions.

"Okay, Sarge," Clark said with a salute. "We do things your way."

Anderson was serious, but Clark's antics did not offend her. She was convinced that these two men needed her assistance and would yield to her expertise in how to get things done.

"One more thing," Anderson said. "I've got a computer expert I use on the sly. No one knows about him, but me. His name is Jacob Greenleaf, but he goes by the handle of "Wireless." I use him to unlock a whole bunch of things for me. I'll never tell him I've met with you both, but I'd like to still use him, as needed, to assist."

Gatlin and Clark both agreed.

"Okay, if we're settled on all of this, then I repeat my initial questions. You want me to try to get through certain doors. What are you talking about?"

Gatlin took a deep breath, then spoke slowly. His focused his eyes downward.

"You said it yourself, Kerry, I'm flying blind. I have no idea what's behind this whole thing. Some of the answers I need are within the walls of the DEA Headquarters in Arlington. I don't know what you can do or how you'd go about getting some answers. I'm not going to pretend I know how to do your job. I mentioned Special Agent William Falwell as someone that Max Bradford reported to and Colonel Shirley at Fort Huachuca had contact with. I can't imagine why Falwell, whom I never met, didn't corroborate my claims to be an undercover agent supervised by Bradford.

There's something else. Best I could tell, Max Bradford was a strong healthy man. Kind of strange that he dies suddenly at such a strategic time. Then, there's that trooper in Arizona investigating the highway accident we were in. Has he come up with anything else that might help identify the men who shot at us on the highway and had to be the ones to kill Palmer and Nunez?

And what about the reporter who discredited the young man who helped me pull one of the agents from the burning vehicle... "

"Yes, the young man named Walter Vaughn," Kerry said.

"So, what prompted that reporter? Why did he do that? Did someone feed him a bunch of negative stuff about Vaughn? If so, who?"

Kerry Anderson smiled.

"Hmm, when we get through all of this, Brett, you might consider taking a job at the Washington Post."

Gatlin and Clark both laughed along with Anderson.

"Let us drive you home, Kerry," Roger Clark said. "It'll take you out of the crowded metro system and give us a little more time together."

"Okay," Kerry said, "that'll also give me time to ask a few more questions and gather some additional info."

Kerry smiled, put her hand out towards Clark, and waited as he placed her phone in her outstretched hand.

"Okay, let's make a list of agents in the DEA with whom you had any extended contact," Anderson said.

Gatlin rattled off several names.

Kerry took the time to inform Brett that she had met with his mother and sister. She saw his eyes fill with tears. Kerry knew that Gatlin wanted to ask more questions about the welfare of his family members, but he was too overwhelmed with emotions to do so.

As Clark focused on driving, Kerry focused her eyes on Gatlin. His expression changed. His lips were pressed together in a slight grimace. He was silent as a pensive expression dominated his face. Anderson reached over and touched Gatlin's arm. As she did, a jolt of excitement surged through her body at the first contact she made with him.

"What's bothering you, Brett? What's on your mind?"

Gatlin appeared to be struggling for the right words. His eyes shifted between Kerry and Roger Clark.

"I appreciate you both more than I can adequately express," Gatlin said, "but, I don't like the fact that I'm dragging you both into this... I don't know... this web of whatever that I'm caught up in. I know I'm innocent of what they say, but for some reason, I'm a target. I'm not the safest person for either of you to be involved with."

"Hey, chill, my friend," Clark said. "This is rather healthy for a guy like me. I need a little adventure in my life. I mean I can't get the same adrenaline rush helping you that I got whenever I was in the F-22 cockpit, but it's better than sitting in my apartment doing sudoku puzzles and drinking beer."

Anderson and Gatlin both laughed at Clark's remarks.

"You just used the phrase 'dragging'," Kerry said, " like you've dragged me into this. But, you haven't dragged me into anything. This is my choice. This is what I want to do or, should I say, I have to do, if I have any sense of decency in me."

"Right on," Roger said. "A guy like me needs to do at least a little something decent once in a while if I want to keep my membership in the human race."

Everyone laughed again.

"Also," Roger said, "I agree with Kerry. You haven't dragged me into anything. I'm in for the long run, so get used to it."

The conversation lightened as they headed for Anderson's condo. They talked about traffic in the nation's capital, the weather, some of the buildings they passed, and the local Major League Baseball team. It wasn't until they neared Kerry's home that everything changed. Kerry was initially surprised when Roger drove past the entrance to Kerry's building.

"Three o'clock," Roger said, "the white van."

"I see it," Gatlin said. "Windows are tinted. Can't make out for sure how many are in there and what they look like."

Gatlin turned towards Anderson and noted the confused look on her face.

"You've got company, Kerry."

CHAPTER 25

OPENING DOORS

Special Agent Mike Wright was glad that his wife, Penny, was out of town with the children. Penny's youngest sister, Mandy, and her husband, Dennis, just had their first child. Penny was going to spend a few days with Mandy, helping her get some extra rest and get acclimated to having a little one around.

Wright would use the time alone to think hard on what he was going to do. Mike was the agent who first introduced Gatlin to the RRT program at the DEA and to Special Agent Max Bradford. Wright maintained an ongoing interest in Gatlin. He tracked Gatlin's progress as he successfully completed RRT training. He did not know specifics related to Bradford's special ops team, but he did know that Brett Gatlin was invited to be a member and had accepted.

Wright kept quiet when the news of a scandal involving Gatlin broke. He was deeply concerned for the safety of his family should he deign to say anything contradictory to the fact that Brett Gatlin was a traitor. He was never specifically warned not to speak nor was his family directly threatened. But, when the news broke about Gatlin, William Falwell met with Wright.

"You got some people with the crazy notion that Gatlin was working undercover for more than four years," Falwell said. "You and I both know, Mike, that we don't keep people undercover in a solitary assignment for that long a period. Messes up their minds. You gotta watch out for people that try to make our agency look bad, you know? Undermines the good work we're all doing and helps the enemy to succeed. We need to be careful that we don't put the wrong idea in people's heads, you know?

Hey, you and your wife got those two little ones to keep you busy, huh? A boy and a girl. I respect guys like you, Mike. Working a dangerous job while always making sure that your wife and children are safe. Not an easy task, my friend. Not an easy job at all."

Mike Wright was troubled. The things being said about Gatlin didn't ring true at all. And the sudden death of Max Bradford was a shock to him. Bradford never shared specifics with Wright, but Mike was more than likely the only person not privy to the confidentiality of Bradford's team's activities that Max ever said anything to. Shortly before Max died, he told Mike Wright that all their hard work was finally coming to an end. Max seemed happy, pleased that all was well. No, he never specifically mentioned Gatlin, but he told Mike that the team had all worked long and hard for more than four years. There was no indication that anyone on Max's team had gone AWOL.

Mike Wright despised his silence at a time like this. That just didn't seem like something his friend and mentor, Max Bradford, would ever do.

Kerry Anderson's face turned ashen as Roger and Brett spoke to her about the white van strategically placed outside her condo. The thought that her home might be bugged represented a gross invasion of privacy to her.

"So, how do we get those things out of my home?" Kerry said.

"We don't," Gatlin answered. "We leave them there and use them to our advantage."

"What? How?" Kerry said. "Why not just make a move on who-ever is in that van?"

Brett reached over and took Kerry's hands in his. He spoke calmly to her, first encouraging her to slow down for a moment and take a deep breath.

"Second question first, Kerry. Got to believe those men, who-ever they are, are hired men. They have a single contact who com-municates with them. They would have no idea who they're really working for.

That also means they're low men on a totem pole who can't get us where we need to go. As far as using them to our advantage, you have the benefit of these guys not knowing that you're aware they are listening in. So, when you're home, at home, the plan would be for you to say things we want them to hear, things that we can use to our advantage."

"Right," Roger said. "From now on, you never say anything at home that you don't want the wrong people knowing about. Same goes for your cell phone. You talk on it always knowing someone will be listening in. I have my phone and acquired a second one for Brett to use. We'll get a disposable phone for you now, Kerry."

Kerry was breathing normal again and the color had returned to her face.

"We'll drop you off in the area where you'd normally come out of the metro station so you can walk to your condo."

"Kerry," Brett said, "I need to know that you're okay. Nothing is more important. If you prefer, we can call this whole thing off now."

Kerry smiled and shook her head.

"I'm fine. In fact, I'm more than fine."

Kerry then turned towards Roger Clark and winked.

"As someone recently said, I'm in for the long run, so get used to it."

⤝ ⤜

Kerry's plan was simple. She intended to make the DEA uncomfortable about upcoming articles she planned to write and give them an opportunity to refute things before they were in print. She studied the DEA org chart and was making determinations as to who to contact first when she received a phone call that changed everything. Kerry let the call go through to voicemail.

"Ms. Anderson, my name is Michael Wright. I'm a Special Agent with the DEA, working out of our Arlington Headquarters. If you want to talk about Brett Gatlin, call me at this number. Don't try to come see me."

Wright left a phone number and Kerry called him back on her disposable cell phone. She introduced herself and waited as Wright said he wanted to move to a better location. The gap in time caused Kerry to wonder if the call had been disconnected, but when she looked at her phone's screen, she could see that it had not. She waited until she heard a voice again.

"Sorry about that," Wright said. "I wanted to get to a more private location.

Hmm, his voice is strained. He's nervous, uncomfortable talking with me. Probably has battled within himself over whether he should even take a chance and call me.

Kerry sensed that the man was fragile. She would say nothing to spook him.

"I appreciate your call, Agent Wright."

"Yeah, well, Max Bradford was a friend of mine. He was my original trainer. The man was legendary, best I've ever known as an agent and a person. When Max had responsibility over agents—and he always used the word responsibility not authority, you know—Max cared about the people under his charge. That's just the kind of man he was."

Take it easy. The man's really struggling. Don't push him. He's babbling, but be patient with him. This guy's a wreck inside. He may be a trained agent and have a whole lot of experience, but whatever he's battling with now is deeply personal to him, combined with the fact that he's scared.

"I'm so sorry," Kerry said, "that I never had the opportunity to meet Special Agent Bradford. Everything I have heard about him points to the fact that he was outstanding."

"Yeah, and let me tell you, Ms. Anderson, the guy had guts and integrity. He would never back down from the truth, no matter what it might cost him. The truth meant everything to Max, you know? What about you, Ms. Anderson? What are you after?"

"I realize that you don't know me, Agent Wright, but I assure you that I'm interested in only one thing and that is to find the truth in anything I'm investigating as a reporter."

Wright paused and once again the gap of silence caused Kerry to wonder if the man was still on the line. He was.

"I'm willing to talk with you, Ms. Anderson. Got some things you ought to hear. Only, we need to meet at a private location and I need your assurance that everything and anything I say is off the record—completely confidential. Is that clear? Is that something you can and will do?"

"Yes, of course, you have my word, sir. I often work under circumstances of confidentiality. Keeping my word is one of the reasons why people have come to believe they can trust me. You have my word that it will be as if we've never met."

Again, an extended time of silence, again a moment when Kerry remained silent so as not to somehow push this man away.

"Tonight, at seven," Wright said, "there's a diner on E Street Northwest, in D.C. I'll meet you there."

Kerry arrived at the diner shortly prior to 7:00 p.m. She waited, but Special Agent Mike Wright never showed up. Early the next morning, the Post newsroom was buzzing with the story that three people were shot randomly while driving on the E Street Expressway in the nation's capital. One of the victims was a DEA Special Agent named Michael Wright. The shootings took place less than two miles from where Anderson and Wright were to meet.

⋙⋘

Once again, Roger Clark hooked up with Kerry when she left her workplace. And, once again, Clark made sure that they were not followed. This time, Gatlin was behind the wheel in the Jeep parked on a side road. Clark directed Kerry to hop into the front passenger seat and he entered the rear seat. The moment she saw Brett, that fluttering in Kerry's stomach returned. When he reached out and took her hand in greeting, a tingling or electrical jolt pulsed through her body. Kerry was particularly glad that in the darkness of the vehicle, neither man would be able to spot the flush in her cheeks.

The small nondescript motel where Clark and Gatlin were staying was in Arlington. On the way, they stopped to pick up some sandwiches, chips, and drinks.

"Sorry that meeting in a motel room is the best we could come up with, Kerry," Gatlin said, "but we did our best to make sure the place was nice and clean."

They were seated in the room and already eating their food when Kerry provided the men with an update. She informed them about the proposed meeting with Special Agent Mike Wright.

Gatlin gulped in some air. His head was tilted to the side. His brows were furrowed.

"I knew Mike Wright. He was my initial trainer and the man who influenced me to go for RRT training. He and Max Bradford were close."

"I'm afraid that's not the only thing I've learned that is troubling," Anderson said. "Brett, I've done some follow up on Max Bradford's death and your infamous drug meeting in the Sonoran Desert. You told me that your team communicated with encrypted messages set up by your team member Danny Nyguen."

"Yes, that's right," Brett said. "We were texting each other under the system Danny created."

"And your last communications were just prior to the meeting in the desert?"

"Yes, we last communicated the night before." Kerry took a sip of her iced tea before responding.

"Max Bradford was on those last communications?" Kerry asked.

"Yes, of course. In fact, as team leader, he spearheaded all our discussions. Why are you asking this, Kerry?"

Kerry shifted her position, flipped her hair, then shook her head.

"Brett, Max Bradford was already dead at the time of your last discussions. He died the previous day while still at the office in the evening. I don't know who was communicating with you all just before the meeting in the desert, but it wasn't Max Bradford."

Roger Clark's mouth fell open, then he jerked his head back. Brett Gatlin's body stiffened, his muscles were rigid, his head was shaking.

"W-what about Falwell?" Brett asked.

"Haven't been able to reach the man," Kerry said, "and there's something strange about the responses I've received. I'm never given the opportunity to leave a message. No one will tell me when Falwell might be available. I was going to ask Wright about this when we met."

"Someone's working hard to keep us from finding out more," Roger said.

Gatlin continued to shake his head. His eyes had a faraway look when he next spoke.

"Yes, even if it means killing two completely unrelated people while targeting a hit on federal agent Wright."

CHAPTER 26

CONSTANT ROADBLOCKS

Roger Clark drove Kerry back to the neighborhood of her condo, leaving her where she could walk a short distance to the building entrance. He used binoculars to watch her enter the front door. He also used them to spot the white van, still poised nearby.

When he got back to the motel, Brett was sitting at the edge of one of the beds. His eyes were squinting, his hands were clenched tightly into fists. He did not turn to acknowledge Roger when Clark entered the room.

Roger tossed the keys to the Jeep, tossed his wallet, and placed a bag on the desk. He sat down in a chair without saying a word. He'd give Gatlin whatever space he needed to work through whatever was tormenting his mind.

The few minutes of silence seemed much longer. Then, Brett spoke, although, once again, he did not even turn to look at Roger.

"This entire thing is a nightmare. I've tried, but I can't make any sense of it. And how the hell can we stand against an entire agency? We don't have the manpower. We don't have the tools. We don't have whatever it would take to fight against all of this? Seems like every step we do take, whoever is behind this is one step ahead of us."

Brett finally turned and looked directly at Roger.

"We're dealing with people who're playing for keeps, Rog. They've already killed, even killed federal agents, and we've got every reason to believe they'll keep on killing until … "

"Until what?" Clark interrupted. "Until they find and kill you? You know, I've been thinking, Brett. What makes us think it ends there? Maybe we're not just fighting for your life. I'm starting to realize we're likely fighting for a whole lot of lives. When I joined the Air Force and, even more so, when I became a Raptor pilot, I was making a commitment to die, if necessary, for my country. You did the same. You raised your right hand and took an oath when they gave you your shield. You underwent a hell of a taxing training program. You did all that knowing you were putting your life at stake for your country. Guys like you and me were willing to risk everything for the opportunity to somehow help make this old imperfect world we live in a better place. I'm thinking this might just be one of those opportunities."

Brett chuckled softly, nodded his head, and gave a thumbs-up to the man he met one night in a Norfolk downtown bar.

"I hear you, Rog. I know you're right. Thanks, man. As a friend of mine once said, I'm in for the long run, so get used to it."

Both men laughed as they stood up, fist bumped, smacked their hands together in a high five, and hugged each other.

Roger then reached back to the desk for the bag he placed there and unveiled the six pack of beer he had picked up on the way back to the motel. He opened two bottles and handed one to Brett. The two men clinked their bottles together in a toast.

"To whatever it takes," Roger said.

Brett nodded. "Whatever it takes."

❖ ❖

He was taking a chance and he knew it. A wrong move on his part could cost him his career. Then again, why did he choose a career as a federal agent to begin with? If he was willing to play politics and keep his mouth shut until he retired, there were a lot of other jobs he could have taken, some of which were a whole lot less dangerous and paid better.

Well, he'd already taken the step and made the appointment to meet with her. Guess it was time to put up or shut up.

"Good to see you again, Martin."

Hennessey, a forty-two-year old single mother of two was five feet eight inches tall, had short blonde hair, brown eyes, high cheekbones, and a dimpled smile. She was both attractive and formidable-looking—an intelligent woman who should never be taken lightly. Barb Hennessey had developed a reputation for being a fair, but tough taskmaster.

Hennessey had overcome much to reach the position she was now in. She had to overcome the stereotype that a male normally filled the position she was in with the DEA. Others who'd been passed over as Hennessey climbed the Agency ladder questioned whether her looks or even sexual favors had enabled her to land the position she was in. Of course, none of that was even remotely true. But, to accept things as they were, many would have to acknowledge that Barb was simply better than the men she beat out to end up where she now was.

Special Agent Marty Gaela smiled and mumbled something in return. See him again? He'd only seen Special Agent in Charge Barb Hennessey one time since she stepped in to head the Phoenix DEA office with authority over Gaela's home base in Tucson. Yeah, they spoke on the phone a few times and exchanged emails, but that was it. As he sat in front of her ready to put everything on the line, it struck Marty Gaela once again that he honestly did not know Barb Hennessey at all.

"So, what can I do for you, Martin?"

"I came here hoping I could take some time to talk with you about this "Gatlin Case." I'm having a difficult time balancing some things. It's been that way from the get-go."

Hennessey's face displayed a radical change in color—there was none, as she reacted to what Gaela said. She rose from behind her desk and gestured towards a door that led to a small adjoining conference room. Galea stood and walked with her into the room.

Hennessey lifted the phone that was on the conference table.

"Mary, would you please bring in some coffee for Agent Gaela and me?"

She hung the phone up and stared across at the agent under her command who had more experience than any other. Barb had gone through Gaela's file several times and each time she did, her respect for the man increased. His service record was outstanding. Beyond that, Hennessey had reviewed several case files where Gaela displayed strong skills in uncovering evidence which would eventually stand up in court and help lead to a criminal conviction.

Beyond that, there were several cases where Barb became convinced that Gaela might well have been the only agent who would have solved things and discovered what he did. She based this upon the fact that Martin Gaela possessed uncanny intuitive skills. When he interrogated people, it was as if he could see inside their mind, uncover what they were thinking, detect if they were lying or speaking honestly.

The newness of her position and some initial demands and adjustments kept Barb Hennessey from following up more with Gaela, but she had every intention of doing so. She even wanted to talk more with him about Brett Gatlin, but she knew she had to be careful. She just did not know the man well enough to gauge whether she could trust him. But now, the man was seated with her in a conference room and the opportunity to probe deeper with him was right there before her. She'd worked hard to get to the position she was now in and aspired to rise even higher in the DEA hierarchy. She never chose the career she did for personal gain or to satisfy an ego. Damn shame that she was being tested so soon after a recent promotion.

⤜⊹ ⊹⤛

Kings Dominion Theme Park in Doswell, Virginia, replete with coasters, kids' rides, and its Soak City park, is a great place to escape from the hot D.C. humid days. Located eighty-five miles from the capitol, it was also the next place where Gatlin, Clark, and Anderson chose to meet.

"Let's just be clear up-front," Kerry said, "there's no way I'm getting on a roller coaster, unless you both are interested in how I'd look with green skin."

Everyone laughed.

"I've got a feeling," Gatlin quipped, "you could put Roger on one of those coasters upside down in a car and he'd never feel a thing. If anything, he'd probably be disappointed that he's not dealing with some major g-force."

Clark laughed.

"Since I'm among friends, I'll make a personal confession. I used to get car sick when I was a kid."

They all laughed again. It was good for each of them to have an opportunity to laugh, considering the pressure that was continually mounting against them. Kerry's news was once again fraught with dead ends and negativism. She began by informing Brett and Roger that she had contacted Allan Kingsley, Chief Counsel for the DEA.

"I informed the man that I was preparing to write another article and wanted to give the DEA an opportunity to refute some of the things I was about to say. I asked if he would be open to an interview with me and somewhere along the line mentioned that I was having difficulty reaching Special Agent William Falwell.

That's when Kingsley dropped the bomb telling me that Falwell's on some kind of extended personal leave. I had my guy, Wireless, digging in to see what he could find about any activity by Falwell. Wireless, through means that it would be best I not share with you... "

Anderson laughed.

"Whoa, leave me out of this," Clark said with feigning seriousness. "Sounds like she's got her computer geek engaged in illegal snooping."

Everyone laughed again, but the laughter ended when Kerry completed her statement.

"Wireless tracked Falwell's cell phone and some credit cards and found absolutely no activity. The guy has vanished."

Gatlin and Roger looked at each other and simultaneously gestured with a finger slicing the throat.

"Yeah, that's what I'm thinking. It's very possible that Falwell is dead," Kerry said.

It was while the three of them were still together that a call came in to Anderson's phone. She let the call go through to her voicemail.

"Ms. Kerry Anderson? My name is Patricia Kenworth. I work at the DEA offices here in Arlington. I worked closely with Special Agent Max Bradford. Ms. Anderson, I need to speak with you."

Kerry replayed the message for Brett and Roger to hear it.

"Okay," Brett said, "this time we make sure that Patricia Kenworth has an opportunity to meet with you before anyone else can stop her. I've got a plan, but we're going to have to move quickly on this and there's no room for error."

CHAPTER 27

DIGGING IN

"What can I say, Barb? Guess I'm going for broke here to-day. If there's anything, at any time, you don't want to hear, you stop me and I won't say another word. I want you to know that I'm not trying to put you in a position of compromise."

"Well, I must say that's one heck of a caveat," Barb said. Then, she shifted in position and leaned towards Gaela. "Look, Martin, I appreciate the fact that we have not had a great deal of time to get to know one another, but I want us to have a better foundation than one of tiptoeing with each other and skirting issues. Please, feel free to be honest with me. I'll do the same."

Gaela was relieved, even though he was still unsure about the level of honesty Hennessey could deal with. He began by telling her that his impressions of Brett Gatlin were highly inconsistent with the man being portrayed as a traitor and a druggie.

"If the guy was enough of a user to end up betraying his oath and his country, he did a miraculous job in completely sobering up with none of the latent side effects and symptoms of a heavy user," Marty said. "And we haven't had any access to the medical tests they took at the hospital. Was there evidence of drugs in Gatlin's system? And there's no doubt in my mind that Gatlin forsook his opportunity to escape and risked his life to save two of our agents who were trapped in a burning vehicle. I've listened to the man, observed him, talked with him. Brett Gatlin does not fit the profile of the wanted man that every law enforcement officer in the country is anxious to shoot on sight.

At one point, when the conversation reached the point where Gatlin escaped from the custody of Gaela and Watkins, Barb interrupted.

"From the report I received, Brett Gatlin had a gun pressed against your head."

"And I did not believe for a moment that he ever would have pulled that trigger. He could have killed Rick Watkins and me then, but the man never even threatened to do so. I'm telling you, Barb, Brett Gatlin is one hell of a tough guy and I'm not doubting that the man can be lethal. But, he's not a threat to us and I don't believe he's the rogue agent that some are claiming he is."

Hennessey was shifting in her seat. Her face was pale and her eyes were focused away from Marty Gaela. For a moment, she held back on her next comment. Then, she lifted her head and stared back at Gaela.

"Martin, you realize that the initial reports about Gatlin came from our headquarters. Do you fully comprehend the consequences of claiming something contradictory to our own agency?"

Gaela's dropped his head, shrugged his shoulders, then lifted his head again.

"Look, Barb, I've considered the possibility that the reports were erroneous. That somehow with Special Agent Bradford dead and unable to speak directly on the issue of Gatlin's status, things got a bit muddled."

Hennessey turned her head towards the conference room window and stared out.

"But, you don't really believe that, do you, Martin?"

Gaela sighed before responding in a voice not much above a whisper.

"No, no, I don't believe that."

The silence that followed was deafening. The empty gap created an awkwardness that, like two master chess players contemplating their next move, would only be broken when one of the two people sitting in this room was willing to gamble and say more.

Marty Gaela stood up, walked away from the table, placed both hands in his pockets, and stared out the window.

"I'm neither a crusader nor a rebel, Barb. Nor do I have any personal interest in going to bat for this man, Gatlin. But, two fellow agents were murdered while I sat with my partner and state trooper in a Tucson ER. And, you know something, Barb? If Gatlin is not responsible for any of this, then I think somebody needs to be fighting hard to determine what is going on?"

Gaela turned back towards Hennessey. He walked towards the table and sat down. His face bore a pained expression. His eyebrows were furrowed, his eyes were cast downward, his hands were clenched in fists.

"Nearly eighteen years ago, I raised my right hand and swore to uphold the Constitution and, I guess you could say, always stand against injustice. I don't recall anyone ever saying that the promises I made don't apply if the people involved in criminal activity happen to work in the same federal agency I'm in or may even be my superiors. I'm no hero, Barb, nor a candidate for sainthood. But, I always believed that if the day ever comes when I can no longer live out the commitment I made when I first became a federal agent, then it's time for me to surrender my shield and do something else with my life."

Hennessey's body was tight. Gaela spotted a slight trembling of her lips. Her hand shook a bit when she lifted her coffee cup and took a sip.

"Agency Headquarters sent two Arlington agents to Fort Huachuca to take custody of an agent there. They completely bypassed the Tucson office. They never notified me. From that point on, Martin, I was suspect. I was especially concerned when all of this occurred following the deaths of so many American and Mexican agents in the Sonoran Desert."

Barb Hennessey leaned in closer to Gaela.

"You're not alone, Martin. I'll stand with you. But, I want full and complete disclosure of everything you do, plan to do, and uncover. I'll do what I can by taking a closer look at things in Arlington. What we discussed here today stays completely between you and me, Martin. Are we in agreement?"

If ever there was a moment in his career as a federal agent that Martin Gaela was filled with a renewed sense of pride in what he had committed his life to, this was that time. He stared at Hennessey's outstretched hand and clasped it.

"Yes, Special Agent Hennessey, we are in complete agreement. You have my word on that."

"One more thing, Martin. Your partner, Rick Watkins, do you trust him?"

"Completely," Gaela said.

"Then I'm going to trust you to make a judgment as to if and how deeply he can be made privy to what we are saying here today."

Hennessey bore a slight smile on her face. She nodded her head, then reached back out and grabbed Gaela's right wrist.

"I'm sure that I don't need to tell you, Martin, we need to proceed with the utmost precaution. I don't believe that I can possibly emphasize that strongly enough."

⇥ ⇤

It was already dark when the taxi pulled up in front of the DEA Headquarters. As instructed, Patricia Kenworth waited for the cab to arrive before she walked out of the building. Kerry Anderson exited the back seat of the cab, leaving the door open, and greeted Kenworth. She ushered Patricia into the rear seat of the cab with her. Kenworth was a woman in her late-fifties. She stood at five feet seven inches, wore thick dark-rimmed glasses, and had light brown hair.

The moment the cab pulled away, Kerry spotted the black Chevy Impala that was following them. She punched a number in her phone, stated "Yes," then disconnected. Based upon a previous discussion Kerry had with Kenworth, neither women said a word to each other while in the taxi. Kerry did reach over and take Patricia's trembling hand in hers.

It was a four-minute drive to the Virginia Highlands Park where the taxi pulled in. The cab stopped, the two women exited, and walked towards a wooded area of the park. Gatlin and Clark were tucked away behind some trees and shared a fist-bump when the two men jumped out of the Chevy and began their search for Kerry Anderson and Patricia Kenworth.

Within minutes, Gatlin and Clark each had their arms tightly grasping the neck of each man from behind. Gatlin took the weapon from the man he was holding. The man that Roger had in his grasp was able to reach the weapon he had in a shoulder holster. He thrust his hand forward to press it against Roger's stomach. Brett quickly knocked his man to the ground. Then, he stepped between Roger and the man with the gun making himself vulnerable. But, before the man could fire, Brett grabbed his wrist, twisted and turned, until the man, in obvious pain, was rendered helpless and down on his knees.

Roger stared into Brett's eyes. He nodded and whispered a thank you. Then, he reached down, pulled the man Brett had knocked down up and fastened his arms around the man's neck.

Neither man could see Gatlin or Clark.

"Who the hell are you guys?" Gatlin's victim said.

"Uh, uh, my friend," Brett said. "I think you got things a bit confused here. You don't ask questions. We do."

Brett squeezed tighter. The man he was holding was also now down on his knees.

"Who are you working for?" Roger said. "You be good boys and cooperate and we might be willing to let you go before we break your freakin' necks."

"You go to hell," the man said to Clark.

"You know, Mortimer," Roger Clark said, "I just don't believe these boys are gonna play nice at all."

"I hear you, Zeke," Brett Gatlin said. "Maybe we should just keep on squeezin' here. I ain't had the pleasure of killin' nobody all day. I'm gettin' kinda anxious, ya know?"

Roger laughed, as both he and Brett tightened the grip on the necks of these two men.

The man that Gatlin had a hold on, gasped, choked, grunted. Neither man could speak even if they wanted to. Brett loosened his grip just a bit. Roger did not.

"Ya got something ya want ta say?" Brett said.

The man coughed and attempted to gulp in more air.

"We-we d-don't know who hired us," the man said.

Brett began to squeeze tighter.

"W-wait… I-I can't breathe… what're you doing? You crazy? I told you, we d-don't… "

Brett began to tighten his grip again.

"H-hold it. I can't breathe. You squeeze any tighter, you gonna kill me, man."

"Well, Einstein," Brett said. "that's precisely what I had in mind."

Brett tightened his grip and, again, the man gasped and called out for Brett to stop.

"W-wait, man. I'll tell you what y-you want to know. Wait."

The man Roger was holding was trying even harder to get free. Roger loosened his grip.

"Shut up, Bo. Don't say anything. You'll get us killed."

Bo, the man Gatlin was holding, may not have been a Rhodes Scholar, but the man was at least smart enough to know he could die right now at the hands of the man holding him or take his chances later by talking now.

"Man's name is Gotschild. PI named Andrew Gotschild. That's who hired us."

The two men were left unconscious in the park. They did not have wallets. Brett and Roger considered a quick search of their vehicle, but chose to return to the Jeep and get the two women out of the area. Kerry and Patricia were already inside the Jeep waiting for the guys to come and drive away.

CHAPTER 28
BREAKTHROUGHS

Kerry Anderson changed taxis and was now seated with Patricia Kenworth at a small diner just outside of D.C.

"Ms. Kenworth, I appreciate your willingness to come forward and speak with me," Kerry said. "May I ask what prompted you to do so?"

"Max Bradford was an incredible man, Ms. Anderson, notwithstanding his status as an outstanding federal agent. I was honored to work with him. You know, I worked under him for more than fifteen years. When Max died, so suddenly, so unexpectedly, I was devastated."

Patricia stopped speaking. She was struggling with what she was about to say next.

"I have no factual basis for what I'm about to say, but I found myself questioning the circumstances of his death. After Max was gone, Mike Wright was the one person that I believed I could fully trust. He and Max had a long-time friendship and I know that Max very much trusted Mike."

Kenworth's eyes were teary now and her voice was strained. The two women had already ordered coffee and pastries and each had a glass of water provided by their server. Patricia reached for her water. Kerry momentarily placed her hand on Patricia's left hand.

"Please, take as much time as you need. I know this must be difficult for you."

Patricia nodded her head and finished sipping from her water glass. She wiped her lips with a napkin and then dabbed at the corner of each eye.

"Thank you, Ms. Anderson."

"Please call me, Kerry."

Kenworth nodded and asked in return for Kerry to address her as Patricia.

"This thing with Agent Gatlin all broke shortly after Max had died. I was much too shaken and preoccupied initially with grief to say or do anything. But, I'm telling you, Agent Gatlin was not AWOL. He was not some kind of rogue agent. Gatlin was in good standing with Max at the time of Max's death."

Kerry interrupted.

"May I ask how you know that, Patricia."

"I know it because Max told me. I was privy to the undercover team Max was overseeing. Very few people knew that *Subterraneo* even existed—that was the name of the special ops team that Gatlin was a member of. The team had been working together for more than four years. My job was to help coordinate supplies, personal needs, things of that nature for the team members. I handled the payments on certain items related to the work they were doing and the expenses generated by team members. For example, Gatlin had an apartment in Mexicali that was kind of a retreat place for him. You'll never find a record of direct payments identifying that place. Suffice it to say that I made sure things got paid without them ever being directly identified or traceable. Our goal was to do everything to assure that there was never an identifiable link between any of the team members and the DEA.

Bear in mind, I was never privy to the specific actions or strategy the team was involved in. Those things were kept at a highly-confidential level.

On the night before he died, I went into Max's office to see if he needed anything before I left for the day. Max was happier than I'd seen him in months. He'd been under a great deal of pressure. Anyway, Max smiled at me, offered me a high-five, and I'll never forget what he said.

"Missy Pat," that was a name Max would use just between the two of us, "Missy Pat," he said, "in just a few days, years of hard work is gonna lead us to everything we've been working for over the past four years. I'm finally gonna be able to bring my guys back home. I'm telling you, Pat, I don't know if any agent ever had a better group of men, dedicated, loyal, so willing to sacrifice. More than four years ago, I handpicked six men and every darn one of 'em has been even better than I ever would have imagined. I am one very lucky man.

When this thing is over, we are all gonna celebrate together and I don't care if I've got to foot the bill myself on everything."

Kenworth paused as tears began to fall from her eyes.

"Max really cared about anyone who worked for him. I mean, don't misunderstand me, he was a boss who expected you to do what you were supposed to do and all. But he would always say that authority, genuine authority, is simply another word for having responsibility."

"Patricia, I take it you believe that Agent Wright also might have questioned Max's death?"

"Mike didn't know details about Max's team, but he knew Max had one and even knew some of the team members. Mike was particularly fond of Agent Gatlin. Max made mention of that to me."

"Did you know that Mike Wright contacted me and was on his way to meet with me when he was killed?" Kerry asked.

Kenworth's face turned ashen. Her eyes rolled to the top of her head, then closed shut. Kerry moved closer for fear that Patricia was about to pass out. When Kenworth opened her eyes, tears poured down her face.

"Oh, my God! Dear Lord! They killed him, just like they killed Max. Dear God, what is going on? What is happening?"

Kerry did move her chair closer to Patricia Kenworth and placed her arm around the woman's shoulders.

Kenworth lifted her tear-filled eyes and stared directly at Kerry.

"No, I didn't know Mike had contacted you. I should've guessed it. There was no way Mike could have kept quiet. What am I going to do, Kerry? Am I next? Are they going to kill me?"

Kerry held Kenworth even tighter.

"Patricia, I want to tell you that no one will ever know what we've talked about and what you suspect. But, it's clear that whoever these people are, they know you have contacted me. I am so sorry, Patricia. I am so sorry."

Kenworth stiffened her posture. She clenched her jaw, shook her head, then reached out and touched Kerry's face.

"No, Kerry. No. I did what was right. I did what Max would have done and what Mike did do. I could never have kept my mouth shut and pretended that I didn't feel what I do. I'll go away. I won't even go back to work tomorrow. I'll be okay. You just let me know how we can stay in touch, when needed."

"What can I do to help you, Patricia?"

Kenworth curled both hands in fists and held them up towards her shoulders.

"You can find out who's behind all of this and you can help make sure they pay for what they've done."

⊨+ +⊨

With increased fervor and a refusal to hold back any longer, Marty Gaela was seated now with State Trooper Carlos Aguilar. Carlos clearly sensed that Gaela was no longer on the fence when it came to a willingness to question and take a stand against his own agency.

"I'm glad you've come to me, Marty. I finally got a breakthrough and have something on the men who, I believe, killed your two agents."

Aguilar told Gaela how he'd finally tracked down a deep ocean blue metallic current year Chevy Silverado truck 100 double cab.

"Found it in an off-airport parking lot and got a real break when the lot had functioning cameras. Caught some rough pics of the two men who, under a false identity, left the vehicle there. Only one man's pic was even good enough to use for a search. Took a while. I turned what I had over to the FBI."

Aguilar stopped speaking.

"No sense lying to you, man. I've been hesitant to reveal too much to the DEA—the people you'd think I'd most be working with. Anyway, you're here now, so that's good.

Finally got a facial recognition on one of the men. Guy by the name of Charlie Hough. Got himself a rap sheet for burglaries, served forty months in the pen. Appears to be clean for the past three or so years. Couldn't get a positive ID on the other man, but we believe he's Luke Munson, who's been known to hang around with Hough. Munson's got some priors, too. We haven't found these two guys yet. No evidence they boarded any flights."

With the help of Kerry Anderson's computer geek, Wireless, Gatlin and Clark were not only able to locate Andrew Gotschild's Bethesda office, they also had his unlisted condo address. They made the trek to the PI's condo in slightly less than thirty minutes.

Based upon Gatlin's superior stealth, Roger and Brett agreed that Roger would stay with the Jeep, while Brett would enter and explore the man's home. Wireless instructed Gatlin how to bypass the condo security system. The computer geek also confirmed that Gotschild was twice-divorced and apparently lived alone.

A phone call to Gotschild's office confirmed that the man was currently there. That placed him some eight miles from his condo. Brett gained access to the condo in no time at all. Brett was unsure whether there would be anything of value at the man's home, but he would use this opportunity to glean whatever he could about Gotschild and his activities.

Brett was inside the condo and had just closed the door when the blur of a body came straight towards him. Brett's quickness enabled him to avoid most of the brunt of the man's charging body. As Brett quickly moved aside, the man's thrust of the knife he was wielding missed Gatlin entirely. The man was tall, thin, dark-haired, and had a dark mole on his face. He held the knife in his left hand.

A wry smile crossed Gatlin's face as he stared at his attacker.

"My, my," Gatlin said, "you look a bit confused. You must have been waiting and expecting Andrew Gotschild to walk in the door. Sorry to disappoint you, friend."

A sneer covered the man's face.

"Well, I have no idea who you are, but, under the circumstances," he said, as he continued to swipe with his knife and miss his evasive target, "you'll do just fine."

Gatlin laughed.

"Can't say how you'd have fared against the PI, but I assure you, my friend, you just got the raw end of a deal here."

The man lunged forward. Gatlin stood still, waited until the last moment, grabbed the man's extended arm, and twisted and snapped it. The man cried out in pain, as the knife dropped to the floor. He would not be using his left hand again. But, to the man's credit, he followed the knife to the floor, avoided a kick from Gatlin, and used his right hand to slice Brett's leg.

Both men were on the floor now. The wiry attacker was on top of Gatlin pressing the knife down towards Brett's throat.

Gatlin had the man's wrist held tightly and was pushing back against his forward thrusts. From the moment Gatlin encountered this man, his goal was to incapacitate him and do whatever it took to keep him alive. He wanted to gain insight as to who the man was and who sent him to Gotschild's residence. Now, that goal had changed. Brett would kill, if needed. It also changed the tactics Brett would use in fighting this stranger.

Brett spun to his side, dragging the man with him. Holding tightly to the man's wrist, Brett bit the man's neck. He twisted the man's hand so that the knife was angled towards the assailant's body. The man tried to spin free. In the course of movement, Brett was now on top of him and the knife plunged directly into the man's heart, killing him instantly.

CHAPTER 29

WHEN TOMORROW COMES

"Okay, so let's go over what we know and what we don't," Gatlin said. He was together with Roger Clark and Kerry Anderson at a locally-owned motel in Fredericksburg, Virginia. They had booked two rooms and would spend the night in this city located slightly more than fifty miles from Washington, D.C.

"I'll start," Kerry Anderson said. "Based upon what Patricia Kenworth said, we know that Bradford was excited about the major buy that was to take place in the Sonoran Desert. And he, up to the last minute, was still identifying Brett as a loyal member of his team along with all of the others."

"Right," Roger said, "so that tells us something of major importance." Roger was now facing Brett as he spoke. "Whatever happened causing you to be labeled as a rogue agent all started after Bradford was dead. Of course, we would have expected that none of that ever came from Max Bradford. But, I'm wondering whether it was not necessarily an original strategy. And, if not, what prompted it."

Roger paused and focused interchangeably on Brett and Kerry. "I'm assuming I'm not the only one here who finds the timing of Bradford's death highly-suspicious."

Kerry and Brett both nodded in agreement.

"Problem is," Kerry said, "no one within the DEA seems to suspect anything, so no one looked closer at everything and anything leading to Agent Bradford's death."

Brett stood, walked towards a room window, and stared out.

"Now that we've learned that Max was dead before we all met in the Sonoran Desert, the plan was likely that every one of us in *Subterraneo*, including Max, had to be dead. Then, no one could adequately question what happened that day in the desert. Rog is right. My survival generated the need for a Plan B. They devised a plan to discredit me and make it look like I helped bring everyone down."

"Sure," Roger said, "so even before they could kill you, they had already discredited you and anything you might possibly say."

"I'm also thinking," Kerry said, "that we need to better understand what happened out there in the desert."

"Doesn't take a rocket scientist," Roger said, "to figure out that the explosives that killed the American and Mexican federal agents were inside the Hummers, planted there, before the vehicles ever arrived on the scene."

"And there was no way a timer could have been used. Someone there that day had to detonate them causing all four vehicles to explode simultaneously," Gatlin said.

"Which means that someone associated with a Mexican cartel was in on the plan," Roger added.

"From what I have learned," Kerry said, "it appears that Garcia and his cartel did receive the knockout blow. Word is that a cartel headed by a drug Lord named Caesar Hidalgo Monterro has taken over."

"It was a changing of the guard," Brett said. "The plan was not merely to take Garcia down. It was also to put Monterro and his cartel in power."

"What we don't know is who's behind all of this and why," Kerry said.

"Monterro could never have accomplished this on his own," Gatlin said, as he returned and sat down with Roger and Kerry. "Someone aware that Max's team had a major drug deal set up involving Garcia's cartel used that to launch their own agenda."

"Means we got us some snakes right here in our own country," Roger said. "And at least some of them are in the DEA."

"We've been looking at this entire thing wrong," Kerry said. "Brett's right. The plan was to put Monterro where Garcia was."

"And Brett kind of messed things up by failing to die along with everyone else," Roger said.

Gatlin had a faraway look.

"The men who came after me in Mexicali—they weren't Garcia's men. They were part of the Monterro Cartel."

"And the only people who even knew about your place there were in your own Agency," Roger said.

"As best I know, only Max was aware I had that apartment," Brett said.

"As tight-lipped as Max might have been, there was always a chance someone else in the DEA found out about it," Kerry said.

"Rog is right," Gatlin said. "This was never about me. It was supposed to look like a plan gone bad. It was supposed to appear as if two Mexican Cartels were embroiled in a territorial war and the lawful authorities of the United States and Mexico got caught in the middle. Without any survivors, there would be no reliable witnesses to tell a different story. When I survived, they had to adjust their strategy."

Brett, Roger, and Kerry were all silent. More puzzle pieces were coming together than ever before.

Kerry broke the silence.

"Okay, then we need to be viewing everything we know, everything we suspect from this new angle. We're dealing with a conspiracy. We have several tentacles involved here. We have layers with a common purpose and, at a minimum, everything is centered on a great deal of money that will come in from the drug trade."

"Money," Roger said, "that people here in our own country will undoubtedly share in.

Okay, shifting our focus for a minute, we sure as hell also know that Andrew Gotschild was a marked man." Roger turned towards Brett. "The guy who attacked you in Gotschild's condo was obviously waiting for Andrew Gotschild."

"But, Gotschild heads up a questionable investigative organization," Kerry said. "The kind that important people with big money hire to do a job."

"And, if Gotschild doesn't deliver," Brett said, "they replace him."

"But," Roger said, "they need to remove the guy because whatever he knows is too much to leave hanging out there."

"So, we assume that after Brett left, Gotschild returns home, finds a dead man in his condo, and no matter how confusing that may be, he has to figure that the man was sent there for him?" Kerry said.

"Yes, I believe that's the case. That also means," Brett said, "we're dealing with people who are bent on leaving no traces behind. Powerful people with unlimited resources. And, the people working for them only have a limited window to get the job done before they end up changing positions from predator to prey."

Kerry reached over to a nearby chair, grabbed her sweater, and put it on. The temperature in the room had not changed, but Kerry was shivering.

Brett sensed the fear that had moved into the room. He tried to relieve some of the oppression that hung in the air, by redirecting the discussion to potential strategies they could choose to take.

"We need to also remember," Gatlin said, "that the highway accident in Arizona and the murder of two federal agents in a Tucson hospital are ongoing investigations. We don't know what anyone has uncovered, but at least someone, somewhere, is involved in something other than just trying to find me."

Kerry lifted both hands, palms up, and shrugged. "So, where does this leave us? What do we do now?"

"There are answers out there," Brett said, "but they're not all in the same place. Some of the key things we need to know are inside the DEA. Another source of info could come from the State Trooper, Carlos Aguilar, whose investigation is linked to the highway accident and the murders of the two federal agents. And, a third source of info is with this PI, Gotschild, and what he knows."

"That's a whole lot of territory for us to cover," Kerry said. "How in the world do we do that?"

Roger read the look on Brett's face and knew where Gatlin was headed. He chuckled before commenting.

"I believe that Special Agent Gatlin is talking about the basic principle of divide and conquer, only it's not our enemies that need to be divided."

Kerry tilted her head to the side, pursed her lips, then turned her palms upwards and shrugged.

"Would you care to explain that to me?" Kerry said.

"Roger's right. I think we should split up for now. You, Kerry, are the best person to concentrate on infiltrating the DEA. I'd never make it two steps before I'd be arrested or end up on a slab in some morgue. As a reporter, it makes sense that you would have questions for folks in the agency.

Rog, if we could come up with a solid angle as to why you're interested, you might be the one to reach out to Trooper Aguilar."

"And you?" Kerry said.

"Well, needless to say, I've got to be the least visible," Gatlin said. "I'm thinking I'd like to try to track down Gotschild. As we said, he's got to be on the run. If I can catch up with him, maybe I can squeeze things out of him."

"But, you have no idea where Gotschild is," Kerry said. "Where do you even start?"

"Kerry," Brett said, "if you could have Wireless dig up everything he can on Andrew Gotschild, maybe I can use whatever we put together to make some determinations on where the guy might go at a time like this."

"Consider it done, Brett."

"I've got an idea as to how I might gain some access to this trooper," Clark said. "What if we say I'm working with Kerry? Won't identify me as the press, but could indirectly open some of Kerry's doors to me."

"I like it," Brett said.

"Yes, works for me," Kerry said. "My biggest concern is you, Brett. You'll be out there wandering alone."

"Ah, I'll be okay. I'll stay in the shadows. Keep a low profile."

"Why don't we discuss all of this while we eat?" Roger said. "We can go over the logistics of how we handle things, answers we need to get, how we'll stay in touch, things like that. I'll run out and get us food and drinks. We can eat here, since we have a certain someone, who shall remain unnamed, who, as he, himself, stated, must not be visible."

Everyone laughed. Brett offered to stay behind if Kerry and Roger wanted to go to a restaurant.

"What? And miss the excitement of eating in a dingy motel room that smells like moth balls and some kind of cheap cleaning product?" Roger said.

Everyone laughed.

CHAPTER 30
BRETT AND KERRY

Roger left, leaving Kerry and Brett alone. As they sat and talked together, Brett bore a curious look on his face.

"There's something I've wanted to ask you for a while now, Kerry. What was it that prompted you to write that first article? What caused you to question what was pretty much universal consensus that I was a traitor and somehow responsible for what happened in the desert? You didn't know me. We'd never met. The info you had must have been sketchy and limited at best."

Kerry smiled.

"My daddy used to tell me to listen with my own ears and not someone else's. He used to say we should listen for what we are not hearing and not simply rely upon what is being said.

Yes, I heard all the accusations that were being made against you, Brett, but there were some key things, primary elements, about which I was hearing nothing at all. We're talking about things such as motive. Why would a man like you suddenly choose to go in the completely opposite direction to everything else in your life? No, I initially didn't know about your brother, Derek, and the impact his death had on your life-changing decisions. But, you underwent some of the most extensive, even brutal training, the DEA has to offer. Why would a man do that, then suddenly flip? As I began to explore more, there were incidents, such as what you did in an attempt to save the lives of Agents Nunez and Palmer. That didn't fit the profile of a man willing to aid in the deaths of more than two dozen federal agents. And, nothing about you seemed to support the possibility that you were a substance abuser, hooked on illegal drugs.

I could go on and on, but simply stated, Brett, it was all the things I wasn't hearing. It was all the gaps in between the uproar and clamor that bore a different slant on things. I was having difficulty believing that what everyone else was saying was the truth."

Brett sat and stared at Kerry. His mouth was open. His brows were furrowed. He shook his head.

"Amazing stuff, Kerry. Simply amazing."

"And, since then," Kerry said, "the voices I'm hearing have only gotten stronger. By the time I met with Patricia Kenworth I already believed in your innocence. But I want you to know that talking with her and hearing all that she had to say was encouraging to me. It reminded me that the truth is out there somewhere. Our job, certainly *my* job, is to find it and uncover it for all to see."

Brett turned his eyes away from Kerry and stared towards the window. He continued talking without looking at her.

"I appreciate all you're doing, Kerry. It all started with you. And now, without you and Rog, I honestly don't know where I'd be."

Kerry's cheeks were blushed. Her heart was beating more rapidly.

"Well, I just want you to know that I care, Brett."

Gatlin continued to speak without even looking at Kerry.

"I've been living in a dark world for more than four years now, Kerry. It's a world where your friends are people that you are programmed to hate and destroy. You laugh, slap backs, and pretend that the things these people say and do are acceptable to you. You do that while you're hating everything about them. You watch every word you say, monitor your own reactions, learn to laugh along with others at some remark that, in your heart, you find offensive. Your greatest fear is that one day someone is going to detect a gesture, a momentary reaction that reveals your true feelings. And through it all, you can never forget that the people you're dealing with every day were at least indirectly responsible for the death of your kid brother. There are times when it takes all the strength you can muster not to place your hands around someone's neck and squeeze the life out of them.

Nothing in your life is normal. You don't even dare to think that anything could be. So many little things in life are things that you never get to do. You can sense the hardness developing in your own heart, but you just can't seem to prevent it. It's the only way you're going to survive, so you keep shutting out anything good, anything clean, bright, or hopeful.

To be perfectly honest with you, Kerry, by now, I haven't got a clue what it's like to have someone care for me."

Kerry reached over and placed her hand on Brett's. As she did, he spun his head towards her and their eyes met. He took her hand and held it within his. In that moment, as he stared into her eyes, she appeared to be so pure, innocent, and vulnerable to him. Kerry Anderson was one tough reporter. She was also someone who possessed the power to stir his imagination and dare him to believe that his life could still have promises and dreams to be fulfilled.

As Brett and Kerry kept their hands clasped together and their eyes focused on one another, neither of them was ready to admit the feelings that were alive within them. Kerry did not want to confuse Brett, especially at a time when the priority was to do everything possible to clear his name. She had no idea whether Brett would even entertain any feelings towards her and she most certainly did not want him to feel obligated to her. She was not doing all that she was because of her attraction to him nor as a favor to the man. She was a reporter living up to her calling in life. She was someone engaged in a fight on behalf of a man she believed to be innocent.

To Brett, Kerry was beautiful, inside and out. But, he did not want to do anything to put her in any more danger than she already was. He was concerned that adding deeper emotions into the situation they were in was not the thing to do. It concerned him that Kerry and Roger were risking their own lives by linking themselves to a man who was being sought for reasons even he didn't understand by people he could not even identify.

"So, you knew at an early age that you wanted to be a journalist?" Brett said.

"Yes. Well, I always loved to write. When I was a little girl I would make up stories, write poems, and started to keep a diary. I still have a journal that I write in every day. I guess you could say that I've always had a vivid imagination."

Kerry smiled broadly. Brett leaned over.

"And what would you say was your strongest childhood fantasy?" Brett said.

Kerry blushed and Brett laughed aloud to see her reaction.

"Oh no. You're just going to think I'm looney or something."

Brett reached over and took Kerry's hand.

"No. I would never think that. Come on. Tell me, Kerry."

Kerry dropped her head, turned her eyes downward, then looked up into Brett's eyes.

"I used to imagine I was a princess who lived somewhere high above the clouds in a land filled with luscious green meadows and an array of beautiful flowers. I had a white unicorn that I rode every day. I named her Starshine."

"Starshine? That's a great name for a unicorn, I'd say."

"Whenever I was frightened or troubled, I would go to my land above the clouds where things were always joyful and peaceful.

During that time I told you about when my daddy was being falsely accused, I'd spend a lot of time in my special land."

Kerry turned her head slightly away from Brett.

"Silly, I know. The fantasies of a young girl with an overactive imagination."

"No, not silly at all, Kerry. And I must say, you make a perfect princess, Your Majesty."

Brett smiled, bowed his head, lifted Kerry's hand, and kissed it. Kerry laughed loudly.

Ah, but as he sat transfixed upon Kerry, his hand holding hers, Brett was lost in a moment unlike any he had ever known—even before his four years working undercover. He was overwhelmed with the desire to hold Kerry in his arms, breathe in the fragrance of her body, and kiss her full, pouty lips. He wished he could whisper softly in her ear and tell her just how beautiful, how uniquely special she is.

Two knocks on the door broke the spell that both Kerry and Brett were under. They heard the sound of a key unlocking and the door opening. A beaming Roger burst through, carrying bags of food, goodies, and drinks.

"He comes bearing gifts," Roger said with a big smile. "It's not exactly a fcast, but we can all pretend."

CHAPTER 31

FROM BLACK AND WHITE TO COLOR

Sitting together and strategizing on their next moves infused a new jolt of excitement for Brett, Roger, and Kerry. Nothing had changed since they began outlining their plans, but the fact that they were taking the offensive and not just sitting back had already made them feel as if they were accomplishing much.

Roger would fly into Tucson. Kerry would fly to Phoenix. She had contacted Agent Gaela and he agreed to meet with her at the Phoenix office. Roger would concentrate on Arizona State Trooper Carlos Aguilar. Kerry had already called Wireless and asked him to put together a portfolio on Andrew Gotschild for Brett. Gatlin would use the Jeep.

In order to provide Brett and Roger with access to the computer genius, Kerry called Wireless and introduced Brett and Roger. Even though she was confident that Wireless was completely trustable, she did not want to put him in a compromising position so she introduced Brett as Riley.

That evening, before Kerry retired to her adjoining room, they all sat together one more time and rehashed their plans. In the morning, Brett would drive Kerry and Roger to the airport. He had already received a dossier on Andrew Gotschild which he hoped would provide him with some insights as to where the man might retreat to now that he was on the run.

Brett hugged Kerry before she retreated to her room. When she closed the adjoining door, Roger turned towards Brett and smiled.

Gatlin sat at the end of one of the beds. Roger grabbed a beer for himself and Brett and sat on the other bed.

"Why don't you just let go and let her know how you feel about her, Brett?"

Gatlin swallowed his beer, started to deny his feelings for Kerry, then remembered he was dealing with Roger.

"Should have known you'd pick up on things," Brett said. "Look, Rog, I don't want to do anything that adds confusion to what we're all doing. The last thing I want is for Kerry to be distracted in any way."

"I hear you, man," Roger said. "But, I also see how it affects you whenever you're around Kerry."

Brett nodded his head.

"Man, you got that right, Rog, whenever I'm around Kerry it's like... oh hell, you're gonna think I'm crazy."

"No, go ahead, man, tell me. I already think you're kind of nuts anyway."

Brett laughed before continuing to speak.

"It has to do with the classic movie, *The Wizard of Oz*—you probably never saw that movie in your life."

"Are you kidding me. Saw it a zillion times. That movie is one of the reasons why I became an Air Force pilot."

Gatlin stopped and stared at Roger.

"The tornado, man. Are you kidding me? Flying through the air like that. Landing in some place over the rainbow. Man, after seeing that movie, I was more than ready to fly, baby."

Brett laughed, shaking his head at Roger's humor.

"Whenever I'm around Kerry it's like in that movie when the whole world suddenly changes from black and white to color."

"You deserve color in your life," Roger said, "and so does Kerry."

Roger smiled and clinked his beer bottle against Brett's in a toast.

"To a world of color," Roger said. Each man took a slug before speaking.

"So, you're okay with the strategy we have, Rog?"

"Yeah, man. I like the fact that we're all on the offensive, ready to turn over some rocks, and find things we need to know. My only concern, Brett, is with you."

Brett shrugged. His brows were furrowed along with a slight head shake.

"Me? How so, Rog?"

Clark stared at Gatlin, pointed his finger, and shook his head.

"The idea of you wandering around having to do everything yourself, risking exposure at every turn, concerns me, man. People have seen your pic on television, in the newspapers. Hell, don't forget I recognized you the night we met in Norfolk."

"Okay, first things first, Rog. You're not the average guy. I've been around you long enough now to see how aware and observant you are. You don't miss much of anything. Secondly, remember that I traveled all the way from Arizona to Virginia where you and I met and I did pretty good keeping a low profile. More importantly, Rog, I promise you, I'll be careful and won't take any chances. Besides, if I tagged along with you or Kerry, I'd just have to stay hidden somewhere while you guys did your thing. Plus, you'd be worried about me."

A big grin crossed Brett's face as he spun his head back towards Roger.

"Hey, it just struck me. You really care about me, Roger. You really like me, don't you?"

Brett roared with laughter and Roger laughed along with him.

"Don't get too confused by everything just because I, as a responsible person, express some concern about your welfare, Special Agent Gatlin."

Then, Roger and Brett laughed again.

"Okay, so maybe I do care," Roger said. "Guess you've kind of grown on me over time. Let me tell you, I don't have a whole lot of friends, Brett. Maybe that's why I was always happiest when I was isolated alone in a cockpit thousands of feet in the air. So, yes, you'd better be damn careful out there. I didn't invest all this time to lose a friend."

Brett smiled. Then, his face took on a much more serious look.

"Same goes for you, Rog. We're dealing with people who seem to have no problem, whatsoever, eliminating anyone who, to any extent, might be a threat to them."

"I hear you, Brett. From what you've told me, I feel pretty good about this Arizona trooper I'll be dealing with. I just don't see him as a player in this dirty mess."

"I agree. He's simply a state trooper charged with patrolling the Arizona highways who was on duty when the accident I was involved in occurred.

And as far as Kerry dealing with Agents Gaela and Watkins, I may be crazy, Rog, but I believe that Gaela was already conflicted by the discrepancies in what the DEA was saying about me. He could prove to be a good source for Kerry."

Roger nodded. Then, he responded to something that had been unspoken between them.

"Don't worry. I'll never be all that far from Kerry. I'll be there if she needs me, Brett."

Roger shrugged, lifted his palms up, and chuckled.

"Truth is, between you and me, that young lady may be the toughest of all. She's more than capable of taking care of herself."

Brett smiled. "I hope so, Rog. I sure hope so."

Barb Hennessey and Marty Gaela were seated together again in the small conference room that adjoined Hennessey's office.

"I was able to use my past communications with Bill Falwell as the basis for why I was trying to get in touch with him," Hennessey said. "I told one of the administrative aides to Falwell that I had followed up on some additional info he wanted."

Hennessey took another sip of her coffee. Gaela did the same.

"Good coffee," Gaela said.

"It's a brand I became familiar with when I was stationed in southern Louisiana," Hennessey said. "Popular brand in that area. Anyway, I got a return call from Special Agent Phillip Marlowe. Said he was handling all matters related to Falwell while the man was out on leave. You familiar with Marlowe?"

"Isn't he the guy," Gaela said, "who several years back came under scrutiny when another agent claimed Marlowe had tampered with some evidence and suggested keeping some of the drug money they recovered in a raid?"

"One and the same," Hennessey said. "They never could substantiate any of those charges and eventually the matter was dropped."

Barb lifted her coffee mug again, but spoke even before taking a sip.

"Look, Martin. I'm not buying this claim that Falwell is on some kind of personal leave that folks either know nothing about or don't care to talk about. And, I'm sure as hell not ready to start talking with Marlowe, unless I can think of an angle where I can try to get something out of the guy."

As Barb looked over at Gaela, she saw that his face was ashen and his mouth was open.

"What is it, Martin?"

"Okay, so I told you two days ago that State Trooper Aguilar had identified the highway shooters and possible murderers of Agents Nunez and Palmer as Charlie Hough and Luke Munson.

And, as we both know, the FBI has been informed and are aiding in the search for these two men. But…"

Gaela gulped in some air and continued to shake his head.

"I spent hours doing my own searching and came up with something I was about to tell you today. At first, I wondered if it meant anything at all."

Hennessey spotted that Gaela's hands were slightly trembling.

"Back when Marlowe was under investigation, his attorney used a PI who came up with a bunch of negative stuff on Marlowe's accuser and identified a drug dealer willing to testify that members of his own gang had set things up to make it look like Marlowe was guilty."

"Right," Hennessey said. "And to this day, you've got people who swear the PI paid that thug to come up with that story."

"Anyway, Barb, the PI was a guy named Malcolm Strickland. The man has some roots here in Arizona. Once was a second-string linebacker for Arizona State's football team."

A wry smile covered Barb Hennessey's face.

"And you said all of that to say?"

"Charlie Hough was on the same high school football team as Malcolm Strickland. And, here's the hook, Barb. Hough's mother and Strickland's mother are sisters. Hough and Strickland are first cousins. It's indirect, I realize, but there's a link between Special Agent Phillip Marlowe and the man suspected of killing two of our agents."

CHAPTER 32

UNTIL THEN

Brett drove Roger and Kerry to the airport. Everyone agreed to maintain contact with each other and each of them had access to Jacob Greenleaf, Kerry's computer whiz also known as Wireless.

Brett embraced Roger and the two men then fist-bumped and nodded their heads. Kerry hugged Brett tightly and kept her alluring blue eyes locked into his. She softly kissed his check and whispered in his ear.

"Promise me, you'll be careful, Brett, and not take any foolish chances."

Brett smiled.

"I promise, Kerry, and you need to be careful yourself."

As Kerry pulled away, she momentarily left her hand clasped within Brett's and smiled.

"Until then," she said.

Her eyes never left his until she turned and headed for the door. Even then, Kerry turned back one more time and smiled.

Brett stood for a moment, watched Kerry and Roger enter the airport terminal, then hopped in the Jeep and drove away. For years, Brett had spent an inordinate amount of time by himself. Until the day he met Roger Clark, Brett had journeyed from

Arizona to Virginia by himself. Yet, now, as he put the Jeep in gear and drove out of the airport, it was the first time he genuinely felt as if he were alone.

⋖+ +⋗

Andrew Gotschild had a great deal of experience before he established his private investigator firm. As a Purple Heart recipient and a decorated member of the Marine Raiders special operations combat force, Andrew had been in life-threatening situations. As the head of an investigative agency, he had been involved in unraveling a good many mysterious situations.

But, when he returned home and found a dead man in his condo, he was at a loss to explain who the man was and who had killed him. Andrew was, however, astute enough to know that the man was likely sent there to execute him. Things had gone from regretting he ever took this job to realizing that the people who hired him now wanted him dead. He had no explanation, whatsoever, how a corpse ended up dead on the floor of his home, but that was not his most imminent priority. Getting away from there as quickly as possible was.

Gotschild picked up a stash of extra cash he kept at his place. He was frustrated that he had dipped into the emergency funds he kept at home to place a few sure-fire bets that didn't pan out. No problem. He still had means available to him to withdraw money or otherwise pay for things without anything being traced back to him. Andrew also gathered up a few extra weapons and his passport and headed out the door. He correctly surmised that whoever sent this man to execute him would follow up when too much time elapsed and they never heard from the killer. When they would find their man dead, they would likely assume that Gotschild had bested his assailant.

They'll get rid of this body and clean this place up to look as if nothing sinister ever happened here.

The people who once relied upon Andrew to do their dirty work would now be hunting him down with the express purpose of killing him. As he raced away, Gotschild could not help but laugh at the irony of it all.

⋙ ⋘

As Hennessey and Gaela sat together, the things they were uncovering about their DEA colleagues constituted the most enigmatic case either agent had ever encountered. Gaela felt as if someone had turned down the room temperature. Hennessey reached for a sweater she had placed on the back of one of the conference room chairs. Although neither of them expressed it, they both had a sense of foreboding that whatever they were discovering would only lead down a much darker path.

Barb Hennessey spoke first.

"We've got to find a way to get a better handle on what Phillip Marlowe is up to. If I can get him to believe that I've come up with something of real interest to him, something I was going to pass on to Falwell, then maybe I can get the guy talking to me."

Hearing Hennessey speak so freely with him bolstered Gaela's confidence and generated a sense of protectiveness in him.

"Barb, you know you'd be putting yourself in a precarious position."

"Yes, yes, I realize that," Hennessey said. "But, we've got to get deeper into the DEA Headquarters and get a sense of who's playing dirty and who's not. There's no way I'm going to be able to penetrate deeper unless I come up with a bone that entices a follow-up starting with Marlowe. He's got to think I have something of real interest to him and his partners and that I suspect nothing is awry at the home base."

"I don't like you making yourself that vulnerable to people who've already murdered two federal agents, may have also killed

Falwell, and would attempt to kill Gatlin before he ever made it to Arlington."

Gaela paused, cupped his chin with his right hand, then lifted his head and made direct eye contact with Hennessey.

"If you're going to be at risk, put me there too," he said.

"I'm not sure I'm following you, Martin."

"We come up with some basic follow up info that you had promised to provide Falwell when the two of you initially talked. Then, you drop the hint that you're having a bit of a problem with one of your agents who is expressing some strong doubts about Gatlin's guilt and raising questions about what is going on within our headquarters. That'll be me, you're talking about. You can act like you've already pushed back against me, but you're keeping an active eye, especially as I seem to be buddying up with a state trooper who is independently investigating everything that occurred on AZ-90.

Let's make these people uncomfortable and get them to make some kind of move."

⇒⟨⟩⟨⟩⇐

For everything that Andrew Gotschild had previously done that was good before he turned to the dark side, Jeremiah Barkley had only done something evil and unlawful. Armed burglary, grand theft auto, a suspect in several rape cases, the man would still be in prison now if his attorneys had not been able to get his latest conviction overturned on some legal technicality. When Barkley was hired in place of Gotschild, the twofold message was clear. The people hiring him were desperate and they were not playing games.

Barkley would assign two men to seek out Gotschild, but his primary resources would be focused on finding and eliminating Brett Gatlin. A Civil War history buff, Barkley compared his intended approach to General Sherman's March to the Sea. Anything and anyone in his way, anyone who refused to cooperate, would be eliminated.

⇒+ +⇐

Kerry told Wireless that she needed to have false identification documents made for the man she referred to as Riley. Wireless had the right connections to get the job done. He contacted Brett when he had things all lined up.

"They're a bit on the expensive side," Wireless said, "but they're the best in the business. You'll have a driver's license and a passport and you can rely on them anywhere. You gonna have to go, let them take a pic, then you'll be told when everything's ready. They usually can have everything done within twenty-four hours."

Brett wanted to reveal his identity to Wireless, as he believed the guy had the right to know who he was dealing with and whether he wanted to continue to do so. He did not because Kerry believed that Wireless would be better off if he could claim that he never knew he was dealing with a fugitive from the law. Besides, Brett had the distinct feeling that Wireless had already figured out who this Riley really was.

Gatlin had read through the dossier sent by Wireless several times and made a list of potential places that Andrew Gotschild might go. Brett considered that the man knew how to hide. Then again, Brett knew how to find.

A quick call to Wireless confirmed that Gotschild had not made any withdrawals at an ATM, had not used any of his credit cards, and was not using his cell phone. In fact, Wireless was convinced he had destroyed it. But, it would not be long before Wireless showed just why Kerry Anderson believed the nerdy computer whiz was, in fact, a genius.

When Brett's cell phone rang, he initially assumed it would be Kerry or Roger. He quickly learned that it was neither of those two.

"Riley," the caller said using the fictitious name provided by Kerry, "Wireless here. You will recall that I reported to you earlier that Andrew Gotschild had not made use of any of his credit cards. I now stand corrected on that."

"What? I'm surprised. I would have thought Gotschild would be much too smart to use a credit card that could be used to track him," Brett said.

"Well, sir, your assumption is both logical and accurate, but it would only apply to a credit card that had the man's proper name on it. I did a bit of digging. Believe me, you do not want to know how I did it or where I searched to find it. Suffice it to say, that when applying for credit cards in a fictitious name and linked to a bank account with that same name, a person has to utilize contact info and such. I was able to identify in the subject's highly-personal computer files certain names and falsified coordinates he used for credit cards, a driver's license, a bank account, and other documents.

So, a man named Chester Bancourt has used a Visa card within the past twenty minutes. Chester Bancourt is our guy, Andrew Gotschild.

Wireless told Gatlin the last location where Gotschild had been.

When he disconnected from the call, Wireless had to laugh aloud at the fact that the notorious fugitive named Brett Gatlin thought Wireless believed him to be a man named Riley.

CHAPTER 33
FINDING THE PIECES

"There's not a whole lot I can talk about regarding an open investigation," State Trooper Carlos Aguilera said. Kerry had opened the door for Roger by calling Carlos and introducing Roger as someone who worked closely with her as an investigator.

"I understand that, sir," Roger said. "As you may or may not know, the deeper Ms. Anderson gets into her own investigations regarding DEA Special Agent Brett Gatlin, the more convinced she is that the man is innocent."

The two men were sitting together in Tucson at the Arizona Government Building on Tucson Boulevard. They were in a small conference room.

Aguilar sat and stared at Roger, but initially said nothing.

"Do you have a comment on that Trooper Aguilar?"

Carlos shook his head.

"My investigation concerns an auto accident that occurred here on a stretch of Arizona's Highway ninety. And even with that, we have the Criminal Investigative Division leading the charge on this thing. It's not within the purview of my investigation to make any determinations on the guilt or innocence of Brett Gatlin."

Roger knew that he had to approach this man carefully if he had any chance of getting him to open up further.

"Trooper Aguilar, I could use your help, your expertise, off the record, of course. I'm not a law enforcement officer. I don't have the training, the experience, or that certain something you guys either have from birth or develop on the job to see into things even before you have all the pieces. I'm talking about a kind of intuition where men like yourself seem to be able to pick up signals and sense things that many of us lay people are blind and deaf to."

Aguilar was not a particularly narcissistic man, but he as a seasoned and dedicated state trooper, he was proud of his work. Roger sensed that he was getting through to the man, but, once again, he chose to step carefully and move slowly in his approach.

"What is it you are asking me?" Aguilar said.

Roger smiled, lifted his hands with his palms up, and shrugged.

"My boss, Kerry Anderson, has stirred a great deal of response, both positive and negative, by raising questions regarding Gatlin's guilt and the overall attitude of the DEA. From what I understand, you had direct contact with Gatlin when he was involved in the accident you are currently investigating. In fact, we've been told that the State Trooper investigative team are the ones who first identified the fact that shots were fired at the vehicle before it crashed—in fact, likely causing it to crash."

Once again, Carlos Aguilar did not immediately say anything. From the look on his face, Roger surmised that the man did have much to say, but was careful with his words.

"What I'm asking is this, Sir, and I'm asking off the record to help me get my bearings on this entire thing. In your dealings with Brett Gatlin, was there anything you observed that caused even a scintilla of a doubt in you that the man is guilty of all that they say he is? Secondly, we understand that you and your people have identified the shooters, but can you tell me whether you believe the shots were fired at that vehicle to assist Gatlin or was he the target?"

Aguilar turned his head away from Roger Clark. His eyes were focused on a distant window. He bore a wry smile on his face. The trooper breathed in, exhaled, then leaned forward towards Clark and spoke.

"Okay, we're off the record?"

"Absolutely," Clark said. "You have my word on that."

"In answer to your first question, yes, I immediately was conflicted with the reports that Gatlin was guilty of criminal activities and may have been involved with a Mexican drug cartel. The man's actions during the highway accident were not those of a man seeking to escape. Hell, they weren't even the actions of a man concerned only for his own safety. If anything, what he did was heroic in his efforts to save the lives of two men who had custody over him.

Now, I'm also speaking based upon my own observations. I believe the shots were being fired at Gatlin to kill the man. They were not fired by people trying to help the man get free."

Roger stiffened his body, nodded his head, and leaned back in his chair.

"Thank you, Trooper Aguilar. That's exactly where I keep ending up every time I go through this whole thing in my mind. The pieces just don't fit. I've tried to make them fit, convince myself that my thinking and that of Kerry Anderson is wrong, but all I do is end up where I started. I mean from what we've learned, people from Gatlin's own agency have refused to corroborate his claims that he was working undercover as a member of a special ops team and have supported the claims that the guy was AWOL, a rogue agent who betrayed his shield."

Aguilar shook his head. He had his arms crossed over his chest. His nostrils were flared.

"I don't know what's going on with that federal agency," Aguilar said, "but when we learned the identities of the two men we believe are responsible for shooting at that vehicle and later killing two federal agents at the hospital, we turned all of that over to the FBI and did not initially go to the DEA with what we had."

Aguilar's hands were tightened into fists. His jaw was clenched.

"Like I say, right now, all I got is some uncomfortable vibes, but, I'll tell you flat out. I've got no tolerance at all for anybody with a badge or shield who crosses the line."

Aguilar began to open and close his mouth as if struggling to find the right words. In truth, he was struggling with whether to say anything at all. He began to blow his cheeks out, then slowly release the air.

"I'll tell you what, Clark, maybe there is something you can help me with and, in return, I'll give you whatever I can. It's difficult for me to get anywhere when it comes to the DEA. I work for a statewide organization that doesn't want to rock the boat with the feds. I already took some slack for turning things over to the FBI, rather than the DEA. But, you don't have to deal with that kind of politics. I need some better insight on what's going on inside that federal agency. They got an agent here out of the Tucson office," Aguilar said referring to Marty Gaela, "who's a good man. I'm sensing that he's got some real questions about his own agency. But, hell, he's in a tough spot too.

You do some digging and maybe you and I can play ball together."

⊫⊹ ⊹⊨

Marty Gaela had spoken with Kerry Anderson before she published her first article and followed her reports since that time. He would not credit Kerry with initially putting doubts in his mind regarding the guilt of Brett Gatlin, but her news reports substantiated what he suspected all along. So, when she contacted him requesting a meeting, he agreed.

"Only thing is, Ms. Anderson, I'm temporarily working out of the DEA office in Phoenix," Gaela said.

On her way to the Phoenix office, Kerry reflected on her first contact with Special Agent Martin Gaela. Back then, her intuitions told her that the man had serious doubts about the charges raised against Gatlin. And, Kerry's instincts were normally spot on. If she was correct, Gaela could be of great help to her in penetrating, at least to some degree, the DEA.

When Kerry entered the Phoenix office, she first encountered Agent Marianne Pacheco, who inquired as to why Kerry was there.

"Okay, if you'll just have a seat, Ms. Anderson, I'll contact Agent Gaela for you."

Within minutes, Gaela came out to the area where Kerry was seated and escorted her to the very conference room that adjoined Barb Hennessey's office.

"So, what brings you back to me, Ms. Anderson?" Gaela said.

"Special Agent Gaela, I appreciate your willingness to meet with me. I need to be completely honest with you, sir. From the start, since the time I first started covering this situation regarding Special Agent Brett Gatlin, my questions regarding the DEA have only continued to increase. I'm not here to put you on the spot, sir, as I respect the precarious position you are in as a DEA Agent. I need answers before I report on some of the issues I am dealing with when it comes to your agency. I do have a great deal of respect for the DEA and I'm not anxious to cast any undue negative aspersions on a federal agency. But, I will not hold back saying anything if I have to do so."

"Well," Marty Gaela said, "I'm not sure just how I can assist you, Ms. Anderson, but I'll see just what I can do. But, yes, there are some serious implications in what you're saying. What I can tell you is that if something is going on within the DEA that should not be, I want to know."

"Agent Gaela, I have information derived from very reliable sources that directly contradicts what some within your agency have claimed regarding Special Agent Gatlin. My sources state unequivocally that Gatlin was, indeed, working undercover as a member of a special ops team headed by Special Agent Max Bradford. And, sir, everyone states he was in good standing with Bradford right up until the end. I am prepared to report that reports emanating from the DEA that Gatlin betrayed his position as a federal agent are not only unsubstantiated. They are lies, pure and simple."

Gaela sat impassively, saying nothing, but listening intently to everything that Kerry Anderson was saying. He was aware that this young reporter could not be ignored. Yes, she had come to speak with him. Yet, at the same time, she had come to provide him with advanced notice that she was prepared to release a scathing report questioning the integrity of the DEA. Marty Gaela rose from his chair.

"Ms. Anderson, would you wait here, please, while I take a moment to check and see if Special Agent in Charge, Barb Hennessey, might be available? I'd like her to hear some of the things you are saying."

The call was made with a cell phone from an empty office within the Phoenix DEA building. Even so, the caller barely spoke above a whisper and did not intend to remain on the call for very long.

"She's here now, in a conference room just outside Hennessey's office with Marty Gaela. They've been in there close to a half hour already."

"Excellent. Well done keeping your eyes open and letting us know. There'll be a little something extra in your envelope for this.

Now remember. We expect you'll stay on top of this and keep us apprised of all developments."

"Will do. I'll let you know what I dig up,"

CHAPTER 34
BEHIND THE SCENES

It concerned Agent Rick Watkins that his mentor, Marty Gaela, was spending more time working out of Phoenix and hobnobbing with Barb Hennessey and Rick was not privy to any of it. From the day Watkins came on board, Gaela had been his "go-to" and the person who taught him more than anyone else. Now, for reasons he did not understand, Rick felt as if he was on the outside.

Watkins pretty much expressed these thoughts on the day that he took a call from the DEA Headquarters in Arlington that was originally intended for Gaela. The call had come in from Phillip Marlowe to the DEA Tucson office. While Gaela was out-of-pocket, his calls were being directed to his partner. Marlowe began by saying that Gaela had reached out to him and Phillip was reaching back.

"Well, sorry that we've never yet had the opportunity to meet. We're gonna have to get you up here in Arlington for a visit," Phillip Marlowe stated. "I've already heard some good things about you and the work you're doing, Watkins," Marlowe lied.

"Thank you, sir. I appreciate that. Really enjoying my work with the DEA. To be honest with you, I consider it an honor to be working with a man like Marty Gaela. I've already learned so much from him."

"That's good to hear. So, you say that Marty has been working out of Phoenix lately?"

"Yessir," Watkins said. "He's been spending a lot of time working with Special Agent in Charge Hennessey. Tell you the truth, I have no idea what they're working on. It's all been kind of hush-hush, like they don't want anyone else to know."

"Hmm," Marlowe said. "You'd think he'd at least let his partner know what's going on."

"Well, sir," Watkins said, "Marty might be trying to protect me from being involved in things, you know? He's always watching out for me."

"Protect you? Not sure I understand. Protect you from what?"

Watkins hesitated, then considered that he was speaking with someone who Marty had already called and reached out to. That gave Rick a confidence that Marlowe must be someone that Marty trusted.

"Can I be honest with you and speak freely?" Watkins said.

"Of course, you can, Agent Watkins. That's what a guy like me is here for. In fact, I want you to be completely free and honest with me."

"Well, sir, Marty's been troubled about things he feels aren't right inside the DEA. He thinks someone's not been honest about Special Agent Brett Gatlin. He's been real concerned that there's something real suspicious going on. Marty told me he was going to Hennessey in Phoenix to 'lay his cards out on the table,' so to speak. He didn't know how Hennessey would react, but he said he was going to tell her he thought Gatlin was innocent and our own agency was not."

"Very interesting, Agent Watkins. I appreciate your forthrightness and assure you that this will remain between you and me. We need more good men like you in this Agency."

The call went through after the third ring.

"Yeah, Marlowe here. We've got some trouble brewing out in the Phoenix Division. I'll need to talk with the man."

"He's not available right now. You can do your talking with me."

"Well, I'll tell you what, Marvin. You let him know I'm wanting to talk with him whenever he can find the time in his busy schedule to fit me in."

Marlowe disconnected from the call, leaned back in his chair and smiled. It was a good feeling to be in control of things, at least, once in a while.

‡ ‡

Brett had already driven for nearly ten hours on I-81 and I-40 when he reached Nashville, Tennessee. In another four hours he'd be in Jackson, Mississippi where, according to Wireless, Andrew Gotschild was presently holed up in an old hotel. Gatlin rested a bit in Nashville, then pressed on. He'd get all the rest he needed later. At the moment, catching up with Gotschild was his priority.

Now, Brett was seated alone in room number 412, where Wireless determined Mr. Chester Bancourt was staying. Hah, the rooms still had old-fashioned locks that were opened with a key. Gatlin was able to unlock the door within just a few seconds.

As he sat silently in the dark room, Gatlin thought about how much his life had changed from chasing Mexican drug dealers to tracking down sinister Americans involved in something Gatlin did not even fully comprehend.

Brett's adrenaline began to pump through his body when he heard the key in the lock, opening the door. Gotschild was in with the light turned on and the door closed before he ever spotted the man with the gun pointed directly at him.

"Come on in, Chester," Gatlin said with a smile. "I heard tell that you were desperately looking for me, so I figured I'd come to you. Keep your hands where I can see them."

Brett quickly patted the man down and removed the handgun that he was carrying. Gotschild's shocked expression changed to a smirk.

"I'm afraid my days of searching for you ended a while back," Andrew said. "At the moment, I'm more occupied keeping people from finding me. I'd suggest you do the same, Agent Gatlin. I hear tell the new guy they hired is a man named Jeremiah Barkley. He's about as cold-blooded a killer as you're ever gonna encounter. Word is the guy likes to kill as much as some people enjoy apple pie and ice cream."

"I'm not interested in killing you, Gotschild. I just want to know who the people are who hired you."

"Can't help you there," Gotschild said, "because I don't know. I'd get my orders by phone. Money was directly deposited in an account for me and my team. So, you see I never knew who hired me. Oh, I have my suspicions. I mean I am a PI, so you'd expect that I'm pretty good at tracking things, but even then, I can't be sure. If I'm right, however, you've got some powerful people looking for you, my friend. And people like that have connections that men like you and me can't always account for. Guess what I'm saying is it's just a matter of time before they get you, Gatlin, just a matter of time."

Gatlin and Gotschild were both startled when the door burst open and two men with guns raised entered the room. With their weapons, both of which bore sound suppressors, pointed directly at Gatlin, the taller of the two men spoke.

"Uh uh, Agent Gatlin, I'd drop that weapon if I were you."

Brett dropped the gun on the floor. He already had Gotschild's weapon tucked in his pants. If these men wanted to immediately kill him, they'd have entered the room firing. Brett wanted to see and hear what their next moves would be.

The shorter stocky man had his cell phone to his ear.

"We got 'em both," he said, "Gatlin and Gotschild. You want either of them alive?"

The man nodded and smiled as he turned to his partner.

"Seems that Gatlin's got a little more time to live," he said. Then, he turned and shot Andrew Gotschild in the head killing him instantly. "Unfortunately for the PI, his time had expired," the man said, as he and his partner chuckled.

"The boss and a team are headed to Arizona where they say the girl is meeting with some feds. He don't want me and you killing Mr. Gatlin here. He's got a few people with shields. Wants them to take him out, so's it looks like he was trying to escape from the law when he got himself killed."

At the reference to Kerry being in Arizona where this man, Barkley, and his thugs were headed, a cold chill passed through Gatlin's body.

"Okay, Gatlin, we gonna have to take a little ride together. So's, I need you to stand, keep your hands where I can see them." The man turned to his partner. "Pat him down."

As the tall man approached Gatlin, Brett whirled and moved so quickly that his body appeared to be a blur. He had the man's weapon, stood behind him, and shot the man's partner. In what seemed like all in one motion, Brett used a knifehand strike to the man's neck to fracture his hyoid bone. The knee to the man's groin, as he started his fall to the floor, was likely of little consequence, since the fractured neck bone would be the man's cause of death within minutes.

Brett quickly searched all three men and found Gotschild to be the only person with a wallet. Brett considered that the three thousand dollars in cash would be handy as he raced out the door. A cold wave permeated his body and he had a momentary ringing in his ears. Dear God, he needed to get to Arizona as quickly as possible. By his calculations, he still had another nineteen hours to go before he would reach Tucson, before he would be with Kerry again. There was a pressing urgency with no time to waste. He had to stay alert. He needed to push his body as hard as he possibly could.

Brett made a quick call to Wireless.

"The man we're interested in now is a thug named Jeremiah Barkley."

"I'm on it," Wireless said. "Just give me a little time and I'll have everything you need to know about this dude."

Gatlin had to stay close to the speed limit for fear that if a trooper stopped him, he'd likely be recognized. But, there was no time to waste. At least he'd gain two hours on the way.

"According to Colonel Shirley at Fort Huachuca," Kerry said, "Falwell was the man who informed him that Brett Gatlin had never worked undercover and Max Bradford never had a special ops team." Kerry was seated with Barb Hennessey and Marty Gaela. "Falwell was the man who referred to Gatlin as a rogue agent who was in bed with a Mexican drug cartel. What I consider to be reliable sources have directly refuted everything that Falwell said.

Yet, now, it appears that William Falwell has disappeared off the face of the earth. And these are just some of the questionable things that have arisen out of the DEA."

"And you've tried to reach Falwell, I assume?" Hennessey said.

"I have and I not only have never reached the man, I have never been provided with any possibility that I will be. Allan Kingsley, Chief Counsel for the DEA, gave me a story about Falwell being on some kind of personal leave. At other times, I've been referred to an Agent Marlowe."

"Are you familiar with Phillip Marlowe's past?" Marty Gaela asked.

"Yes," Kerry said. "I'm at a loss as to how or why the guy is still with the DEA."

Hennessey was careful as she considered how to word her next question.

"Ms. Anderson, if you have had any direct contact with Agent Brett Gatlin, are you aware that you could be brought up on criminal charges ranging from aiding and abetting a fugitive from the law to obstructing justice?"

Kerry stared back defiantly at Hennessey.

"Special Agent Hennessey, if you have reason to believe that there has been wrongful criminal conduct within your own Agency and you refuse to disclose or take any action against it, what might you be guilty of? If such action is not deemed as criminal, might it not at least be a breach of the oath you took and the very nature of what you are committed to do and be as a federal agent?"

CHAPTER 35

THE CHASE IS ON

It was a three-way call between Brett, Kerry, and Roger with each of them reporting on what they had done and learned. Brett was talking while continuing his marathon drive to Tucson. Kerry was making the nearly three-hour trek towards Fort Huachuca. Roger had already booked an adjoining room for Kerry at the motel where he was and where the three of them would stay. He left his motel room and headed to the place where he would be meeting with Trooper Aguilar.

Roger and Kerry were particularly upset at what they regarded as a genuine threat to Brett's life in the hotel room with Gotschild and two of Barkley's men.

"Hey, I appreciate your concern," Gatlin said, "but it probably sounds worse than it really was. I never believed things had gotten totally out of control. Of much more importance than me having a tussle with a couple of thugs is the fact that Barkley and his mobsters are apparently headed your way. And, in particular, these guys made mention of you, Kerry. I'm still driving now, but I've got a good way to go before I get there. You, both of you, need to be careful."

"Copy that," Roger said. "I could have said 'roger' but, for obvious reasons, I find the use of that word rather clumsy."

Clark laughed as he said that, but Brett did not.

"Rog, I'm serious, man. I saw one of Barkley's Neanderthals shoot Gotschild in the head and they both acted like it was just another day at the office. No big deal. I've got a feeling that Barkley's the worst of the lot."

Roger breathed deeply, exhaled, then spoke again.

"Don't worry, Brett. We'll be careful, I promise. Same goes for you, buddy."

"Before he was killed, Andrew Gotschild told me that he took the assignment without ever knowing for sure who he was working for. He received instructions by phone. Money was transferred to him by wire to an account—all of which would be untraceable, I'm sure. But, he said he had his suspicions about who was behind all of this and who hired him. He said they were powerful, dangerous, and pretty much unbeatable."

"I'm speculating now," Kerry said, "but based upon some of the things I sensed from my time with Special Agent in Charge Barb Hennessey and Special Agent Marty Gaela, I believe they've accepted the fact that we're dealing with a conspiracy. They both recognize there are individuals within the DEA Headquarters and elsewhere who are involved. Hennessey was careful with her words, but I believe she's on board with the fact that you have been framed, Brett, and people within her own organization are involved.

I learned something of interest when I was with Agents Hennessey and Gaela. We know that someone had to rig the Hummers that killed the agents. So far, we've been focused on the DEA agents in Arlington, but those Hummers were military equipment from Fort Huachuca. It had to be there, at the Fort, that someone planted those explosives in those vehicles in a way that no one would detect that they were hot."

"Hmm, and the DEA does not have a presence at Huachuca," Roger said.

"Somebody there has to know something," Gatlin said, "but the question is who had access to those vehicles."

"Exactly," Kerry said. "I'm headed there now. I'll be in the area tonight and head to the fort tomorrow morning."

"Trooper Aguilar is convinced the DEA has some dirty players," Roger said. "He also is not buying into all the things Brett has been charged with. He's turned some things over to the FBI, but, like anyone working in any federal or state position, he seems to get some real pushback from his own superiors when he wants to go deeper into investigating anyone within an agency like the DEA."

"One area that we don't seem to have any handle on," Brett said, "is what's behind this whole thing. Is it purely a money game or is it also money to be used for something else?"

"Bingo," Roger said. "I can't seem to get away from thinking that there's a goal even greater than pulling in some big bucks by cavorting with a Mexican drug cartel. If we can get a handle on that, we'll have a major puzzle piece right there."

"We need to keep in mind that whoever we're dealing with," Gatlin said, "they have some really big outstretched arms. We were in Jackson, Mississippi when two of Barkley's men caught up with Gotschild. Then, they were talking about two federal agents coming to Jackson to take care of me before I escaped. These guys are all part of a network. They could show up anywhere."

"I'm gonna have to break off from this call," Roger said. "Carlos Aguilar is meeting me this evening. We're gonna have a bite to eat and take in some beers. I'll see how much I can share with him and see if maybe we can get any backup support from any of his guys. You be careful driving in, Brett."

"Will do, Rog."

Brett and Kerry stayed on the phone while Brett continued to drive.

"Are you sure you can keep driving on so little rest, Brett? Should you stop somewhere and get some sleep?"

"Well, I'm pretty stoked on black coffee and a whole bunch of caffeine. So far, I'm feeling pretty good, Kerry."

"Please, Brett, if you have to stop and sleep somewhere, just do it. You can only push yourself so far."

"Okay, Kerry. I promise you. If I can't make it, I'll stop somewhere."

"I… uh… I want you to know, Brett, that I'm really looking forward to seeing you again."

"Same here, Kerry. I'll be back there with you before you know it."

"Great," Kerry said. "Until then, Brett."

"Yes, until then, Kerry."

Walter Vaughn, commonly known as Woody, was headed towards the garage of his friend, Arthur, where the band had a practice scheduled. Woody's hands had healed well since he had been burned at the scene of the highway accident. Today was the day he would wear some latex gloves and see how well he could play guitar. His temporary replacement as lead guitarist was currently sitting in jail following a drug bust, so Woody and his bandmates hoped they would be able to get their man back in time for their next gig in six days.

Woody had just climbed into the driver's seat when a man approached the car window. The man had a smile on his face and was carrying a map, looking at it interchangeably as he approached Woody's car.

"Hey, sorry to bother you, son," the man said, "but I guess I got turned around a bit and can't seem to find my bearings. Wonder if I could get some directions from you."

Woody laughed.

"Don't mean to sound disrespectful, sir, but there's your problem," Woody said, pointing to the map. "Nobody uses them things anymore. Don't you have a GPS in your car or your cell phone?"

The man laughed along with Woody.

"Well, you got a good point there, son. You're right. I do have a GPS. Use it all the time. I really do," the man said. "This map is really just a prop."

"A prop?"

"Yes, it just enabled me to get close enough to you without you being suspicious. You see," the man said as he drew his weapon, replete with silencer, and pointed it directly at Woody's head, "I'm here because of some unfinished business that was supposed to be taken care of some time ago."

"Hey, man, w-what're you doing? You crazy? Don't point that thing at... "

Two quick snaps, sounding much like a staple gun, completed the task and Woody's body slumped against the steering wheel. Jeremiah Barkley smiled as he holstered his weapon and joined the driver waiting nearby in a dark sedan.

"Feeling good, my friend," Barkley said. "Looks like another job messed up by Andrew Gotschild has now been properly executed. And I do mean executed," the man said, as he and his partner drove away roaring with laughter.

Edmund Foley was the Chicago Tribune reporter who originally published a story that discredited Walter "Woody" Vaughn as a known substance abuser and claimed that he fabricated the stories about his and Brett Gatlin's heroism at the scene of the Arizona highway accident. Foley published yet another story that received top billing at his home base newspaper and was quickly picked up nationwide. With a headline, "Where's Brett Gatlin Now?" Foley's article cited the murder of Woody Vaughn as resulting from a local drug dispute. He also stated that he had reports from reliable sources that the investigation into the deaths of so many federal agents in the Sonoran Desert was leading many experts to believe that Agent Brett Gatlin had assisted the Monterro Cartel in getting away with a huge amount of money and drugs.

"Authorities are convinced that it was an insider who made it possible for twenty-nine American and Mexican federal agents to be killed that day. Only one federal agent walked away from the bloodiest slaughter of federal agents in history and that agent was none other than Brett Gatlin."

Foley quoted Allan Kingsley, Chief Counsel for the DEA, as saying, "Our agency maintains twenty-one domestic field divisions with two hundred twenty-one field offices and ninety-two foreign offices in seventy countries. The DEA employs over 10,800 people, including 4,600 Special Agents and 800 Intelligence Analysts. And, we are convinced that overall our people carry themselves with integrity and serve their country with honor. We are saddened by the possibility that one of our specially trained individuals has allegedly dishonored his shield. We look forward to a meaningful resolution to this and some much-needed closure for the families of our agents and the Mexican agents who died in the line of fire."

Foley went on to warn readers "not to fall for the fancy rhetoric of a young female reporter striving to make a name for herself by casting doubts that Gatlin is the man who betrayed his oath and aided in the slaughter of so many dedicated law enforcement individuals."

Stating that the Bible itself declares that Satan can appear as an angel of light, Foley stated, "be there no doubt about it. Brett Gatlin is neither an angel nor a bearer of any light, whatsoever. The blood of many innocent people in the Sonoran Desert and on those who purchase illegal drugs on dark street corners throughout our land can be found on the hands of a man whom our government once entrusted with a shield of honor and lawful authority. Americans cannot rest and the souls of the innocent dead will continue to cry out until Brett Gatlin is brought to justice."

CHAPTER 36

BACK TO ARIZONA

A major accident on I-10 W, just as Gatlin was entering the State of Arizona, slowed things down. It also concerned Brett that he would be forced to slowly pass State Troopers in a single lane, increasing the risk that someone might identify him. To his knowledge and great relief, no one had linked Gatlin to Roger Clark and the Jeep that Brett was traveling in. Nevertheless, he was some 275 miles from Tucson and anxious to get there.

A lone Arizona State Trooper stood at the front of a single file of vehicles waving the cars through and away from the area where the accident had occurred. The trooper was standing just to the side of a vehicle driver's window. When Brett saw just how close this man was to each driver, a bolt of fear shot through his body. If Gatlin was recognized, his journey, his every effort to help clear his own name, his ability to reach Kerry and Roger would end right here at the border of The Grand Canyon State.

Beads of sweat had already formed on Brett's upper lip. His grip on the steering wheel was so tight, his knuckles were white and his hands were cramped. If this law enforcement officer recognized him, Gatlin's options were minimal. He could accelerate and attempt to race away, but, in addition to any troopers who could quickly pursue from the location of the accident, they could and would also radio ahead. Other troopers in vehicles, copters summoned to fly overhead, Gatlin would not get very far before he was apprehended. Also, the Jeep would be identified eliminating Gatlin's last means of transportation other than stealing vehicles again.

Ever so slowly, Brett moved the Jeep forward. He held his breath. It seemed impossible that the trooper would not recognize this high-profile fugitive. The man was waving, constantly summoning each vehicle to move past this one spot where they would soon afterwards be free to utilize any of the three highway lanes and resume normal speed.

Just as Brett reached the man, the trooper received a call on his radio and bent his head downward towards his left shoulder where his radio was fastened. For that moment, the man's eyes were not on the driver of the Jeep. And just that quickly, Brett slipped through. Gatlin breathed a sigh of relief.

By the time Kerry reached the Sierra Vista area, the sun had already set. It was a dark, moonless night. A cool breeze, preceding a front that was moving into the area, rustled through the trees causing Kerry to shiver as she approached her car. But an impending storm was not the only presence on this night. The air was also filled with a sense of foreboding and the wind itself seemed to be whispering a warning that a portent of evil was in the air.

When her phone rang, the screen simply displayed that it was an unknown caller. Kerry chose to answer. The voice Kerry heard was disguised by a professional voice changer device. There was no question about that.

"Good evening, Ms. Anderson. There's an old abandoned warehouse on Chester. There's going to be an exchange of money there tonight. Guess you might say that what you've been searching for happens there tonight at 7:00."

"Who is this?" Kerry responded. "Who will be there? Who are you?"

Kerry was greeted by silence. When she checked her screen, she could see that the call had been disconnected. The caller's solitary goal of delivering a message to Kerry had been fulfilled. Now, the burden had switched to Ms. Anderson. The sensation that everything was moving too quickly to process dominated Kerry's mind. She was desperately searching for answers. Was this a hoax, a trap? Or might this be a major breakthrough in the case? Her mind was racing. The caller mentioned the word "payoff." If there was a conspiracy between a group of Americans and Monterro's cartel, they could choose a location like this to meet and exchange cash just as they would do with any drug deal. If the caller was right and there was a meeting tonight, this could be Kerry's opportunity to get a lead on who was involved on this side of the border. For too long, she, Brett, and Roger had been flying blind and even, at times, following potential leads that quickly vanished.

Kerry's hands were shaking as she punched in Wireless' number on her speed dial. She explained what had occurred and listened as Wireless' fingers raced across the keyboard.

"Yeah, it's an off-premises property that Fort Huachuca once used for storage," Wireless said, after he provided the exact location to Kerry. She was twenty minutes away and the caller said the meeting would take place in twenty-eight minutes, at 7:00 p.m. "Looks like they had it on the market three years ago, but, best I can determine, they never did sell it. From what I can see, the place is empty now and in considerable disrepair. It's a bad, dirty, dark neighborhood located in an unincorporated area just outside the southwest border of Sierra Vista."

When Kerry said nothing more, Wireless spoke again.

"Hey, you're gonna need some backup to even consider going near a place like that," Wireless said.

"Okay, thanks," Kerry said. "I'll get on that now."

But, there was no time for that. Both Brett and Roger were too far away to make it in time. Besides, Kerry had no intention of entering the building. She would place herself within range where she could view things and take pictures using her night vision binoculars that also had a built-in camera. If her hunch was right, Americans would meet with representatives from Monterro's cartel. Kerry needed to know who these Americans were.

Kerry did make a quick call to Roger's phone and left a message on his voicemail informing him that she was out getting something done and would be back at the motel sometime later.

Wireless' statement that the area was dark and dirty was, if anything, an understatement. The building itself had bricks missing from the outside, cobwebs filled most of the windows, shingles were missing from the roof, and garbage was strewn along the front of the building. The chain link fence that once surrounded and protected the warehouse from intruders was missing major panels and the front gates hung loosely and open.

Kerry assumed that Wireless' assessment that the area was bad needed no additional evidence. A secret meeting between members of a Mexican drug cartel and Americans dealing with them was enough to label any neighborhood as evil.

Kerry was parked away from the building with her car nestled behind some trees and shrubbery. She had a direct line of sight to the entrance to the old warehouse. The activity began within minutes after Kerry's arrival. The first vehicle she spotted was a black SUV. Four men exited as the driver moved the vehicle further down in front of the building. The men were dressed in slacks, sport coats, and armed with AR-15s. Each of them also carried a lantern which would be the only source of light within the building. If Kerry was correct, these men were all Americans. Well, at least they provided some diversity. Two of them were Caucasian, one was African American, the other was Hispanic. Once again, although this was merely speculation, if Kerry had to label these men, she would say they were all federal agents. Three of the men entered the building. One remained outside standing near the front door like an armed guard. The next vehicle to arrive was an Army Jeep. The driver was clearly an MP, who also carried an AR-15 automatic rifle. His passenger appeared to be a man of rank—a lieutenant, Kerry was quite sure. Kerry had never met Lieutenant James Gilliam.

The next two vehicles to arrive were Hummers. Each contained four men who were clearly Mexican. They each bore an AK-47. Kerry had every right to assume they were members of Caesar Monterro's cartel. As with the American vehicle, the drivers pulled ahead and remained parked behind the black SUV and the Jeep.

Kerry continued to speak into her phone, recording what she was seeing, while taking pictures with the camera built into her binoculars.

"They're all waiting for someone," she whispered into her phone. "Looks like the party hasn't begun yet."

It wasn't particularly cold on this night, but Kerry felt a strong chill as she sat alone in her car. She was convinced that on this night something big, something revealing, was about to occur. Her premonitions were proven true when the black limo pulled in front of the warehouse. Kerry had difficulty holding her binoculars steady, as her hands began to tremble. She struggled to control her breathing. She winced at the tightening in her chest and took a moment to shake her hands and feet to rid them of the tingling sensation that had moved in.

A man exited the front passenger door and came around to open the rear seat behind the driver. Two men stepped out from the rear seat of the limo. Kerry gasped. She shuddered at the sight of them, making sure the pictures she was taking would clearly identify them. This was a major piece of the puzzle. With this kind of power and support behind the illegal activities, it made a lot more sense why they had such difficulty getting the breakthroughs they so badly needed. At the moment, Kerry did not understand all the reasons why things were being done, but she had just uncovered a major who.

Once the men were inside the building, Kerry would not be able to determine what would occur behind the closed doors. But, she had the evidence of the meeting and this would go a long way to help resolve…

Kerry gasped. Her body trembled and she began to sob. Her heart was beating so fast, she imagined that it might explode within her chest. One man was standing outside her driver's window. Another was at the front passenger seat window. Both men had their weapons pointed directly at Kerry. A third man stood at the front of her car with his AK-47 pointed at Kerry from there. The fourth man with the broad grin covering his face and nodding his head swung the tire iron he had and shattered the driver's window. Kerry screamed. Shards of glass covered her body. Kerry's screams were stifled as the man reached in and grabbed her throat. He pushed her down on the seat to make sure she would not be in position to start the vehicle up and attempt to drive away. Her face was flushed against the car seat making it difficult for her to breathe.

"Well, good evening, Ms. Anderson, good evening," the man said. "You and I haven't had the pleasure of meeting before tonight. Although, I dare say, meeting me under these conditions, hell, meeting me at any time, would never constitute a pleasure for you, ma'am. My name is Barkley, Jeremiah Barkley, and, I must say, finding you here tonight is kind of like winning the lottery for a man like me."

Then, Barkley roared with laughter.

CHAPTER 37

SHATTERED DREAMS

"We're gonna stay in the area," Barkley said as he spoke on the phone. "Like I been saying, I got me a strong feeling that Gatlin and the reporter lady have been working together. I got me a hunch that with the pretty lady coming here, our boy is gonna show up, also."

"The man doesn't pay you for your hunches, Jeremiah. We expect you've got better methods of finding someone than using a crystal ball or some other enchantment. Need I remind you that Andrew Gotschild didn't fare very well when he failed to deliver?"

"The day's coming," Barkley said, "when I'm gonna get my hands around your scrawny little neck and watch you plead for your life. Believe me, that's when you'll take any kind of magic you can find in the hope that it'll somehow help to spare your life."

Barkley smiled as he pictured the man he was speaking with pale and trembling at Jeremiah's threats. He could sense the difference in the man's voice as he next spoke.

"L-listen, Barkley. I'm just saying, okay? The man, he doesn't like failure and he doesn't care for delays. I'm just reminding you what you're up against."

"I don't need no reminders, not from you or anybody else, you hear? The man don't like failure or delays? Well, Jeremiah Barkley, he don't like threats unless he's the one giving them. The sooner you get that, Marvin, the better it'll be for your own personal health. I generally don't like to waste my skills killing somebody without getting paid, but get under my skin enough and I'll be more'n glad to make an exception in your case."

⤙⤚

Lieutenant James Gilliam had been stationed at Fort Huachuca for eight years. Until recently, he considered the assignment to be nothing more than a dead end that stifled his career. When the opportunity was presented to him to not only make some good extra cash, but also align himself with future political powerhouses, Gilliam's attitude towards his Huachuca assignment changed overnight.

"One of them was a State Trooper, man named Aguilar," Gilliam said. "He was the on-scene patrol officer when the accident on Highway Ninety occurred. The other man was a guy named Clark, Roger Clark. He said he was working with Kerry Anderson. I did some background checking. Learned he's been a fighter pilot with the Air Force until some health issues grounded him. Nothing much to show since then. Seems to be just wandering around probably wishing he was back in the cockpit.

Clark was asking a lot of questions about who worked on the specialized Hummers that were used in the incident in the Sonoran."

"This is rather disconcerting. You realize, of course, Jim, that the man gets very uncomfortable when people keep coming around asking too many questions?" the caller said.

"Yeah, I get that. I gave them nothing. Told them that any number of soldiers work on something like that and that we have the most stringent safeguards and checklists utilized on any military equipment that ever is handled here in the Fort."

"I suggest you keep a sharp eye on things, Lieutenant. There's no room here for mistakes. I am assuming you do not need to be told that the man will want to know if anyone comes by again asking questions."

Brett drove straight to the motel where Roger was staying. As he did, he noticed that the parking space in front of Roger's adjoining room was empty. Brett knocked on the door and a bleary-eyed Roger eventually opened it.

"Hey, Rog."

Clark embraced his friend.

"Is Kerry not in her room?"

Roger's face turned pale. "Huh? She sent me a text. Said she had something she needed to do and would be back afterwards. Guess I fell asleep, man. Never noticed she wasn't in."

At 2:00 in the morning and no idea where Kerry might be, the two men were initially at a loss to know where Kerry might be. They began calling Kerry's phone, but never got an answer. Their concern heightened. Ultimately, they took a chance and called Wireless. That's when they learned that Kerry was going to the old warehouse when she last spoke with the tech genius.

Roger and Brett were quiet as they drove towards the place where Kerry had last reportedly been. Each of them conjured up places where she might now be and why she had not yet returned to the motel.

When they reached the warehouse, Roger was the first to speak.

"I don't like the looks of this place at all, Brett. We're going to have to be real sharp when we enter a place like that."

We're going to need some light, Rog."

"I've got a flashlight in the glove box," Roger said, as Brett reached in and grabbed it.

With guns drawn, Roger and Brett slowly approached the old warehouse. There were no vehicles in sight. No one appeared to be in the building. There was no immediate sign of Kerry.

The two men entered the building, clearing the way for each other. Everything was pitch black. They did not turn the flashlight on until they were more assured that no one was lurking in the darkness. Then, Brett clicked on the light and they began a search for Kerry.

Despite the condition of this building, they came upon an area where there was a table and folding chairs. Cigarette and cigar butts further confirmed that people had recently been in this area.

"Wireless said that Kerry suspected Monterro's people and others were meeting here tonight. Looks like she may have been right," Roger said.

"This place is huge," Brett said, "but, she's certainly not anywhere in this immediate area." Brett then handed the flashlight to Roger. "If you continue searching in here, I'll go outside and see if I can spot anything that might help us figure out where Kerry might be."

Brett stepped outside in the cold night air. The ground was soaked from the hard rain that had passed through earlier. Brett saw enough tire tracks in the muddy area at the front of the property to indicate that several vehicles had, indeed, been onsite earlier. He stepped away from the front of the building and looked around.

When he first spotted a vehicle parked at a slight distance behind some trees and shrubbery, a sudden coldness hit at the very core of his body. He gasped and bent over in an effort to restore his breathing. Then, Brett ran as fast as he possibly could, hoping, above all else, that the car he spotted had nothing, whatsoever, to do with Kerry Anderson.

His gun was drawn as he reached the driver's side of the car and spotted the shattered window. The rain had soaked the interior of the vehicle, including a portion of the body that was strewn on the front seat. Brett froze and stood as one paralyzed staring inside the car. He initially tried to convince himself that the person lying across the front seats was not Kerry or that, if it was, she was still alive. He opened the car door, reached in, then desperately searched for a pulse that he knew he'd never find. Then he moved the body, sat in the front seat, cradled Kerry in his arms, and sobbed. His body shook uncontrollably. Tears poured from his eyes—more tears than he had ever shed before.

"No, no, no," Brett cried out, in the midst of his sobbing. As he stared at Kerry, she was as beautiful in death as she had been in life. To Brett, she looked like an angel, sleeping peacefully or, perhaps, a princess who lived somewhere high above the clouds in a land filled with luscious green meadows and an array of beautiful flowers.

Brett rocked Kerry in his arms as he held her and gently rubbed her face. He bent down and kissed her again and again. His heart ached. He could not stop crying. He didn't want to stop. In a moment of time, Brett felt as if his own life had ended, also. In a very real sense, he wished it had.

He continued to gently rock Kerry. By now, her body was cold, lifeless, empty of the soul and spirit that defined who Kerry was. He traced his finger along her lips and continued to gently rub her face. He knew Kerry was gone, but another part of Brett's heart and mind spoke softly to her as if he could somehow awaken her from a deep sleep.

"I-I n-never got to t-tell you, Kerry, that… that I… I had f-fallen in love with you. Oh, my God, Kerry, I-I never told you that."

"She knew, Brett. She knew that you loved her."

Brett spun his head towards the car door and spotted Roger standing there. His eyes were also filled with tears. The tears ran down Roger's face. He wept for Kerry. He wept for his friend, Brett, and the knowledge that Brett's heart was shattered.

Roger reached in and placed a hand on Brett's trembling shoulder.

CHAPTER 38

IT'S NOT OVER

Brett and Roger had no choice but to anonymously call the authorities and give them the location of a car with a dead person inside it. They were not in a position to identify themselves or explain how it was that Kerry ended up where she did. Brett was a known fugitive from the law. Roger could not stand alone and explain anything that had occurred. Also, Kerry had long protected Wireless since many of his activities were illegal.

Three days had passed since the news of Kerry Anderson's death went worldwide as the media reported her mysterious death in a deserted area outside of Sierra Vista. The news coverage reported that Kerry's phone and any notes or other devices were not in the car where her body was found.

"Whatever mysteries this young reporter may have uncovered went with her to her grave," one reporter stated. Some of the reports cast blame on Brett Gatlin for somehow pulling Kerry Anderson into a web of evil that eventually cost Kerry her life. Speculation was strong that Kerry was likely killed by members of a Mexican drug cartel who had crossed over into the United States with their products. "If Anderson had not been chasing the myth that Brett

Gatlin was not a rogue agent who had betrayed his country, Kerry might very well still be alive," one news report stated.

In addition to grieving over Kerry's death, Brett and Roger were frustrated that they were forced to sit back and say and do nothing. Following an autopsy by the county coroner, Kerry's body was flown back to Indiana where she and her family were from. A huge crowd attended her funeral. Brett and Roger did not.

"Maybe I should go to the authorities, Brett, and spill out all that we know," Roger said.

"Who can we even trust, Rog? And any evidence we might have was taken by whoever killed Kerry. We have nothing but speculation, nothing concrete. Damn it all, Rog. It can't end like this. It's not over. It's definitely not over."

Clark shook his head. His body was slumped. "Man, I feel so defeated," Roger said. "Listen, Brett, you haven't eaten in days. You need to get something inside you. Maybe if we catch our breath a bit, we'll be able to think more clearly."

Roger was concerned that Brett would do something foolish. He sensed both the grief and rage within his friend. The sun had already set. Roger had not yet bothered to return his leased vehicle. He used it as he ran out to get some food for Brett and himself. As Roger stated, Brett had not eaten since they had found Kerry's body. While Roger was gone, Brett's phone rang.

"This is Wireless. Listen, man, I've just about worn my fingers to the bone and stretched my mind beyond what I thought I could ever do, but I've found 'em. Assuming we're looking for Jeremiah Barkley, I know where the guys are who killed Kerry."

"Yeah, Barkley was headed towards Kerry at the last report we had. He's our man. Tell me what you've got, Wireless."

"There's a house. It's a two-story home standing alone on two-acres of land. The area surrounding it is rural, bunch of farms. The house itself was once a farmhouse, but my guess is the owners died. Anyways, somebody's been renting the place out. A shell corporation named "Huguenot Enterprises" is on the lease. If I had to guess, I'd say the folks behind this whole mess use the place for whomever needs it from time-to-time, you know? Anyways, that's where they are.

Listen, man. I can't tell you for sure how many of 'em are in there. I can't even tell you for sure that Barkley is there right now, but I'm sure the dude's been staying there."

"Thanks, Wireless. Great job."

"Listen, man, can I tell ya something?" Wireless said. "Kerry, she was a special lady. She believed in me when nobody else did. To a lot of others, I'd be nothing more than a weird computer geek. But, Kerry, she treated me with such respect. I didn't work with her just for the money I got paid. I worked for her because she was one of them rare people that sometimes grace this dark, evil world we live in. And, I'll tell you something, man. Once I got to know her, it wasn't just a question of Kerry believing in me. I believed in her."

Wireless paused. Brett knew he was striving to control his emotions.

"I don't know what you've got to do to get these bastards, man, but I am hoping to God you do. Just know I'm here. Off the clock. I'll do whatever I can, anytime night or day, to help you."

After Brett disconnected from the call, he gathered up his weapons, extra clips, and headed out for the Jeep. He would not wait for Roger. There was no need to implicate him in what Brett was about to do. Most people have several friends. Brett only had one and he did not want Roger to risk his life any more nor be involved in something that could not be justified under the law. Roger was much too good a man for that. Besides, Brett was all in. He was willing to die to accomplish what he needed to do.

As Brett drove away from the motel, he realized that he might never return. He wished he could tell Roger one last time just how much he loved and appreciated him.

Roger told me that he was sure that Kerry knew before she died that I loved her. I'm going to have to believe that Roger knows just how deeply I cherish his friendship.

As Brett drove towards the old farmhouse, his eyes were cold, hard, and flinty. He could hear his pulse, his heartbeat, pounding throughout his body. He was grinding his teeth. Even if he had not fallen in love with Kerry, she was, as Wireless had stated, one of those rare people who occasionally grace this planet. Kerry helped to make it a better world simply because she was in it.

I know, I know you would probably tell me not to do what I'm about to do, Kerry. Truth is, I've never known someone like you before. But, I cannot let you die in vain. I can't just sit back and do nothing. Besides, the people responsible for your death need to be eliminated from this world or they'll just continue to destroy innocent lives.

Gatlin switched his mind over to a state of preparedness. He had made his decision. He did not need to engage in thought justifying his contemplated actions. He did not care if what he intended to do was in any manner justifiable. He breathed in deeply three times in a concerted effort to calm his body down. Brett Gatlin had undergone some of the most intense training before he became active as a member of Max Bradford's *Subterraneo* team. Now, he intended to tap into all that he had learned. Live or die, he would leave the blood of these killers in his wake.

It took slightly less than a half hour for Brett to reach his destination. He drove past the house, taking the time to analyze the situation and plan his next steps. The house, as Wireless had informed Brett, was a two-story farmhouse with a white exterior and green shutters. It was set back from the road and surrounded on both sides by fields of corn already growing tall and bearing its crop. Several dark SUV vehicles were parked alongside the house at the end of the long driveway. Brett doubted that anyone was on duty watching the exterior of the house and property, but driving down a shale-covered driveway would surely give the occupants time and opportunity to know that someone was entering. Brett could see lights on inside the building.

Well, looks like someone's home this evening. Guess what, fellas? Company's coming.

It would be nearly impossible to approach the house by driving down its long driveway. Gatlin drove ahead looking for a spot where he would leave the Jeep and travel by foot through a stand of corn to his destination. He knew that he risked the chance of being spotted even by approaching the house on foot, but that appeared to be his best choice. Brett had learned over the course of time that every decision, even those made in a split second, has more than one choice. He also knew that there are times when none of the available choices are free of considerable risks. This was certainly one of those times. He recalled the words of his mentor, Max Bradford. "You get to make the choice," Bradford would say, "but you don't get to choose the consequences." Brett was hopeful that the risks associated with the choices he would be making were at levels that he could deal with and overcome.

When he drove past the house, Brett saw a slight movement near some bushes at the front of the building. Once again, he was glad that he had taken the time to study the situation before taking action. He had been wrong in his initial assumptions. There was a guard or two watching over the house from the outside. What he did not know was that the occupants of the house were always watching for the possibility of an attack by members of Monterro's cartel. The drug lord had always anticipated that a day would come when he would begin eliminating the people with whom he had to share the fruits of his labor. Since Barkley and his thugs worked for those people, it made sense that Monterro would want them out of the way before he took action.

"What are they going to do to me if I break the deal we made?" Monterro once told some of his closest men. "Perhaps, they will sue me in American courts for violating the terms of a contract?"

Monterro said and laughed heartily afterwards. "The people we are involved with think that I need them, but they are wrong. I will always have some who will assist us to assure that our products get across the border. And paying off those people will be a whole lot less than dealing with the others who take such a huge cut into our profits. Well, as I say, now that Garcia is gone and we are at the top of the hill, these others are no longer needed."

Brett was glad that he was wearing dark clothes. He wished that he had camouflage paint to darken his face, but he did not. He reached down and rubbed some dirt on his face and hands and headed towards the house. As he got closer, he laid down on his belly and approached the house in a crawl.

Gatlin spotted the first man standing on the right side of the front door. He pulled a knife from his pocket and continued to move with the stealth of a big cat pursuing its prey. As he drew nearer, Brett was exhilarated. Nothing he was doing would bring Kerry back, but it would assure him that someone would be accountable for sending her away. Also, ever since the travesty in the desert, Brett had primarily been on the defensive. It felt good to be the one taking charge.

Brett's mind was in full gear.

Can't be certain that there's only one man up front, but, I've got to go with the limited knowledge that I have.

Brett recalled the words that Max Bradford used in training his men. *First things first, then the next thing.* He began to formulate a plan of action in his mind.

The way I see it, there's a man in my way and he's got to be removed for me to gain access to the building. So that's my starting point.

Gatlin intended to remove that impediment and he did. Swiftly, silently, he was behind the man, had him gripped by the neck, and deftly slit the man's throat before any sound was ever uttered. Ever so silently, Brett whispered as the man's dead body slumped to the ground.

"Her name is Kerry. Where you're likely headed, you'll never get to see her."

Brett assumed the front door would not be locked, but he wanted to know what other options of ingress were available to him. He silently walked towards the back of the house, careful should there be anyone else standing guard back there. He saw no one.

Brett knew that whatever element of surprise he currently possessed would be lost soon after he entered the house. He walked around towards the windows at the rear of the house and found one that was not locked. He carefully raised it a few inches, then walked away towards where he could cut off the power to the house. His adrenaline was spiked high. This was his mission and he intended to take full advantage of it. He cut off the power to the farmhouse.

In this case, darkness is no one's friend, but mine. It'll serve to even up the odds a bit more.

Brett had a picture of Jeremiah Barkley that had been forwarded to him by Wireless. He didn't know exactly what role Barkley may have directly played in Kerry's death, but it was a detail that changed nothing. As the head honcho, Barkley bore responsibility for her murder. As far as Gatlin was concerned, the verdict was already in.

When the lights went out, the men inside did not necessarily expect foul play. Although it was not a stormy night, there were many legitimate reasons why an old house in the country might lose power. Brett pulled the window open and climbed in.

Another vehicle pulled into the driveway of the old farmhouse, Roger's fear that Brett would do something foolish was now a reality. More men, more weapons, the odds had just increased against Brett Gatlin surviving this night.

CHAPTER 39
A TIME TO KILL

Brett found himself in a laundry room that opened up to a hall-way. The laundry room also was where the circuit breaker box was located and Brett could hear someone headed in that direction now that the power was out. He waited and when the man entered the room, he grabbed him from behind and tightened his grip on the man's neck.

"This is what it's like to not be able to breathe," Gatlin whispered in the man's ear as he choked the life out of him.

Brett moved down the hall and could hear several men talking together in a nearby room. They were seated at a kitchen table and had been playing poker.

"Hey, Fred. You find any breakers tripped?" one man yelled out.

"I'm not sure Fred could find his way out of a wet paper bag," another man said. "I'll go see how he's doing?"

The man rose and started down the hall where Brett was located. It was too late for Brett to retreat back to the laundry room. The man spotted him immediately and Brett fired, hitting the man in the chest. As he fell to the floor, the two men who had been with him jumped up from the table they'd been sitting at, pulled their weapons, and took cover.

The men who had just arrived heard the gunshot and moved quickly. One raced towards the back of the house. Jeremiah Barkley and another man were at the front. Barkley took note that the man who had been stationed out front was lying dead on the ground.

Brett moved towards the kitchen. As he momentarily peered into the kitchen, a shot was fired and the bullet struck very close to where Brett had been. But, he was down on the floor now, on one knee. He fired and struck the man who shot at him. As Brett stared into the kitchen, he did not hear the man who had entered the back door of the house and was moving down the hallway towards him. The man raised his weapon and was prepared to pull the trigger.

Just then, Brett heard a sound. He spun his head around just in time to see Roger Clark snap the man's neck from behind and let him fall to the floor.

"Rog, w-what?"

Clark put a finger up to his lips, then raised two fingers and pointed towards the front of the house, signaling that two more men were coming in the front door. Brett motioned that he had one additional man somewhere beyond the kitchen. So, there was a total of three men remaining in the dark house.

Brett and Roger did not like the position they were in. They could not see any of the men in front of them and would have to step out from the hallway to find them. Also, if someone went around to the back of the house, they could position themselves behind Gatlin and Clark.

Brett signaled to Roger that he would move back to the rear of the house and attempt to leave and circle around to the front. Roger nodded his head and moved a bit closer towards the kitchen. Brett did not exit through the back door. He opened the same window he used to enter the house and peered out. He spotted a man hidden nearby.

No time to waste. If they hear a shot, they might just as soon think their guy picked me off coming out the back door. Worth a gamble to me.

Brett lifted his gun, aimed carefully into the darkness, and fired two shots, dropping the man where he stood. Then, he hopped out the window and ran towards the front of the house.

There were still two men at the front section of the house. One of them was Jeremiah Barkley. They heard the shots at the rear of the house and did assume that their man likely caught the man in the hallway exiting out the back door. At this point, Barkley did not know who had entered the house. He assumed it could be individuals from Monterro's cartel and that there could be more than one man.

"You there, Ike?" Barkley shouted. "Ike? You hear me?"

Barkley's answer came from behind him, as Brett entered the front door.

"Gonna be real difficult for Ike to answer you," Gatlin said. "He's dead."

The man with Barkley whirled, but Brett emptied five shots directly into the man's face. Brett's mouth fell open as he found himself staring directly at Jeremiah Barkley. At the same time, Roger had moved forward and had his gun pressed hard against the back of Jeremiah Barkley's head.

"Well, well, well," Barkley said, "I finally get to meet the notorious Special Agent Brett Gatlin, although not under the best circumstances for me." Barkley laughed heartily. "Nicely done, Gatlin, didn't know you had an accomplice. Is that your grounded pilot buddy?"

"You shouldn't have killed her, Barkley," Gatlin said. "I'd have gone to the ends of the Earth to find you and make you pay for that."

"Tut, tut, my friend, you make it sound much too personal. It's all just part of the course in the business I'm in, you know? All in a day's work. In fact, I killed the young lady myself with my own hands. But, she really didn't suffer—unless not being able to breathe until your body shuts down constitutes suffering. Haha."

Brett lunged forward and pressed his own weapon hard against Barkley's forehead.

" My, my, check out the look on your face, Gatlin. Guess her death was very personal to you, eh? Were you sweet on her? Is that it? She was a fine-looking woman, I must say. You know I had an inkling to maybe enjoy the pretty lady before I killed her, but I never do mix business and pleasure."

"I'm going to kill you, Barkley. You're finished."

"You know? I believe you, Gatlin. You've got that murderous look in your eyes. But, then again, they say you've killed before, eh?"

"I'm going to enjoy watching you die, Barkley."

"Then, do it, Gatlin. Finish me off. Go ahead and pull the trigger. You got your gun pressed against my head. This is your moment. C'mon, man, pull that trigger. Do it."

Gatlin's face was twisted into an expression Roger had never before seen on his friend. Brett was beyond angry. Roger could hear a moaning, wheezing sound escaping through Brett's lips. Then, Gatlin took several deep breaths, held them in for what seemed like an eternity, before expelling the trapped air. A wry smile covered his face, as he tossed his weapon down on the floor behind him.

"You can remove your weapon, Rog. A bullet exploding in this animal's skull is much too light a punishment for who he is and what he's done."

"Ah, too bad," Roger said, "I was looking forward to blowing a big hole in Barkley's ugly head."

Roger removed his gun and Brett threw a punch that seemed to shatter Barkley's nose before it fully landed. To Barkley's credit, he recovered quickly enough to begin throwing a series of punches at Gatlin. But, none were landing. Brett was much too quick.

The two men were out in the center of the kitchen now. Barkley thrust his large frame at Brett as he charged forward like a raging bull. But, his efforts were met with a series of punches and Brett was gone before Barkley even finished his charge. Brett was smiling. Barkley was in a rage. He lifted one of the wooden kitchen chairs and hurled it at Gatlin. Brett moved to get out of the way, but something slippery on the floor thwarted his efforts and the chair struck him with a forceful blow knocking him to the floor. Barkley saw his opportunity and moved forward hurling himself atop Brett's body. He pushed down on Brett's face, in an attempt to twist and snap Brett's neck.

Roger prepared to intervene, but before he could do so, Brett had twisted, turned, and forced Barkley's body over, until Brett was now on top. Brett's punches were fast, hard, and crisp. Within minutes, Barkley's face was unidentifiable.

"Finish him off, Brett," Roger shouted. But, instead, Brett stood up, gave Barkley an opportunity to stand on his wobbly legs and tossed the man his knife.

"Brett! What are you doing, man?"

" Don't worry, Rog. I'm just evening up the odds a bit for Mr. Barkley here."

Barkley laughed, sneered, and, with a somewhat renewed sense of energy, began to swipe and strike at Gatlin. The knife narrowly missed its target several times. Barkley's confidence was up as he moved in for the kill. He had the knife raised and had Brett pinned up against the refrigerator, with his other arm clasped around Gatlin's neck.

"Time for you to die, Gatlin," Barkley screamed. Then, as he began to thrust the knife forward, Brett kicked Barkley in the groin, threw a punch to Barkley's neck, then head-butted the man. As Barkley staggered backwards, Gatlin grabbed Barkley's hand that wielded the knife, twisted it until the man's wrist bone snapped. Jeremiah Barkley screamed as Gatlin plunged the knife into Barkley's face and shoulder.

"Those are a little something special from me to you, Barkley. How's it feel man?"

Barkley was still crying out in pain when Brett moved the knife over Barkley's heart.

"This one's for Kerry."

Then, he plunged the knife deep into Barkley's heart and let it fall to the floor along with Jeremiah Barkley.

"Hmm," Roger said, as he stared down at the lifeless body. "Mr. Gatlin, you can be one mean dude when you get riled up."

Brett was breathing hard. Then, he stared over at Roger with a puzzled look on his face.

Roger shrugged, then raised his hands, palms up, and smiled.

"What? What can I say, Brett? Did I forget to tell you that I had a GPS Tracker placed on my Jeep months ago? Before I ever met you, in fact. What can I say? I've always been a bit of a gadget guy. Hell, you ever look inside the cockpit of a fighter jet?"

Then, Roger laughed.

"What? You thought I was gonna just stay on the sidelines somewhere and let you have all the fun?"

Brett dropped his head and stared at the floor

"Look, Rog, I-I didn't want to get you involved in something…"

Brett focused upon the lifeless body of Jeremiah Barkley.

"I-I was overwhelmed with the desire to get this man and kill him. I had to make him pay for what he did. Nothing else mattered.

I was in a such a fury, Rog. I never felt like that before in my life. I battled just to think clearly.

When I saw Barkley and confronted him, I was filled with a hatred like I've never known before. I don't like what I felt. I don't like what I was when I caught up with the man."

"It's over now, Brett." Roger laughed. "And for the record, I don't think Barkley liked it much either."

Roger placed his arm on Brett's shoulder.

"Now you see why I was concerned you were going to run off and do something crazy. Hey, I know what you were thinking, Brett. I get it, buddy. I also saw the pain, the emptiness in your eyes. Man, my heart ached for you, Brett. Look, you need to remember, she was my friend too. And you and me? Well, we've come a long way from drinking a beer together in downtown Norfolk."

Roger kept his hand on Brett's shoulder.

"To be perfectly honest with you, Brett, I never did make friends all that easily. Maybe that's why I don't treat friendships lightly. Hey, it's no big secret that it's not all that easy for you to let someone else into your life. Guess we sort of have that in common."

Roger smiled, reached over, and lightly tapped Brett's face. "As someone once said, 'I'm in this thing for the long run, so get used to it.' "

The two men embraced, then Brett pulled back a bit and looked squarely into Roger's face.

"Thank you, Rog. I can't thank you enough."

Roger smiled.

" Maybe not, but you can buy me a nice cold beer right about now."

CHAPTER 40

WHO'S WATCHING WHOM?

Before Brett and Roger left the farmhouse, Brett checked Barkley's phone and memorized a few of his more recent calls. One was a cell phone in the Washington D.C. area that he and Roger could not further identify. They turned that one over to Wireless in the hope that he could identify who that phone belonged to. Another number was easy for Brett and Roger to identify, since it was a direct line to someone in Fort Huachuca.

Roger made the call.

"Well, hello there, sir. How are things with you today? So, good to hear your voice," Roger said.

"Who is this? What do you want?"

"Well, Lieutenant Gilliam," Roger said, "what I want is a meeting and a nice chat with you, my friend. Hey, I'm going to give you the off-premises place and time for you to meet with me."

"Why in the hell would I meet with you, whoever you are?" James Gilliam said. "Stop wasting my time and calling me or I'll have you reported to the authorities. They'll track you down and... "

"Uh uh, Jimmy boy, that ain't gonna work at all. In fact, getting the authorities involved is the last thing you'd want to do—especially after I pulled your number from the phone of a professional killer."

Roger could not see the shocked expression on Gilliam's face, but the ensuing silence assured Clark that he had clearly gotten Lieutenant Gilliam's attention. He gave the man the place of meeting and the time.

"How will I know who you are?"

"No problem, Lieutenant, I know you. You just introduce yourself at the front and they'll direct you from there. No problemo. Hey, hope you like Mexican food. They say this place has the best in the area."

Gilliam said nothing.

"Now, don't you be late, Lieutenant," Roger said. " 'Cause that'll upset me and you don't want me irked. Not with what I know about you and your extra-curricular activities."

Roger and Brett had decided to bluff Gilliam by getting him to believe they knew more than they did. It was clear that Gilliam took the bluff. Roger smiled knowing that he and Brett had certainly ruined the Lieutenant's day and had plans to make things even worse for him.

The meeting was set. Brett and Roger would both be there.

⇌ ⇋

"What've you got?"

"Well, Sir, the caller made contact with Lieutenant James Gilliam to set up a meeting with him. The meeting's at 7:00 this evening at the La Casita Mexican Restaurant and Cantina on East Fry Boulevard."

"Damn, how the hell did anyone find out about Gilliam? This messes up everything."

"What do you want us to do?"

"Be there. Time to make a move and finalize things."

⊷⧾ ⧾⊶

Roger had chosen a table towards the back of the restaurant and left explicit instructions that Lieutenant James Gilliam was to be directed to their table. Brett wore a hat pulled low over his face. The men seated at a nearby table were shocked when they spotted Brett Gatlin seated nearby. At the moment, they did not say or do anything.

When Gilliam arrived, he was brought to the table.

"You're the guy who said he was working with the reporter lady," Gilliam said, as he stared at Roger. His mouth fell open when he identified Gatlin.

"I could create a scene right now," Gilliam said, "and have the police come and arrest you Gatlin," the Lieutenant said.

"And I could put a bullet in you from under the table, Lieutenant, before you say another word. I'd be more than glad to trade my life for yours, Gilliam. Go ahead. Make your move, soldier boy. I'm game, if you are. Call my bluff."

"You're crazy, Gatlin."

"C'mon, push my buttons, Gilliam, and let me show you how crazy I can be. And, as far as trading my life for yours, check that, Lieutenant. Maybe I'd be doing a life for a life trade between you and Kerry Anderson."

All the color left Gilliam's face.

"I had nothing to do with that reporter's murder. Nothing."

"Well," Gatlin said, "I'm afraid your phone buddy, Jeremiah Barkley, did. I don't think it's all that far-fetched to draw conclusions based upon links between two people."

Gilliam's lips and chin were trembling. He started shaking his head as if in denial of what Gatlin was saying.

"By the way, Lieutenant," Roger said, "you may be seated."

Gilliam sat. Gatlin and Clark had clearly unnerved the man.

"W-what d-do you want from me? What? Money? Is that what you're looking for? I can pay you. I can do that."

Gatlin's flaring nostrils and the tightness in his eyes served only to heighten Gilliam's fear.

"You're a disgrace to that uniform, Gilliam. I'd like to tear it off your body right about now," Gatlin said. "You think you can buy your way out of this? Is that what you think? You think we want money, just because that's what motivated you to sell your soul? We want names, Gilliam. Who else is involved in this? Who are the players here? Who rigged those Hummers, Lieutenant?"

Gilliam shook his head more robustly.

"I had no idea they were going to rig those vehicles with explosives. I thought maybe they were going to wire them, place some bugs in them for whatever reason. All I did was give them off-hour access. They used their own crew to do what they did."

"Man, you're just Mister Innocent here," Roger said. "We got bodies showing up all over the place while your bank account is obviously getting fatter as time passes, but you don't think you're responsible for anything."

"Barkley and his gang were all criminal low-lives," Gatlin said, "but you parade yourself around in a fancy uniform with a bunch of ribbons and pins to cover up the blackness inside of you. One way or another, Gilliam, you're going to pay for what you've done."

Gilliam bolted from his seat, then stood and glared across at Gatlin.

"Go ahead and kill me, Gatlin. You might as well do it now because, if I say anything more, I'm a dead man anyway. Look, I'm sorry about the girl. I'm sorry about all the things you've gone through. Like I said, I never had any say in any of that. That had nothing to do with me."

"Sorry doesn't cut it, Gilliam," Brett Gatlin said.

Before Gilliam could turn to even attempt to walk away, three men were at the table. They identified themselves as FBI Agents. Gilliam, Gatlin, and Clark were all cuffed and escorted from the restaurant.

⊨⊣ ⊢⊨

Roger and Brett were interrogated separately.

"Mr. Clark, you told Lieutenant Gilliam on the call you made to him that you got his number from the phone of a hired killer. Which hired killer? Were you talking about Jeremiah Barkley? Is that the man you were referring to? How did you get access to his phone? Where is he now?"

Although Roger was silent, his mind was racing with a myriad of thoughts.

Okay, so the FBI was on to Gilliam and apparently had his phone tapped. They heard my conversation with him. That's how they knew we would be meeting here tonight. But, they don't know that Barkley is dead? My God, those bodies are either still at the farmhouse or someone came in and cleaned up the mess that Brett and I left behind?

Clark sat impassively without saying a word.

"Listen, Clark. I don't know where you fit into this whole thing, but you can make things a whole lot easier on yourself if you'd start talking."

"Okay, sure." Roger said. "You were one of the agents at the Mexican restaurant. So, tell me, how'd you like the food there? We ordered our food, but never really even had a chance to eat before you guys interrupted our meal."

The agent got up from his chair and walked out of the room.

Brett Gatlin never said one word, never made eye contact with anyone throughout the entire time that he was questioned. When he was read his Miranda Rights, Roger acknowledged them and declined any need for an attorney. Brett did neither. He sat stoically

253

and, based upon his reactions, might just as well have been a man incapable of hearing anything.

"Talking to Gatlin is like trying to have a conversation with a cadaver," one of the frustrated agents said to a colleague after he left from a session with Brett.

Little did they know that Brett was a dead man inside his mind. The accumulation of all that he had endured had taken its toll. Gatlin no longer cared what any of these people did. From the media, to the conspirators, to the FBI and other legitimate law enforcement officials, Brett was done. He was finished. Kill him, convict him, lie about him, attempt to help him—it was all the same to Brett. He was not interested in any of it.

"We could charge you with aiding and abetting a known fugitive," Roger was told.

"He told me his name was Bertrand Phillips," Roger said. "Should have known better. He kind of had shifty eyes, now that I think of it," Clark said.

"You think all of this is a big joke, Mr. Clark?" one of the FBI agents said.

"No, sir," Roger said. "Only joke I see is that you're wasting your time with guys like me and Gatlin when you know damn well you got yourselves a damn web of people in prominent positions behind a list of felonies that'll keep your paperwork going for months."

"What about you telling Gilliam his phone number was found in a hired killer's phone?"

Roger smiled.

"It was a bluff. Something we made up. Looks like we hit a winner on that one."

Roger would soon be released. He was correct. He was much too small a fish in the pond that the FBI was currently fishing in. They could always pick up Roger in the future if they needed to.

"But, you can be sure we'll be watching you, Clark," he was told.

"That's not a bad thing," Roger said. "Having you guys watch me might just help keep me alive—provided you're also keeping your eyes on the snakes out there that lied about Brett, ordered the hit on Kerry Anderson, and tried to kill me and a few other law-abiding citizens."

Brett Gatlin was held over on charges that he violated his oath as a federal agent which constituted a federal crime. He was also being held on suspicion of capital murder for the deaths of the federal agents in the Sonoran Desert. When Brett heard mention of that, he was filled with disgust. He nearly died that day, along with all of his team members and other courageous federal agents. And what was his reward for his service to his country and willingness to risk his life? An accusation that he was a murderer.

The news of Brett Gatlin's arrest dominated all the wire services and media outlets throughout the nation and was treated as a top news story overseas.

Before Roger was released, he was permitted a visit with Brett. The two men were careful with anything they said, as they were certain that the authorities were listening in.

"Listen to me, Brett, if not to yourself, you owe it to Kerry to continue to fight against all of this. She believed in you, man. Together, we need to finish what she started."

Roger promised Brett that he would visit with Gatlin's mother and sister to confirm that Brett was okay and that Roger would keep them informed as things develop. A visit to Brett might be had in the future, but, for now, Brett requested that they not do so.

"You can bet they've got reporters knocking on their door," Brett said. "But right now, a visit would only place them under an even greater media spotlight."

Neither man ever mentioned Jeremiah Barkley and his thugs, but they were both at a loss to explain why their deaths had not yet hit the news.

"I'll be back to see you after I pay that visit to your mom and sister," Roger said.

"Just tell them I love them," Brett said, "and get Mom to bake a cake and put a file inside it."

Both men laughed.

"And, Rog, love you too, Bro."

"Goes both ways," Roger said.

CHAPTER 41

SPEAKING FROM THE GRAVE

An attorney, Timothy Wakefield, contacted Gatlin with an offer to represent him *pro bono*. Wakefield was closely associated with the Washington Post newspaper owners and a senior editor. Wakefield had once worked for the Federal Bureau of Investigation and over the years had gone from prosecuting cases to defending federal agents who were in trouble. To date, Brett had not yet even said a single word to the man.

"There are many at the Post who are strongly sympathetic to you, Agent Gatlin, and were great admirers of Ms. Kerry Anderson. However, I can't properly assist you, if you continue to choose to not even speak to me," Wakefield said. "I'm here for you, but I need you to help me do my job."

Time and again, Brett said nothing, until the day he relented.

"I will accept your offer, Mr. Wakefield, out of respect for Kerry and the people who believed in her. And, I am very grateful for your generosity, sir. But, I'm telling you now, you can't help me. Throughout this whole ordeal, every witness that existed ended up dead. Every person with the potential to turn state's evidence ended up on a slab in the closest morgue. All of Kerry Anderson's evidence, insights and reports, including things she never even had a chance to share with Roger and me, were taken and presumably destroyed by the people who murdered her.

I know you mean well, but, no, you can't help, Mr. Wakefield. The odds are stacked much too high against me. Hey, one day I'm in the heat of the Sonoran Desert risking my life for my country. Next thing I know, I'm a fugitive running from the law, a man who supposedly betrayed his oath and his country. These people, they're good at what they do. They leave no stone unturned. You can't beat them. Hell, you can't even find them.

I appreciate you wanting to try, Wakefield, but you're wasting your time, bubba."

⚬⚬

Nearly two weeks after his arrest, Brett received a surprise visitor. Gatlin was cuffed, sitting alone in a room at a small wooden table when the tall African-American woman entered. He barely glanced at her, then dropped his head and kept his eyes focused downward.

"Special Agent Gatlin, my name is Delonda Wilson. I'm with the FBI," she said, as she flashed her credentials. Gatlin never lifted his head. "Sir, I understand that you are distraught over all that has occurred of late. I want to discuss some things with you. I also understand that you have endured a great deal, beginning with spending more than four years working undercover as a member of a special ops team."

Gatlin lifted his head and glared at his visitor. His jaw was tight, his body was stiff.

"Understand? You say you understand? I seriously doubt that you do. We've got so many people who sit behind their desks in government offices thinking that they know what it's like to be in the field, doing the work that only a select few people will ever be qualified to do. Those of us who've been in the field, we live in a world most people could never even imagine."

Brett's face was stern and cold. The muscles in his arms were taut. A vein in his neck protruded angrily. His fists were clenched so tightly that Delonda could see his nails biting into the palms of both hands.

"It's a world so dark, Agent Wilson, that you become accustomed to living in shadows where lies are the only truth you'll ever deal with every day. You go along with things you detest, things so contrary to everything you believe in, that, after a while, you begin to question yourself and wonder if maybe you really have embraced the dark side.

It's a world where we have to hope beyond hope that our instincts, our judgment, and our courage are better than others, because we're called upon to make decisions in the heat of a moment where our lives and the lives of others hang in the balance.

And when all is said and done, Agent Wilson, what do we have left? Friends? None. Families? None. Homes? Pets? Nice cars? None. Concerts and sporting events attended? None. Future plans and goals? None. People who appreciate and understand the sacrifices you've made to do your job? None.

You understand, Agent Wilson? I doubt that. I seriously doubt that you do."

As she stared deeply into his eyes, Delonda Wilson saw the pain, the anguish that Brett Gatlin harbored. Delonda had never been a particularly emotional person and over the years, as a trained federal agent, she became even more adept at keeping things in check. But, what she saw in Brett Gatlin was more than Delonda could handle. For a moment, she broke her eye contact with the man to maintain control of her own emotions.

"You loved her, didn't you?" Delonda said. And when she did, Brett's head snapped upwards and a pained expression covered his face. "You see, I loved Kerry too. I've loved her, as more than a friend, as a sister, for many years."

Delonda told Brett how she and Kerry met while in college, were roommates, and maintained a close friendship even up until the day Kerry died.

"You say that I don't understand what a man like you endured working in the field. Perhaps, you're right about that Agent Gatlin. But, I'll tell you what I do understand. I understand that people like Kerry Anderson come along very rarely in life. I'm talking about people with an integrity so genuine, so true, that no one and nothing can ever cause her to bend it or compromise. I'm talking about someone with the courage to stand up when no one else will, when the flow against her is seemingly insurmountable. And when a person like Kerry does stand up, she does it with a willingness to risk her job, her reputation, her safety, if necessary, in order to pursue the truth."

Delonda sighed deeply. "I understand that, Agent Gatlin."

Delonda no longer attempted to hide the tears that had filled and now were breaking loose and falling softly from her eyes.

"And this much more I know," Delonda said. "I know that Kerry had already fallen in love with you, Agent Brett Gatlin. I know that, sir, because she and I discussed it. And I want you to hear one last thing that I understand. Kerry's attraction for you had nothing to do with the reason why she died. If you were someone she had no attraction towards, in fact, even if she particularly disliked you, Kerry would have still done everything she did. She would never turn her back on injustice. Once she believed in your innocence, nothing and no one could ever stop her until she uncovered everything she could to support that belief."

Delonda stood and headed towards the door. Before opening it, she turned back one more time towards Brett.

"You'll be hearing from me again, sir," she said. "I will not permit the work that Kerry was engaged in to end here. Of that, you can be assured."

Then, Delonda was gone and Brett sat with his head buried in his hands and sobbed.

━┤┼┝━

Special Agent Martin Gaela and his family lived in a pleasant three-bedroom ranch house in a well-established subdivision in Tucson. Marty was asleep in his bedroom with his wife, Sharon. The children, Gabe, age fifteen, and thirteen-year-old Pamela were asleep in their rooms. Rusty, the family's six-year old Labrador Retriever, had been asleep laying across the foot of the bed when his low growl stirred Marty awake. It was then that Gaela saw the shadow of a man pass by the bedroom window.

Marty gently shook his wife and whispered.

"Baby, I need you to listen to me now. No time for questions. Slide off the bed and get on the floor now, Sharon."

"M-Marty? What's going on? W-what… "

"Now, Sharon. Quickly. Get on the floor."

Sharon had barely reached the floor when the crashing sound of shattered glass evidenced that the window had been broken. Shots were fired into the room. Gaela had already retrieved his weapon and was kneeling on the other side of the bed returning fire. Sharon Gaela was screaming. Rusty was in a frenzy, barking, growling, placing himself in harm's way as he raced towards the window.

"No, Rusty. Down, boy. Rusty, get back." Gaela shouted.

Rusty leaped out the broken window. Marty could hear the tires screeching as a car pulled away. The dog began chase, but the vehicle would soon reach speeds that made it clear that Rusty's efforts to catch it would be in vain.

Within minutes, the dog was back at home. The children were with Sharon and Marty. The police were at the house investigating the crime. Several neighbors, awakened by the commotion, offered to have the Gaela family spend the night at their home.

Such a violent crime in a normally safe neighborhood shocked the police. Marty Gaela was not. He and Barb Hennessey had set the stage for someone to suspect that Marty was asking far too many questions and, perhaps, making some disturbing discoveries. He never intended, however, to put his family in danger.

He called Hennessey, despite the lateness of the hour, to be sure that she was on notice for her own safety.

Gaela and Hennessey were both deeply shocked and saddened by the death of Kerry Anderson. At the time, Gaela vowed that he would do everything in his power to stay on this case and find out who might be involved within the DEA.

"Barb, you've got to take every precaution to protect yourself and your family. I'll do the same. But, I swear to you, in all my years as an agent, I've never felt like I do right now. I don't know who these people are that we're dealing with. But, I promise you, I'm going to get these people if it's the last damn thing I ever do. They're gonna pay, Barb. We've got to make them pay."

CHAPTER 42

WHEN WILL IT STOP?

The prison officials moved Brett to the United States Penitentiary on South Wilmot in Tucson. The transfer was without incident. The high security USP Tucson federal prison housed more than 1,500 male inmates.

The media interest in Gatlin continued to be high, as news personalities throughout the country vied for the opportunity to be the first to openly interview the man. Attorney Timothy Wakefield strongly advised his client not to grant any interviews. No problem there. Brett had absolutely no inclination or desire to do so.

Gatlin did agree to a visit from DEA Special Agent Marty Gaela, although Wakefield insisted that he also be present for the meeting between the two men.

"The guy's been favorable to me from day one," Brett told Wakefield, "and he was gracious in working with Kerry. I have no idea what he wants, but I'm willing to at least sit with him."

Marty Gaela focused back on Brett Gatlin. He did not know that there had ever been any direct contact between Gatlin and Kerry Anderson.

"Agent Gatlin, I don't know if you ever had the opportunity to meet Kerry Anderson, the Washington Post reporter," Gaela said. "But, the lady was a class act, you know? She gave me the courage to push further in what I believed, even if it meant standing against my own Agency.

I didn't come here today to ask you a bunch of questions, Gatlin. I came here to tell you that I'm not finished. I'm gonna stay on this case until I get the answers I'm looking for—the truth in what really is happening here."

Gaela informed the two men of the night attack against him and his family.

"I got my family protected now," Marty said, "and I'm not backing down."

Galea turned towards Timothy Wakefield.

"You need any help from me, sir," Gaela said while handing one of his business cards to the lawyer, "you give me a call and I'll do whatever I can."

Gaela turned back towards Brett Gatlin.

"There's still a lot here that I don't know or understand, Agent Gatlin, but I've been a federal agent long enough to know when something isn't right. I knew shortly after I met you that the pieces in this puzzle just didn't fit."

Gaela chuckled before continuing to speak.

"My wife, Sharon, and I do those big jigsaw puzzles together. And I gotta tell you, I'm pretty darn good at finding those pieces and fitting them together. There's a puzzle here and I'm not quitting here until the right pieces are fitting together."

Gatlin smiled. "Thanks, Agent Gaela. I appreciate you coming here today."

"You bet," Gaela said, "especially after you did have a gun pressed against my head at one point in time."

Then, Gaela laughed, stood, and shook hands with both men. He turned one last time towards Timothy Wakefield.

"Let's see if we can get this man out of here without him having to press a gun against anyone's head."

⇥ ⇤

Roger Clark had flown into the Nashville Airport, leased a vehicle, and driven to Antioch where Brett's mother and sister lived. The visit was somewhat stilted at first, since Brett's mom and sister had no idea who Roger was. Brett had written a note that Roger brought with him.

> *Dear Mom & Lucy:*
> *It feels so awkward even writing to you, since we've had no contact whatsoever for years.*
> *Yet, you have always been in my heart and thoughts. I long for the day when I will see you again.*
> *Don't worry about me. I'm okay. I've done none of the things they've accused me of. I'd like to believe that I don't even have to tell you both that, but I wanted you to hear it directly from me.*
> *They say that a true friend is the person who walks in when the rest of the world walks out. That is Roger Clark.*
> *Please welcome him.*
> *I love you both.*
>
> *Brett*

Roger left his Jeep at the Tucson Airport and upon his arrival there, he planned to stay in a motel close to the USP Tucson so that he could visit Brett. Visiting hours at the prison were primarily on Friday, Saturday, and Sunday.

The distance from the airport to Roger's motel was less than twenty-minute trip, but things became a lot more complicated when Roger spotted the black sedan that had been parked near his Jeep and was now following him.

Well, well, you guys have now figured out who I am and made me a person of interest. How exciting! Man, I wish this Jeep was an Army tank and I could turn around, ram you guys, and run right over you.

Roger knew that men like these would eventually determine where he was staying, but he didn't want to make anything easier for them. As a result, he did not go to the motel where he had reserved a room. He continued to drive throughout different areas of Tucson with the black sedan doing a poor job of remaining inconspicuous.

When Roger spotted the Tucson Mall, the largest shopping mall in that city, he made a sudden turn and pulled into an outdoor parking area near the J.C. Penney's store. The sedan was delayed from making the turn. By the time they did, the two men spotted Roger slowly jogging into the department store.

They found a spot to park about eight spaces away from Roger's Jeep and followed suit by entering the Penney's store. Both men entering the store to hunt for Roger was their major mistake. It meant that no one was outside in the lot should Roger return to his vehicle. In fact, Roger exited through another door, ran to his Jeep, found the Camillus 7.75-inch fixed blade knife he kept under a seat and ran over to their sedan. Roger saw no one around when he slashed two of their tires, ran back to his Jeep, and drove away. He positioned the Jeep far enough away where he could use binoculars to see them, but they would not be aware of him.

I'm going to get a really good look at you fellas and study your faces. I want to be ready for you when we meet again.

And, Roger did just that. He was too far away to take a meaningful picture, but he was sure that he'd recognize these men the next time and he saw them. He was also sure they'd be around again in the not too distant future.

The federal penitentiary in Tucson had in excess of 1,500 inmates and Brett Gatlin bore the dubious distinction of being the most famous one. Fame in the eyes of the general public or even the media was not an issue, since they did not have access to him. Fame in the eyes of the prison inmates was a major issue. There was always the possibility that an inmate might like to make a name for himself by murdering the infamous rogue agent who had, at times, dominated front-page news. Or there might be inmates who were serving time due to arrests made by DEA agents. Or, there were inmates who hated anyone who or anything that, in any way, had something to do with law enforcement. In Brett Gatlin's case, there was always the possibility that people from the outside could wield enough power to have someone inside the prison off the man. Brett Gatlin was in a precarious situation.

On the third day of his incarceration, Brett was sent to work in the laundry room. He was caught alone by three inmates who approached him.

"Well, if it isn't the famous lawman," one of the men said. "Look fellas, we just bumped into Mr. Wyatt Earp, hisself."

Brett tightened his body. Stood still and eyed each of the men, sizing them up, trying to determine what his options were.

"I'm not looking for any trouble." Gatlin said.

"Maybe you ain't lookin' for it," the largest of the men said, "but, it sure do look like trouble done found you."

He was an African-American man who stood at about six feet four inches and had the body of a professional football linebacker. Brett would later learn that this prisoner pretty much ran things in this area of the prison. The look in the large man's eyes was menacing. He reached out to grab Gatlin. Brett moved to the side, grabbed the man's arm, spun behind him, and had him bent over with his arm firmly twisted behind his back. Every time Brett pushed even slightly upwards, the man cried out in pain. And, every time either of the other two men even looked like they would approach, Brett pushed up on the man's arm.

"What's your name?" Brett said.

The man said nothing and Brett applied more pressure to his arm.

"I said, what's your name?"

"M-Morris, my name's Morris."

"Okay, so, here's the deal, gentlemen," Brett said to the other two men, "make your play, but you move towards me and I'm gonna rip Morris' arm clear off his body—and do know that I'll enjoy every minute of it."

Morris continued to grunt and moan. It was clear that he was in a great deal of pain.

"I don't have all day, fellas. And, I don't believe your friend here is getting any enjoying out of this. What's it gonna be?"

"Let it go," Morris said to his two thugs. His voice was raspy and strained. His face was twisted evidencing his suffering. Perspiration poured from his brows and dripped down onto the floor. "I can't take no more. Do what the man say."

"In that case," Brett said, "I say you two need to clear out of here now. Your buddy and I are going to walk just a little bit farther to the entrance of the laundry room. If I don't see either of you, I'll let him go."

The two men did what Brett told them to do. When he released Morris, he pushed him forward, turned, and walked into the laundry room.

CHAPTER 43

NOT SAFE ANYWHERE

Roger was at the prison during visiting hours. This was the first time the two men were together since Roger paid a visit to Brett's mother and sister in Tennessee.

"Your mom and sister are doing okay," Roger said. "As you'd expect, Brett, they're worried about you. And, I'll tell you, man, they sure didn't need me to convince them that you're innocent. They had no doubts about that at all."

Brett thanked Roger for doing what he did. He listened closely when Roger told him about the car that had followed him from the airport.

"But, I slept really well last night," Roger said. He smiled as he spoke. "Nobody came around looking for me. And, if they had, I was more than ready."

Brett's brow was wrinkled and he was softly biting his lip. His eyes had a distant gaze to them.

"Okay, tell me, Mr. Gatlin. What is it? What's bothering you, man?"

Brett hesitated before speaking.

"Rog, I could never repay you for everything that you've done for me. I'm not sure how I feel about guardian angels, but it wouldn't take much to convince me that you either are one or you were sent to me by one."

Brett's attempt to use humor to soften the impact of what he was about to say was unsuccessful. Roger stared back.

"But, what?" Roger said.

Brett fidgeted in his seat and spoke without looking directly at his friend.

"But, maybe it's time for you to distance yourself from me, man. You know, maybe you should just call it a day and move on. I'd understand fully, Rog. I swear I would. Like I said, I can't possibly thank you enough for all you've done."

Roger glared at Brett, then gritted his teeth.

"That's one hell of a thing for you to say to me, Brett. What's it gonna take for you to get it, man? When are you finally gonna stop acting like you're some kind of remote island that somebody could pass by or maybe even visit for a day or two before moving on?"

"Rog, I didn't mean anything offensive. I just… "

"You just keep thinking that it's your duty to protect me or make decisions on my behalf. Listen to me, Bubba. I'm not here because I got into something and can't get out. Need I remind you, Gatlin, that it was my decision to help you. I came along of my own free will. You didn't freakin' kidnap me.

In addition to believing you are innocent and being railroaded, linking up with you has given me something worth waking up for each day. Since I've been grounded, I haven't had much purpose in my life. Flying was what I lived for. Flying was the only thing that I ever wanted to do. Once that was gone, my life became empty, man. And it was spiraling downward.

Look, I already told you how I feel about you, Brett, but let me make something real clear. Nobody, not even you, Mr. Gatlin, calls the shots in my life. Nobody makes me do something I don't want to do. I do what I want, when I want. If you haven't figured out by now why I never found a woman who was willing to put up with me for too long a time, you now know why."

Both men sat staring at one another in silence before Roger spoke again. He laughed. Then lifted his arms and shrugged.

"Gatlin, do I have to mention that 'in it for the long run' stuff again or is any of this getting through that thick skull of yours?"

It was Brett's turn to laugh now.

"Nah. I get it, Rog. I'm sorry, man. I just couldn't bear to think something bad might happen to you."

"Hey, Mister Field Agent, I've been in the cockpit of a badass plane traveling at 1,500 miles per hour, that's Mach two, and an elevation as high as 60,000 feet. I'm not taking anything lightly, Brett, but, I assure you, I'll be alright."

Gatlin smiled.

"Okay, man. Thanks. I hear you, Rog."

"Good," Roger said, "then drop that guardian angel stuff, too. It's kind of an insult to any real angels."

Both men laughed.

⊱✦⊰

Several days passed after Roger's last visit. Based upon what Brett told Roger about Marty Gaela's visit, Roger made plans to visit the federal agent.

"I'm also gonna check back with Carlos Aguilar," Roger said. "If he hasn't got anything new, at least I'll see if I can sit and have a few beers with the guy."

Brett had just showered. He was wrapped in a towel and getting ready to get dressed. Some other men were still in the shower. Others were also getting dressed, but none were in the same area as Brett. A tall thin man with a sharp shiv slipped in behind him. Brett was unaware that the man was even there. The man had his arm raised and began his descent towards the back of Brett's neck, when Gatlin heard a noise, spun around, and saw that Morris had the man's arm. He twisted and bent it until the shiv fell to the floor. Three other men moved in as Morris directed them to gag the man.

"Now, take this dude someplace nice and private and fix him up real good where he ain't about to bother nobody again for a long time."

The men pulled the man away. Morris stayed. Brett stared at the man, nodded, then thanked him for what he just did.

"Why'd you do that?" Brett said. "Last time we were together, we weren't exactly on the friendliest of terms."

"Friends ain't got nothin' to do with it, Gatlin. The man who come after you is one of Felipe Montez' boys. Would look good if they took down a fed. This dude, Montez, he trying to establish hisself and his gang as the top people to deal with here. That's my gig. I ain't about to let that happen."

Morris started to walk away, then turned back towards Gatlin. A smile crossed his face.

"Besides, I needed you to see that you ain't the only one around here who can twist up somebody's arm."

Roger Clark was seated with Special Agent Marty Gaela at the DEA office in Tucson. Roger and Gaela had never before met, which meant that the federal agent was initially guarded in his dealings with Roger.

"How can I assist you, Mister Clark?" Gaela said.

"Well, sir, you can begin by dropping the Mister Clark label. Anytime someone calls me that, I start looking around the room for my father and I lost him many years ago."

Roger leaned forward.

"Agent Gaela, I'm a friend of Brett Gatlin who believes the man is being framed. The word I got from Brett and his attorney is that we could come to you if we are in need," Roger said.

"So, I assume that you have a need?"

"Brett tells me that you were the victim of an attack at your home. Sorry to hear that, man. Sounds like a harrowing experience for you and your family. I, also, had a couple of thugs following me from the airport when I recently flew back into Tucson. As a result, I've changed motels a couple of times since then. But, there's only so many motels I can go to and, to tell you the truth, packing up and moving around like that gets old real quickly. I never was much for packing suitcases anyway."

Gaela sat quietly, waiting for Roger to reveal what prompted him to come here this day.

"Okay, so you're the expert on this kind of stuff, not me," Roger said, "but I've been thinking. Whoever came after you at your home might be a whole lot more hesitant when it comes to you than they would be coming after me. So, what if we were to set me up as a kind of decoy? Make it real obvious where I'm staying and try to lure these guys to pay me a visit at night."

Gaela's head pulled back as his shoulders pushed forward. His lips were pressed together. He was hearing what Roger was saying and had to admit it could work. But, he would be permitting a civilian to put himself in danger.

"You know you'd be taking a real risk putting yourself in that position," Gaela said, "plus I don't know if I could justify allowing a civilian to be placed in harm's way like that."

"Well, with all due respect," Roger said, "I'm gonna be in harm's way whether we set a trap or not. It's just a matter of time before these goons catch up with me. The way I see it, if that's the case, we might just as soon use it to our advantage. If we can take these guys alive, we might be able to figure out who they are and who they're working for."

Gaela rested his chin on his hand. Then, he leaned back in his chair and closed his eyes for a moment or two.

"Okay, here's the deal, Roger. If we do this, we do it on my terms. I'll set things up, you agree to play by my rules. I've got to know that you won't take any foolish chances or attempt to do anything on your own. Are we clear on that?"

Roger smiled, saluted, then reached out to shake Gaela's hand.

"Like I already said, sir, you're the expert on these kinds of things. You can be the king. I'll just be one of those pawns."

Gaela frowned.

"Look," Gaela said, "I admire your courage and your willingness to step up, but I've got to know you are hearing me and taking me seriously."

Roger paused. He stared into Gaela's eyes.

"I knew Kerry Anderson. The last time she was here in Arizona spending time with you, I was meeting with Trooper Aguilar. I want more than anything to get the people responsible for her death. It's also true that I am convinced that Brett Gatlin is innocent. He's being railroaded and the people involved likely include some folks within your own Agency. I'm doing what I am for Brett and for Kerry. If we do this, I'll do whatever you say. You have my word on that."

CHAPTER 44

TAKING THE OFFENSIVE

"The man is most certainly not pleased. Gatlin's still alive, we've lost Barkley and his organization, and Gilliam has been arrested. We still have Gaela sticking his nose in places where it doesn't belong. Looks to me like we've got work to do."

As the Deputy Attorney General of the United States, Marvin Belgrade was little more than the whipping boy for Attorney General Floyd Harrington. Nevertheless, everyone understood that anything Belgrade said was directly from the mouth of the nation's chief law enforcement officer and head of the country's Justice Department.

Belgrade was sitting with Norman Finley, the man who had the most direct contact with Mexican Drug Lord Caesar Hidalgo Monterro. Finley played a major role in assuring that the final strategy regarding the crucial meeting in the Sonoran Desert was established.

"I understand Harrington's concerns," Finley said, "but these matters are trite when compared to what we have already established. We destroyed the number one drug cartel in all of Mexico and replaced it with a cartel that we have a major interest in— both operationally and financially. We successfully silenced the

Washington Post reporter who had been very effective in gathering evidence that would have been totally destructive to all of us. You do remember, Marvin, that Anderson had photos of you and me at an old warehouse outside Sierra Vista, along with members of Monterro's cartel? Fortunately, Barkley and his men confiscated all of that at the scene."

"Yes," Marvin said. "I know that we have been very successful on many key points, but the stakes are so high in what we're shooting for. That makes every little issue matter. I mean, we're talking about Lloyd Harrington becoming the next President of the United States and when that happens, well, the benefits are immeasurable, my friend. Need I say we'll have the world at our fingertips?"

Finley nodded his head.

"For sure, Marvin. No doubt about it. But, remember also that we've already filled Lloyd Harrington's campaign chest to overflowing with more funds coming in every day. And, we have greatly succeeded in our efforts to make Harrington shine while the president's poll numbers continue to plummet. So, you see, there's a lot moving in a positive direction, my friend."

Finley reached over and tapped Belgrade's hand. He smiled and gestured with a slight wave of his hand.

"But, I am hearing your concerns, Marvin, and I don't want you to be anxious. Now, as you know, my primary function is to keep Monterro in check. That, in itself, is a full-time job. None of us completely trust that man.

When it comes to cleaning up some of these smaller annoyances, why not put some added pressure on Phillip to take care of things. The man can get the job done. Plus, Marlowe has more sordid acquaintances than you or I will ever have."

Finley chuckled at his own statement.

⊷╬ ╬⊶

Roger Clark was in his motel room bed when the doorknob of his registered room began to slowly turn. Two dark figures carrying tire irons were preparing to enter. The room had two single beds. They spotted the figure of a man under the covers in the bed farthest from the door. They entered the room and moved slowly towards their target, pleased that Roger Clark had not stirred at all. So far, the operation was a success. This should not take long. It was even easier than they anticipated. .

Closer still, ready to raise their tools and finish what they'd come here to do, the room lights suddenly turned on. A fully-clothed Roger Clark spun around in the bed and was now sitting up with his weapon pointed at his two visitors. Another man was standing at the door behind the intruders pointing a handgun at them.

"Morning gentlemen," Roger said. "Nice of you to drop by."

The man who had been at the door moved closer.

"Federal Agent. Drop your weapons. Do it now," Marty Gaela shouted.

Roger hopped out of the bed, while continuing to keep his weapon pointed at the two men. One of the men stood at five feet ten, had a slim body, a shaved head, and sported a goatee. The other man was closer to five feet eight inches, was a Latino with slightly darker skin, jet black hair, and a stockier build.

Roger moved closer with his weapon pointed directly at the man with the shaved head, as Gaela cuffed each man. Gaela also took a moment to shove his DEA credentials in each man's face.

"Gentlemen," Gaela said, "I'm going to assume that with each of you bearing tire irons, you're not from AAA coming here with the intent of repairing a flat tire." Gaela smirked, then pressed the barrel of his weapon tightly against the forehead of the Latino man. Roger followed suit with the other man. "That being the case," Gaela said, "I suggest you start cooperating with us right away."

"We know our rights," the Latino said. "You can't make us do nothing."

The man hardly finished the words when Gaela added his clasped hand on the man's throat to accompany the gun pressed against his skull.

"Now, I'm gonna only say this one time," Gaela began, "so I want you boys to listen real closely. Somebody came to my house at night and put me, my wife, and children all in danger. I'm gonna assume that was the two of you. And somebody was tailing Mr. Clark here even before tonight. I'll put that tag on you guys also."

"Hey, we had nothing to do with… " the man with the shaved head started to speak, but Gaela warned him to shut up.

"You guys don't get to talk," Gaela said. "We talk. You listen. So, here's something very important that you boys need to know." Gaela pressed his weapon even harder against his man's head. His eyes were squinted and a smile covered his face. "I never reported in to my superiors that I would be here tonight. Far as my Agency knows, I'm home in bed. That means, I have no problem, whatsoever, killing both of you and dumping your bodies. As far as my friend and I are concerned, we'd claim we never saw you two at all. Isn't that right, Roger?"

Clark smiled. "Hey, I'm like real good at keeping my mouth shut and denying I know a thing. And since we're talking about two men who came here tonight intending to beat me to death with tire irons… ouch… " Roger said, "you know, it hurts just thinking about that. Anyway, I'd be honored to rid society of two lowlifes like these. In fact, I'm thinking we just forget about this cooperation stuff and do it, man."

"You're bluffing," the Latino said.

But, the man with the shaved head stared into Roger's eyes as Roger had the gun pressed so hard that it indented the skin on his forehead. The man trembled when he saw Roger's fingers moving on the gun trigger.

"No," the man said to his Latino partner. "This dude's crazy. He ain't bluffing. He'll kill me, man. He wants to blow my head off."

Roger smiled. "Gotta give you a lot of credit, man. You're nowhere as dumb as you look. You understand real good."

The Latino spoke next.

"What do you want from us? We were just doing a job, you know? If we don't do what they say, we gonna be the ones on the other end of a tire iron. That's all. We just do what they tell us to do."

"Who's the 'they' you're talking about? Who put you up to this?" Gaela said.

"Look, man, we tell you, they kill us anyway. Just like they gonna kill your friend in prison. If they can reach a guy behind bars, they can reach guys like us no matter where we go," the Latino said. "No reason we should talk to you. *No tiene sentido.* Makes no sense."

Gaela called for backup and the two men were brought to the DEA offices in Tucson to be interrogated. Despite the lateness of the hours, he also called Barb Hennessey to report everything to her.

Relying upon their network resources, it didn't take long before the men were identified as William Galt and Fernando Alvarado. Both of them had rap sheets.

"From what we're seeing," Gaela informed Hennessey, "they're both in deep with a local loan shark. Guy named Wade Saffire, who local authorities are convinced is behind several murders, but haven't been able to come up with enough evidence to get a conviction."

"So," Barb Hennessey said, "Galt and Alvarado do what the people who hired them to do and get their debts paid off or they end up dead at the hands of Saffire."

"That's pretty much how we see it, Barb," Gaela said. "Our team is doing everything they can to try to find out just who is behind hiring these guys to kill. And, by the way, we don't have anything yet linking them to the hit on my home."

Gaela paused for a moment before opening the conversation to another point.

"We now have every reason to believe that there's a hit planned against Gatlin at the prison," Gaela said. "I've already notified the prison authorities, but maybe an added push from you would help even more."

"You got it," Hennessey said. "I don't know him well, but I have met Warden Paul Anthony there at the USP Tucson. I'll give him a call now."

"Thanks, Barb. Uh… these two thugs made a statement that I can't seem to shake. They talked about how anyone who could reach behind bars and have someone killed has to be pretty damn powerful, you know?"

"I hear you, Martin. Guess it's time for us to believe that we can be a force to be reckoned with, also."

CHAPTER 45

BEHIND BARS

Their names were not Steve and Matt, but temporarily, those names would do just fine. After all, the two men were not going to be in this role for very long. They had a mission to fulfill, then they would go underground and be untraceable.

When Morris spotted the two men working out in the penitentiary gym, the one thing he knew for sure was that he'd never seen them anywhere around before. With more than 1,500 prisoners it would be preposterous to think that Morris knew every inmate in the place. But, men this big and chiseled were not your everyday prisoners. Morris was the kingpin in his section of the federal penitentiary. These men, he certainly would have noticed.

Each man was taller than Morris' six feet four inches. The man using the name Steve had sandy brown curly hair and brown eyes. Matt had blonde hair which he wore in a buzz cut. It was rare for the gym to be this empty, but Morris was alone when he encountered them.

"Hey," Steve called out to Morris. "We hear tell that you're the head honcho here in this section. We got that right?"

Morris walked over to a set of dumb bells and began pumping. His large biceps stretched the short sleeves of his shirt. He neither acknowledged nor answered the man.

The man walked over to Morris. Matt joined him.

"Maybe you didn't hear me," Steve said.

"Or maybe," Matt chimed in, "you're just impolite."

Morris stopped pumping with the weights and stood staring at the two men. Once again, he said nothing.

The man named Steve turned towards his friend. "Hey, Matt, you ever see such rudeness in a man when all we're attempting to do is have a friendly chat?"

"Nope," Matt said. "This boy is downright ill-mannered, I'd say. Guess his momma never taught him no manners. Probably one of the reasons why he ended up in here. Don't ya think?"

Matt and Steve were nowhere around when Morris' body was found with a barbell pressed against his crushed neck. The man's death was ruled as an accident and cited as another reason why people working out with weights should never handle barbells alone without someone else nearby.

⇥ ⇤

The word of Morris' death spread quickly through the prison. With Morris dead, a new top gun would be established in the inmate ranks. Morris was a lifer with no family members in contact with him for years. One of the chaplains held a memorial service in the prison chapel. Brett attended and spotted a group of men, primarily African-Americans, who had been closely-associated with Morris. Despite the fact that Morris had a great deal of inmates you lived under his protective umbrella, most of them had already moved on after he died.

So many people are only loyal based upon their own needs. When their needs change, their loyalty disappears. Makes me also wonder what would happen if I died in this rat hole. Who do I have in my life? Let's see, there are Mom, Lucy, Roger... uh... Mom, Lucy, Roger. Man, you're talking enough to count on only one hand with a few fingers to spare.

Barb Hennessey did speak with Warden Anthony and put him on notice that there was a report of a potential in-prison threat against Brett Gatlin. The warden believed that his prison had adequate safeguards to assure that a man like Gatlin would be safe. No extra security was needed. He did agree that the word would be passed to the prison guards in the area where Gatlin was housed.

━╪╪━

The prisoners were all out in the yard during some free time.

"Gatlin," the prison guard named Hollingsworth called out, "Warden wants to see you in his office. Head on down the hall. Guards will let you through at the checkpoints leading to the man's office."

Gatlin's stomach was churning. There was a tightening in his chest. Normally, a guard would accompany a prisoner down the halls. Brett was being sent alone. As he walked, Brett could not shake the feeling that he was being watched. He heard a movement just ahead and prepared to make a move, if necessary. Gatlin was not one to be spooked easily, but whenever he suspected something was amiss, it was as if he had an inner button he could push to activate a high alert throughout his body.

The noise was slight. Perhaps, most people would not have heard it. But, Brett Gatlin was not most people. Someone was lurking ahead where the hallway turned to the right. Gatlin was convinced that at least one person was waiting for him. He curled his hands into fists and positioned himself for an attack. He walked a bit slower and just as he turned the corner, the man was there. Brett prepared to strike.

"Whoa, hold on there, Gatlin," the prison guard named Walters said. "Got word the man is wanting to meet with you. I'll escort you to the next checkpoint. You got any idea what Warden Anthony wants?"

"No idea," Gatlin said. "I was told he wanted to see me. That's all."

Walters momentarily fell a step or two behind Gatlin and that was when he made his move. Gatlin never saw the man withdraw the wand he was carrying and strike at the back of Brett's neck. Gatlin fell to the floor when Steve and Matt appeared on the scene. Steve began to kick Gatlin in the ribs, but Brett recovered enough to make a quick move, spin, and rise to his feet. Walters was no longer around.

Still groggy from the blow rendered by the guard, Gatlin was not quick enough to prevent Matt from grabbing him from behind. Steve threw the first few powerful body punches causing Brett to double over. He then threw a vicious uppercut that snapped Gatlin's head upwards followed by a volley of punches to Brett's face. The strategy was clear. These two men intended to beat Gatlin to death and each punch was bringing them closer to their goal.

Gatlin never saw the six African Americans who rushed on the scene and attacked the two men who had accosted Brett. One of the arriving men struck Matt on the back of his skull with a hard object causing the man to lose consciousness and fall to the ground. All six of the others attacked Steve and overpowered him. Now, Steve and Matt were in danger of being beat to death.

Brett was on the ground, conscious enough to hear whistles, shouting, and a rush of activity as prison guards arrived on the scene. Using pepper spray and tasers, they took control over the team that once was committed to Morris and had arrived just in time to save Brett Gatlin's life. These men had sensed something was wrong when they spotted the prison guard sending Gatlin off alone. Afterwards, they would be sent to solitary confinement and face serious charges that would likely extend their prison terms and make it all the more certain that they would never be looked upon favorably by a parole board. But, these men were aware of Morris' actions to save Brett before he died. And, they were certain that their leader died as a result of foul play and not an accident.

They watched as Brett was taken away to the prison infirmary. They knew that what they had just done would cost them in terms of prison discipline, but some things were worth the price. They were met with a great sense of satisfaction. Morris would have been pleased that they played a part in saving Gatlin's life. Beyond that, they had, to an extent, avenged Morris' death.

⇌ ⇌

Brett's attorney, Timothy Wakefield, filed petitions with the court seeking to have his client removed from the Tucson prison and released to a hospital outside the prison system. He also began the process of petitioning that disciplinary measures be taken against the prison officials and guards for failing to adequately guard a prisoner, even after receiving advanced warnings of an impending threat from a ranking federal agent.

Brett had several broken ribs and looked like a professional boxer who had suffered a major loss in his last bout. But, he did not have any fractured facial bones and was expected to make a full recovery. He informed Wakefield of the actions that Morris' associates had taken to save his life and Wakefield promised to do what he could on behalf of these men and force the prison to take a deeper look into Morris' death.

Roger Clark was livid when he learned of the attack on Brett. Marty Gaela and Barb Hennessey assured Roger that they also would actively get involved in support of Brett and would coordinate with Tim Wakefield.

As Brett was healing well in the prison infirmary, charges were already being brought against certain prison guards. Warden

Anthony, although not implicated in Gatlin's attack, was under scrutiny by the prison board for negligence in his duties.

⇒⊹⊹⇐

Due to some strong actions taken by Timothy Wakefield, along with Barb Hennessey, Roger Clark was permitted to enter the hospital infirmary to visit Brett. He leaned over and hugged his friend, as Brett was propped up in his hospital bed.

"What the hey?" Roger said with a slight smirk on his face. "Can't I leave you alone for a little while without you getting in trouble?"

The swelling on Brett's face was subsiding on a daily basis, although he would bear shiners on both eyes for a while. He smiled.

The smirk on Roger's face was replaced by a wrinkled brow.

"Man, I just don't like you being in here. I know Wakefield's working on things. He's even trying again to get a judge to allow us to post bail."

"Don't worry, Rog. I'll be okay. You just take care of yourself. Having one of us a bit banged up ought to be the absolute limit."

The two friends stayed together until Roger's time was up. Little did they know that the winds of change were already rustling and building up some steam.

CHAPTER 46

THE TIMES THEY ARE A-CHANGING

S he was there in his dark room standing beside his bed in the middle of the night. Her voice was soft and enchanting. Her smile was captivating. Her smell was delicious and enticing. She reached out and gently stroked his face and told him not to worry—all was well with her. The glow that encompassed her caused him to suspect that she had come from high above the clouds in a land filled with luscious green meadows and an array of beautiful flowers. She told him that everything pertaining to him was about to change and, as she said that, a broad smile covered her face. She was as beautiful as always and he so desired to hold her in his arms. But, when he reached out to her, she was no longer there.

⊷⊶

Brett, as always, had awakened to an otherwise empty room. The vision of Kerry both warmed and troubled him. God, how he missed her! Her death had devastated him. But, above all else, he couldn't bear to think that she was gone forever. He would never see her again. The very thought of her generated the strongest feelings of sadness and anger he had ever known in his entire life.

Brett's lawyer had not even gotten to him yet when the word was spreading like uncontrollable wildfires throughout the nation. There was breaking news of a scandal involving some agents within the DEA and government officials, some of whom were in the Justice Department. The news interrupted morning television programs and covered the front pages of newspapers and online websites. The more that was revealed, the more questions were raised that were yet to be answered.

What was known was that certain Americans had conspired with the Mexican drug lord, Caesar Hidalgo Monterro, to help make his drug cartel the most powerful in all of North and South America. The conspiracy centered upon a sharing in the spoils of the illegal drug trade. The amount of money involved was staggering.

The arrest of Marvin Belgrade, the Deputy Attorney General of the United States, immediately raised questions as to whether Attorney General and potential presidential candidate, Floyd V. Harrington, was also involved. A strong consensus was already forming that he was. A photo of Belgrade and Norman Finley entering a seemingly abandoned warehouse in Arizona graced the front pages of newspapers across the country and was seen repeatedly on television. There was also a pic of Lieutenant James Gilliam. For weeks and months to come, this story would continue to grow and unfold. The arrest of Norman Finley further implicated the Attorney General.

It was the Washington Post that first broke the story using reports and pictures taken by the late Kerry Anderson. Hidden behind the scenes was a computer whiz by the name of Jacob Greenleaf. Wireless, in agreement with Kerry, had devised a backup system to Kerry's work. FBI Agent Delonda Wilson received data whenever Kerry was recording on her phone or taking pictures. Jeremiah

Barkley's attempt to destroy the evidence Kerry had at the time of her death had failed. Delonda had copies of everything.

Delonda had been extremely cautious. A good portion of material she received had been the product of illegal searches and hacking conducted by Wireless. But, Wireless and Kerry were not law enforcement officials and the courts were ruling that certain Fourth Amendment prohibitions against unlawful search and seizure did not come into play.

In her communications with Greenleaf, Delonda agreed to not expose him. She classified him as a confidential informant.

"I don't care if it gets me in trouble," Wireless told Delonda. "If me coming forward and testifying will help put people directly and indirectly responsible for Kerry's death behind bars, count me in."

Marty Gaela and Barb Hennessey continued in their own investigative work. Now, they were marveling at all that was occurring.

"My God," Marty exclaimed in a conversation with Barb, "Kerry Anderson is still speaking from the grave. Most incredible thing I've ever witnessed."

This breaking news was also rewriting the story of Special Agent Brett Gatlin. America and the world learned that Gatlin had been framed by some members within his own Agency and the Justice Department. Steps were taken to immediately release Brett from prison. Reporters from around the world and every major television network sought an interview with the man who had been betrayed by his own federal employers and maligned by every major news source other than the Washington Post's Kerry Anderson. Brett turned down every request.

For a while, it seemed as if new arrests were being made every day. Added details expanded the story of all that had occurred. In exchange for a lesser sentence and assurance that he would not be charged with aiding and abetting in capital murder, Lieutenant James Gilliam agreed to turn state's evidence. Investigators were striving to identify the individuals who helped rig explosives in the vehicles transporting American and Mexican federal agents.

Although Gilliam could not specifically name any of the individuals he had encountered, he had already identified photos of two of the men involved in the rigging of explosives.

American authorities were making the effort to have Charlie Hough and Luke Munson, suspected of killing federal agents Nunez and Palmer, extradited from Chile where they were currently being held by that government.

Special Agent Marianne Pacheco agreed to talk, after her arrest at the Phoenix DEA offices. Her testimony revealed that there were payoffs, which, in turn, had investigators tracking the money. The New York Times published an article stating that reporter Edmund Foley of the Chicago Tribune had received money from someone within the U.S. Attorney General's office in exchange for Foley's willingness to publish articles discrediting Walter "Woody" Vaughn as a witness to the highway accident. Foley also challenged Kerry Anderson's articles supporting the fact that Brett Gatlin was innocent.

Patricia Kenworth resurfaced and was now openly cooperating with the FBI in their investigative efforts. She revealed what she knew about Max Bradford, his special ops team, and the innocence of Brett Gatlin.

In a conversation with Delonda, Patricia had an opportunity to further express her personal feelings.

"I feel good. I feel free being able to speak the truth. In a small way, I feel as if I'm serving Max, Mike Wright, and Kerry by speaking out."

Phillip Marlowe was a person of interest in the murder of Agent Bill Falwell. The FBI opened a formal investigation into the death of Special Agent Max Bradford, including the exhumation of his body. Initially, a new autopsy revealed that Bradford may have been poisoned in a manner that generated his heart attack.

Day after day, week after week, the reports continued to pour in and add to a story that had the attention of the country and the world. Public sympathy on behalf of Brett Gatlin escalated, but Gatlin did not care. As he stated to Roger Clark, "I always knew that I was innocent and had been framed. Having the world privy to that means nothing to me. It doesn't change a single thing that ever happened and cannot serve to bring Kerry back."

The whereabouts of Jeremiah Barkley, the primary suspect in the murder of Kerry Anderson, remained unknown. The same was true regarding the disappearance of Andrew Gotschild. The authorities had not yet found any bodies.

As the head of the Department of Justice, Floyd V. Harrington wielded extensive authority over several federal law enforcement agencies including the Federal Bureau of Investigation and the Drug Enforcement Agency. As a result, Barb Hennessey and Marty Gaela knew that their willingness to stand against members of their own agency placed them in the direct line of fire with Floyd Harrington. They were spot on. Hennessey received notice that she was being transferred to the DEA Domestic Field Division in Detroit. Gaela was reassigned to the New Jersey Division.

Hennessey and Gaela both viewed Harrington's actions as vindictive and an effort on his part to curtail any aspects of the ongoing investigation that he could. Leaving the DEA would completely remove them from the ongoing investigation. Nevertheless, each of them had separately written and submitted their letters of resignation when they received direct communications from the White House. Since the Attorney General serves at the pleasure of the President of the United States, it was within the prescribed authority of President Creighton Mallory to fire Harrington. President Mallory did just that, although his official statement impugned no substantiated evidence that his Cabinet Member was guilty.

"With a focus distracted by the need and right to defend himself and an unfortunate cloud of suspicion hanging over him and his Department, it is in the best interests of our nation that anyone in such a demanding position be free of anything that might interfere in his or her ability to do a much-needed job," the President stated.

Hennessey and Gaela were both reinstated to their positions in the Phoenix and Tulsa DEA offices.

Allan Kingsley, Chief Counsel for the DEA, was also fired. Although he was not implicated in any criminal conduct, the overwhelming opinion was that Kingsley spent his time defending the image of the DEA, rather than expressing a willingness to determine if suspicions being raised had any validity.

Contrary to Gatlin's refusal to be interviewed or even release any statements, FBI Agent Delonda Wilson did speak openly. She spoke about the shameful dark scandal that betrayed the innocence of someone like Brett Gatlin who had faithfully risked his life in serving his country. She spoke about how this scandal led to the murder of Kerry Anderson. Delonda stated that she rejoiced anytime her work resulted in placing the cuffs on another individual who may have betrayed his or her country or whose crimes resulted in the murder of another person.

"And we will not stop in our work until every last person involved in this hideous tragedy is brought to justice," Delonda said.

CHAPTER 47
CONGRATULATIONS

Several months following his release from prison, Brett Gatlin made his first public appearance. He attended a formal dinner in New York City along with Roger Clark and Delonda Wilson. Executive Director Allison Richfield Valencia posthumously presented an International Women's Media Foundation Courage in Journalism Award to Kerry Anderson.

"Courage Awardees," Valencia said, "are those uniquely gifted and courageous women who rise above threats, intimidation, and even, in some instances, the risk of death in their willingness to uncover and report the truth. Kerry Anderson is an outstanding example of such a person. She is someone who will remain an inspiration to generations of reporters to follow."

The IWMF award was followed by Kerry's alma mater, Indiana University, establishing the Kerry Jane Anderson Scholarship Fund granting a full four-year scholarship for an incoming journalism student. The Washington Post created the Kerry Anderson Excellence in Journalism Award consisting of a $50,000 grant to assist journalists nationally and internationally engaged in a quest to uncover truth against formidable odds.

In each instance, Brett continued his refusal to speak to the press. "These awards place a spotlight on the life of Kerry," Brett stated to both Roger and Delonda, "and that's exactly where the spotlight belongs. I have no interest in drawing even one iota of attention away from her."

The greatest instance of recognition came with the announcement that Kerry Anderson was named as a Pulitzer Prize winner in Investigative Journalism. Brett agreed to celebrate this award by going to dinner in Kerry's hometown of Elkhart, Indiana. It was a gesture that Delonda thought of in tribute to Kerry. It was a private dinner with no fanfare and no notice given to the media.

Just choosing to celebrate in Kerry's hometown had a strong impact upon Brett. Here in Elkhart, he was walking in Kerry's footsteps. This was the city where she was born and raised. She had lived here before completing college in Bloomington and moving to D.C. to take a job with The Washington Post.

As they toasted the wine they were sharing for dinner, Delonda, Roger, and Brett each took a moment to recall an outstanding attribute of a woman who died much too soon. Brett acknowledged that he owed his life to Kerry who came to the forefront and questioned the charges against Brett that everyone else deemed to be true.

"How could I have ever known that Kerry would touch my life and my heart as deeply as she did?" Brett stated.

Delonda asked Brett what he intended to do with his life now that he was a free man. He had already spent time with his mother, Lucy, and Lucy's fiancé. He did not intend to continue working as a federal agent. Brett did have a law degree and would consider whether he could use that in a way that was both rewarding to him and to others. Regardless of what he might otherwise do, Brett and Roger were first making plans to take a trip out west, including a stopover in Arizona to once again thank individuals such as Barb Hennessey, Marty Gaela, and State Trooper Carlos Aguilar.

He was thankful for Delonda Wilson and her efforts to clear Brett's name and free him from incarceration in prison. Yet, in truth, Brett did not feel as if he was a free man. The stigma of the accusations rendered against him would follow him throughout his life. He would always be remembered as the rogue agent accused of betraying his country and his oath as a federal agent. Some would always believe that Brett Gatlin was somehow responsible for the deaths of his federal agent team members and four Hummers filled with American and Mexican federal agents. The bitter taste of betrayal that he suffered at the hands of those who should have been the first to declare his innocence and attest to his loyal service to his country would always be something he would remember. The saddest thing about betrayal lies in the fact that it never comes from your enemies.

Beyond all else, Brett believed that everything he had ever desired, in an opportunity to share in love with a woman, disappeared the day Kerry Anderson died. He was very familiar with people talking about encountering and sharing life with their soul mate. But, what do you do when your soul mate is stolen away by death before you ever have the opportunity to share a romantic moment with that person? Hah, Brett remembered hearing that true love does not have a happy ending because true love has no ending at all.

"So, what does that mean in my case," Brett said to Roger. "Am I now doomed to live the rest of my life wallowing in the shadows of 'what might have been?' Do I just spend my days fantasizing about what I might have shared with Kerry had she lived? Truth is, Rog, that pretty much sums up how I feel."

Brett bore a bitter taste in his mouth when he reflected upon his years as a federal agent. He never regretted the choice he made nor the reason behind that choice. But, he believed that he had nothing of any real value to show for more than four years of sacrifice living in an existence that defied everything he valued and everything he otherwise believed in. From the onset, Brett never expected that many others would ever even know the sacrifices he would make. He realized that his willingness to forego his own dreams in order to fight for a cause that would offer hope to countless others was something personal. But, he never imagined that everything he ever did while hidden underground, away from the eyes of all but a very few, would, through no fault of his own, end up negative and twisted. Having the good and noble things you've done never fully recognized by others was one thing. But, having everything you've ever done maligned and destroyed was quite another thing. And why? Because others whom you had every right to trust had established their own evil agenda? That was a bitter pill to swallow.

Brett sat alone on the banks of Percy Priest Lake catching fish and tossing them back in. Roger would be arriving on the following day. As he sat contemplating all that he had experienced over the past years, Brett could not help but think of others who were dedicating their lives to a work that is so often underappreciated.

He stared up at the sky and attempted to look behind the white puffy cloud that gently glided overhead. His mind reverted back to a moment he shared with Kerry. He told her that after years of working undercover, "I haven't got a clue what it's like to have someone care for me."

Then, Kerry reached over and placed her hand on his and their eyes met. He took her hand and held it within his. In that moment, as he stared into her eyes, he knew that Kerry possessed the power to stir his imagination and challenge him to believe in so many thing he had lost sight of.

Kerry was the one person who changed his black and white world to color. The very thought of her reminded him that not everything in life was dark and evil. Perhaps, in keeping Kerry alive in his heart and mind, he could, indeed, learn to believe that life still possessed unfulfilled dreams and promises.

The End

www.ingramcontent.com/pod-product-compliance
Lightning Source LLC
Chambersburg PA
CBHW062125170626
46813CB00002B/574